A NineStar Press Publication

www.ninestarpress.com

Franklin in Paradise

Printed in the USA

ISBN: 978-1-64890-292-5

First Edition, May, 2021

available in eBook, ISBN: 978-1-64890-291-8

WARNING:

k contains sexual content, which may only be
r mature readers. Depictions of death of family
(off page), death of animals (off page), scenes
ve auto accidents and multiple dead bodies,
ounted domestic abuse resulting in death (ref
d recounted accusation of sexual assault (ref
to past).

Life is good for eighte the spectrum, structuring and organizing his days, avoiding messy situations and ambiguity. But what he really wants is a boyfriend.

Twenty-one-year-old Patrick has a past he can't seem to shake, and a sexual identity that's hard to describe—or maybe it's just evolving.

When a manmade virus sweeps the globe, killing nearly everyone, the two young men find themselves thrust together, dependent on each other for survival. As they begin to rebuild their world, their feelings for each other deepen. But Franklin needs definition and clarity, and Patrick's identity as asexual—or demisexual, or grey ace?—isn't helping.

These two men will need to look beyond their labels if they are going to find love at the end of the world.

FRANKLIN IN

PARADISE

Paradise, Book

John Pat

T
in
in
ac
eve

All
repr
phot
perm
all ot
or wel

Also

This boo
suitable fo
members
of massi
scene of re
to past) an

This book is dedicated to the memory of my brother-in-law, Harry, and to my sister and nieces who had to endure loss and grief in a year turned upside down by a virus.

Chapter One

I finished cleaning my bedroom before lunchtime. Not that it needed it. I'm not the kind of guy to leave his dirty socks and shorts lying around. But I dusted behind the headboard and vacuumed the corners of the ceiling in my closet, removing the neatly labeled boxes from the top shelf first, before dusting those, too, and restacking them in alphabetical order: beads, crystals, fly hooks, etc., all the way down to screws.

I tugged the bed aside and vacuumed the carpet underneath, carefully nudging the bed frame back into the existing carpet indentations when I was finished.

I was ready.

Right after my parents left that morning, I even shaved. Not that there was any real need for that either. Even though I'll be eighteen in a couple weeks, I'm hardly rocking the facial hair, just a few soft black wisps curling under my chin.

Nothing to do now but wait for Tyler.

I walked to the picture window in our living room and stared out into the gloomy March evening. Across the dirt road, Mrs. Knudson's front porch lights came on. If I leaned forward and craned my neck to the right, I could almost see the intersection with State Highway 27. I waited at the window until I saw a sweep of headlights illuminating the deep forest along the road, silhouettes of oaks and pines picked out one by one as Tyler's pickup bounced through the ruts.

I stepped away from the window and moved to the front door. The throaty rumble of his truck died, and a moment later a door slammed. Footsteps on the side deck were followed by a shout of "Yo, open up." I silently did a slow three-count, then opened the door.

"Dude, here, take these. Back in a sec." Tyler thrust three large pizza boxes into my arms and headed back to the driveway. I carried the boxes across the living room to the counter separating it from the kitchen, the scent of hot cheese, tomatoes, onions, and pepperoni filling the air. By the time I laid out each box in a neat row on the counter, Tyler was back, kicking the door shut behind him.

He had a gym bag looped across his shoulders, and he was carrying a case of Sam Adams.

He came around the counter and into the kitchen, put the beer on the table, and dropped his bag on the floor by the counter. "Woo-hoo! Sweet Sixteen!" he said, as he shrugged out of his jacket.

Sweet Sixteen? What...? Oh, right. March Madness. Sweet Sixteen round. That's what we're doing tonight, right?

"Your folks get off okay?" he asked.

"Yep, they got there already and texted me an hour ago. It's 75 degrees in Puerto Rico right now."

"Good for them, man." Tyler used the opener on his key chain to pry the caps off two bottles. He handed me one. "And they're good with us doing this?"

"Yeah, of course. You've slept over lots of times." Even as I said that, I felt a blush rising in my cheeks. I hoped tonight would be different than all those other times. "Besides," I continued, "Mrs. Knudson will be keeping an eye out. She knows I'm alone this weekend, and my folks told her I wasn't allowed to have any parties." I was embarrassed my parents had asked our eighty-year-old neighbor to spy on me. "How about your folks? They know you're staying the night, right?"

"Right. No problem. They just don't know we're alone." He waggled his eyebrows.

*

Tyler and I have been best buds since fourth grade, but lately, I've been thinking about him in a...well, I guess romantic way would best describe it. I was pretty sure he felt the same about me, too, because more and more, Tyler has been lightly touching me. A pat on my head, a tap to my arm. He knows touching is a "thing" for me, and he's been really good about too. Signaling it would happen so I could be prepared without making a big deal about it.

Two years ago, my first and only girlfriend, Maya, let me know I was gay. I hadn't thought about it, one way or the other, up until then. I didn't like the whole idea of dating. Turns out she was right, of course. She was so pushy when it came to the physical stuff, even though she knew I was...sensitive...to that kind of thing. "We don't have to do anything you don't want to do," she'd say. But then she'd try to kiss me or grab my hand.

One night, the last time I saw her, we were sitting in her parents' basement, and she asked if she could hold my hand. I didn't want to, but I knew this was what boyfriends and girlfriends did, and I was trying so hard to be *normal*, so I let her. Before I understood what was happening, though, she guided my hand down to her thigh and under her skirt. When I discovered she wasn't wearing underwear, I'd gasped and yanked my hand away, waving my fingers in the air as if they'd been burned. I might have gagged a little too.

"Uh-huh. I thought so," she'd responded immediately. "You're gay, you know, Franklin. Right? You do know that? I'd hate to see you waste the next couple of years 'struggling' to understand yourself. You should just blow your buddy Tyler right now and get it over with."

Fair enough. But I didn't blow Tyler, and as much as I was convinced we had a future together, I was pretty sure I didn't want to blow him, or at least not yet. But I'd been thinking about kissing him, and although it made me a little uncomfortable, I thought I might be ready for that.

*

We settled on the couch. We both took a corner, leaving plenty of room between us. We went through the first pizza as we watched the game and started in on the second. It was a good matchup, and although I wasn't much of a basketball fan, I was sort of enjoying it. But I was enjoying watching Tyler more. He was wearing his silky green athletic shorts, even though it was cold out with snow expected overnight. Every now and then he'd stretch his legs in front of him, the soft golden hairs on his thighs glinting in the light of the television.

During a commercial break, he leaned back and stretched his arms behind his head, then out wide to the sides, one hand briefly brushing the back of my shoulder. He glanced over at me. "Dude, your hair is getting really long." He tugged on a curl hanging over the back of my collar. I was surprised to find I didn't mind the unexpected touch. In fact, an electric jolt ran through me. Was this it? Was he going to kiss me? But no. He let go, stood, and walked into the kitchen. He popped open two more beers, his fourth and my second.

On his way back into the living room, a local newscaster came on the screen. "Good evening, Bangor. Here's what we're covering for our eleven o'clock broadcast. Tonight's snowstorm is now looking more like an ice storm for areas just inland from the coast. Central and Northern Maine could be hit hard. Sandra will have the timing and the details. Also, our national affiliate in Washington, DC, will be updating us on breaking news out of Asia, following unexpected and provocative actions by North Korea. See you at eleven."

"Did he say an ice storm tonight?" asked Tyler, handing me a beer and sitting back down on the couch, closer to me this time.

"Yes. Maybe we'll be stuck here." I liked the idea.

The game resumed, and we made our way through more pizza. I got up to use the bathroom, and while I was there, I remembered that you're supposed to fill containers of water if you might lose power. I filled the bathtub for toilet flushing, then went into the kitchen and filled several containers and buckets for drinking water.

When I returned, I sat even closer to Tyler, our legs just inches apart.

He punched my arm, using an exaggerated slow motion so I could see it coming, and called me a Boy Scout. "Doesn't hurt to be prepared," I said. At one point, he twisted toward me and leaned over to set his beer down next to me, even though there was also a table at his end of the sofa. His knee rubbed tightly along my thigh.

A newscaster interrupted the game. "This is CBS Breaking News. Our Washington desk is following disturbing developments out of Asia. China has, without warning, closed its borders and airspace and disabled its internet. The US State Department is trying to determine the status of tens of thousands of US citizens currently in that country. The move by China comes immediately on the heels of word that North Korea is readying several missile launch sites and has also closed its borders and airspace. Additionally, we've been following an escalating health crisis in South Korea, with unconfirmed reports that hospitals in Seoul have been overwhelmed with victims of a newly circulating, deadly flu.

"Our Asia experts are here to discuss the situation and possible connections between the events unfolding there."

Tyler leaned forward and picked up the remote from the coffee table. He muted the sound and turned to me. "You want to see something?"

"Sure."

He rose from the couch and went to his bag, still on the floor by the kitchen counter. He squatted and rummaged inside for a second, then pulled out a DVD case and held it up so I could see it. "My cousin down in Portland gave this to me." He walked back to the couch, grinning.

I took it, and a twinge of anxiety twisted in my stomach when I realized what it was.

"Porn," I said, studying the case. There were pictures of naked young men. Just men. "I didn't know you were into that."

"Not just porn. Amateur stuff. My cousin says there's a guy in Portland who pays guys to do things on video. Mostly just jerk off together, you know?"

"Huh." I didn't know what else to say. The whole idea made me uncomfortable. I've seen porn on the internet, of course, but I didn't like it. It struck me as messy and fake. Plus, I wasn't good at what Dr. Levy called "reading" people, so when I *knew* people were only pretending, I had difficulty figuring out what was going on.

Porn left me confused and anxious—the opposite, I guess, of how most people responded. So, no, I didn't want to watch porn.

"Anyway," Tyler continued, "my cousin says this guy is looking for guys to work together. Opposite types, you know? He says we'd be great together. You're dark and stocky; I'm tall and blond..." he trailed off, apparently waiting to see how I'd react.

Absolutely not was my first thought, but I held it back. What did Tyler want to hear from me? Was he really suggesting this, or just leading up to watching the DVD together? So instead I said, "Uh...don't you need to be eighteen to do that kind of thing? On film, I mean."

"I *am* eighteen. And you will be in just a couple weeks." He took a swig from his beer. "Maybe we can watch this disc so you can see what it's all about. It's pretty tame, like I said." He stood up, turning the case back and forth, looking at me. "It's just guys, though... That won't bother you, will it?"

Would it? I *am* gay after all, so it shouldn't. Although I'd rather Tyler just kiss me and put the porn back in his bag. But if this is what Tyler wanted...maybe it wouldn't be so bad. I could just focus on Tyler, right? I wouldn't have to look at the video at all. "Oh, uh, no...that won't bother me."

"Great! This'll look amazing on the big screen." He pried the disc out of the case and headed toward the DVD player below the television. The sound was still muted, and the screen was showing a shaky video of what looked like lines of dead bodies in a hallway somewhere. A banner reading "unconfirmed footage" scrolled across the bottom.

"Hold on," I said. "We can't watch that here. There's no curtains and Mrs. Knudson might see in."

"Dude, that is so whack! You live on a dirt road in the freakin' middle of nowhere, no other houses around for miles, except this one old lady who lives *right across the freakin' street*! What is with that?"

"I know, right?" I thought of all the cleaning I'd done earlier. "Maybe we can watch it on my laptop in my bedroom?"

Chapter Two

I was pulled out of a troubled, anxious sleep by...a noise? A voice? The last tendrils of a dream were dissolving: I was being stoned as a punishment for something, but the stones were too small, pebbles really, handfuls being thrown by Maya and Tyler. Tyler!

I tilted my head to the right, but of course he wasn't there. Why would he have stayed after the fiasco last night? I only hoped he hadn't left and gone home. We needed to talk about what had happened. Or, I guess, for my part, what *hadn't* happened. What the hell is wrong with me?

I rolled over to look at the clock on my desk: 4:40 a.m. I wasn't used to beer. I felt a little dizzy and needed to take a whiz. I quietly entered the hallway and was relieved to hear snoring coming from the living room. It was bright in there too; Tyler must have left the TV on. I went into the bathroom and pissed for what seemed like an hour. I had a big drink of water and simply stood there, staring at Tyler's bright-blue toothbrush lying over the edge of the sink, at an odd angle that I immediately fixed to align it with the faucets, and to point the bristles down rather than up.

I went back down the hallway, passed my bedroom, and stepped into the living room. Tyler was stretched out on the couch, tangled in a blanket, his blond hair shining silver-white in the bright light from the window. Wait, what? I glanced at the dark TV. So where was that light coming from? I moved farther into the living room to look out the window and noticed that all Mrs. Knudson's lights were on.

That was odd; she was never up past 9:30. Why would she have all those lights on in the middle of the night? I walked to the picture window. A gust of wind drove a smattering of sleet against the glass. The ground was covered in a thin, gritty layer of white. The sleet must have been what woke me. Tyler shifted on the couch but didn't open his eyes.

I looked across the street and could tell from the shifting blue and silver shadows inside her house that Mrs. Knudson's television was on. Another burst of sleet was driven into the glass in front of me. *Tap, tap, tap*. It reminded me of a dream I'd had, but I couldn't recall the specifics. I went back to bed.

*

Several hours later, I woke to a loud clanging sound. An alarm? No, it was intermittent and familiar somehow. My phone? I lifted myself onto a shoulder and looked at my bedside table where my phone sat silent and dark. The sound went off again, and I realized it was coming from outside my bedroom. I stumbled out of bed and into the hallway. I heard Tyler getting up in the living room.

Was it *his* phone? Did he have one of those funny ringtones that mimicked what old phones used to sound like?

"What *is* that?" Tyler called from the living room, sounding disoriented. Oh, of course! The landline.

We kept an old-fashioned wired phone in my dad's office for emergencies, and it was ringing now. "I got it," I said to Tyler as we stumbled past each other in the hallway, him heading to the bathroom, me to the office at the other end of the hall. Tyler turned slightly away from me as he passed, but not before I noticed his morning erection pushing against his shorts. My stomach dropped at the reminder of my failure last night.

I fumbled my way into the office, missed the light switch, but finally reached the desk. The landline was rarely used, so the phone sat on the floor just beside the filing cabinet, and it took me another moment to find it. I lifted the handset to my ear as I sank to the floor. "Hello?"

"Franklin! Are you all right?" my mother asked, breathless and worried. Scared, even.

"Yes, yes, I'm fine, of course. What's wrong? Why are you calling on this phone?"

"We might not have much time. The lines have been going in and out. We're coming home as soon as we can. Your father is at the airport now trying to get us on the next available flight, and I'm heading there to join him right after this call."

"Coming home? Why? What's wrong?"

There was a lot of noise in the background, shouting and angry voices that sounded very close.

"You need to turn on the news. The North Koreans sent nukes into space to take out a bunch of satellites. There's no cell service. And there's lots of people dying in Asia. All over. No one's sure what's going on because the communication satellites were destroyed. The US has shut down international flights, but we should still be able to get home on a domestic flight." All of this was offered in a rush, as if she'd given thought to what to say as quickly as possible.

I pulled the phone away from my ear when an abrupt banging sound came through the line. Distantly I heard my mother say "No!" in a harsh tone, before she was back. "I have to go. We love you, Franklin. We'll try to get home by this evening."

"I love you too. But what's happening there? Should I call anyone or try to change your flights from here..." But I realized I was talking to dead air. "Mom? Mom?" I tried a couple of times and waited, but nothing. I hung up. Then I picked the phone up again and heard a fast pulsing tone that didn't sound like what I thought a dial tone was supposed to be.

Tyler stood in the doorway; I was still sitting against the wall. "Dude, I gotta go," he said. "The storm is getting bad out there. It's going to be impossible to drive soon." He walked into the living room, and I rose and followed him. He pulled on his jeans and a sweatshirt, then began throwing his things into his bag. He picked up his coat.

"But, there's some sort of emergency out there with the Koreans or something. You should stay here. Have breakfast."

He swiped at the screen on his cell phone, not listening to me. "Damn it," he mumbled to himself. "Out of juice." He looked around the room to see if he'd missed anything.

"No, it's the satellites," I said. "They've been blown up."

He looked at me like he might ask a question, but then shook his head. "The sleet has changed to rain, but it's still below freezing. Soon it'll be sheer ice everywhere." He turned and headed to the door.

"Wait," I began. "About last night..."

But he was already opening the door. The sound of a drumming rain came swirling into the room with the cold. "Hey, no biggie. You weren't into it. It happens. I'll call you." And then he was gone.

*

I went into the kitchen and opened the refrigerator. The bacon and eggs I had planned on making for Tyler sat unopened on the top shelf. I removed the carton of orange juice and the tube of biscuit dough, then turned the oven on. The clock on the wall read 7:30 a.m., 29 degrees outside. I poured myself a glass of juice and took it to the window in the living room.

The sleet had changed to a driving rain. Every tree shimmered in a layer of ice, swaying back and forth under the added weight. It was beautiful in a way, but even as I stood watching, an enormous limb from Mrs. Knudson's front-yard pine broke from the tree with a loud crack, then thudded to the ground. I looked more closely and noticed many good-sized sticks and branches littering our yard as well.

I sat on the couch, placed the orange juice glass on a coaster next to one of Tyler's beer bottles, and turned on the television.

I wasn't born yet when 9-11 happened, but this is what I think it might have been like. Worried newscasters trying to retain their professionalism even though it's clear something big and really, really bad might be going on. There were lots of windows open on the screen showing different things, but what caught my eye was the one in the lower left corner.

It displayed a video of a street scene somewhere in Asia, filmed by someone riding on a scooter directly behind another scooter overcrowded with several people hanging on to each other, all wearing masks, the kind we all wore a few years ago when COVID started circulating. The two scooters swerved through the streets, dodging what looked like...wow, yes...bodies, lying on the sidewalks, propped against walls. The five-second loop ended each time when the young girl on the scooter in front simply fell off, as if she'd fainted.

It was replaced by a second video, this one, based on the angle from above, filmed by a security camera inside an airport terminal. The banner across the bottom of the screen read "Shanghai." The terminal was filled with bodies. Stretchers lined the hallways as if an emergency medical response had been underway before being overwhelmed by what was happening.

In the main portion of the screen, three newscasters sat at a round table. I recognized one of them from the nightly news my parents watched. "Of course, communication has proven very unreliable without satellites, and none of these videos have been independently confirmed. But if what we are seeing is true, it indicates that whatever is spreading through Asia—"

"And now Australia and India," one of three interrupted.

"—is highly contagious and deadly," finished the first.

Before she could go on, the third anchor raised a hand to interrupt. "Sorry. Hold on..." He was reading intently from a handheld device. "Based on what's crossing the wires right now, an emergency has been declared at London's Heathrow Airport, and the region—wait, is that right?—yes, the entire metropolitan area has been quarantined." A gasp could be heard from off-screen.

A quarantine of London? That was one of the lessons from COVID. As soon as you see a new virus, lock down right away. Still, how could it be happening there and in Asia at the same time?

"Well...uh..." The first anchor stumbled a moment, then continued. "Earlier this morning, our military expert on North Korea speculated that there is a possibility a manmade pathogen, perhaps a virus, was released either intentionally or unintentionally." The newscaster's hands were shaking, and she looked relieved to cut to video. "Here's a clip of that conversation."

From outside, there was another loud crack, followed by a second shortly after, and then a booming, crunching sound. The house shook. Shit. I stood and went to the picture window. More branches and limbs had come down, but I couldn't see what had caused the sound. I moved to the other side of the room and looked through the window in the front door. A large oak tree had fallen across the driveway, crushing the front half of my Jeep. Next to my mangled car was a black patch of asphalt, covered in slick ice now, where Tyler's pickup had been.

The strong smell of newly cut oak filtered into the house, and a light dust drifted down from the ceiling. I'd have to clean that.

From behind me, in the living room, a high-pitched single tone interrupted the news broadcast, followed by a repeating series of three klaxon-like alarms. In my head I immediately provided the words that had always followed that sound, 'This is a test of the emergency broadcast system...' But it wasn't a test, was it?

I turned back toward the television. The screen displayed an order to "Shelter in Place Immediately." A recorded voice repeated the message: "A national shelter in place order is now in effect. Take shelter indoors immediately until further notice."

A faint blue flash lit the room, and the power went out.

*

I sat on the couch and stared at the dark television. A silence came over the house, an absence of sound that only makes itself known when all the little motors and compressors go off. Ice-cloaked trees swayed and moaned outside. I looked into the kitchen and saw the cardboard tube of biscuit dough sitting on the counter, partially twisted open with the dough pushing itself out between the seams.

I stood, intending to put the biscuits in the oven while I figured out what to do next. But then I remembered— electric oven—so that wouldn't work. I went to put the package back in the refrigerator and paused. I should keep the refrigerator closed as long as possible to keep things cold. But how long would the power be out?

A large dry-erase calendar affixed to our refrigerator door had "Happy Birthday, Franklin" written on a circled date a few weeks out. We had a reservation at the fancy

Italian place in town. Surely this would all be over by then?

I went into my parent's bathroom and pulled a package of face masks out of the linen closet. Masks, hand sanitizer, and toilet paper are the three things my mother will never, ever run low on again. I walked back to the living room window. Mrs. Knudson's house was dark too. I wondered if it was just our two houses that were out. I wanted to go outside and look toward the highway, see if there were downed wires, but what about the shelter in place order? And how can that make sense for a whole country, anyway? For now, I decided to stay inside.

I started pacing. There was so much to consider. I went into my bedroom and grabbed my phone. There was no cell service, so I powered it down. I noticed my laptop on the floor by my bed, and the empty DVD case sitting next to it. The disc itself was still in the machine. Great, no internet, but I could watch porn if I wanted. Super.

I powered the laptop down, too, then went back to the office to see if the landline was still working. It wasn't, so that meant the phone lines were also down.

Well, hopefully, my parents would be home by this evening. Part of me realized that was unlikely. After all, even if the shelter in place order didn't extend to Puerto Rico, what would they do once they landed in Portland? How would they make it all the way back up to Northwood?

I decided to build a fire. We had a nice stack of logs next to the wood stove, and many weeks' worth of wood in the mudroom leading to the screened porch. There were even more on the screened porch, but could I go out there or would that violate the shelter in place order? Hopefully, I wouldn't need to worry about it.

I tidied the house, collecting the empty beer bottles, rinsing them, and placing them neatly along the back wall of the counter next to the sink. I collapsed the empty pizza boxes, after picking off the remains of dried cheese, meat, and crust, and stored them on the shelf in the mudroom. It bothered me that I couldn't put them where they belonged in the garage, but to get to the garage I would have had to go outside through the screened porch.

I took another look at Mrs. Knudson's house but didn't see any movement. I figured if the power still wasn't on by this evening, I'd put the battery-operated lantern in our window and tape up a sign asking her if there was anything I could do for her. I got a good fire going, grabbed a leftover slice of pepperoni, and settled in to wait for the power to come back.

Chapter Three

But the power didn't come back, and, very slowly, the hours turned into days. I spent the time just...waiting. And cleaning up as much as I could, of course. Tyler had the annoying habit of peeling the labels off his beer bottles, and even though I'd rinsed them and lined them up neatly, it bothered me, a lot, that some had peeled labels and some didn't.

I told myself it didn't matter, but, well, it really did. So, on day two, I carefully peeled the labels off *all* the empty bottles, and after an hour's work, had eight pristine green bottles arranged in perfect order underneath the dish cabinet. They sat there for a week before I decided to dust them.

Sometime in the middle of the second week, I cleaned the bottles again and moved them to the kitchen island. But I'd gotten used to seeing them under the dish cabinet, so I moved them back. I reread my favorite books but decided against computer games or watching movies in order to preserve my battery.

The one eventful thing that *did* happen during those first couple of weeks was that Mrs. Knudson died. Right on her front porch. That was early on, but I don't know exactly when. She wasn't there when I went to bed, but she was there when I looked across the street the next morning, sprawled halfway down her porch steps, front door wide open.

She was definitely dead. I could tell through my binoculars. Otherwise, I think even with the whole shelter in place thing, I would have gone over to see if she was hurt. I hope I would have, anyway. But no. The eyes, the mouth, definitely dead.

But why had she gone out on the porch? And was it going outside that had killed her, or had she known she was dying and headed out anyway? Maybe she'd been feverish? Maybe she'd been headed over here for help? It made no sense that there could be something in the air that would kill you as soon as you stepped outside. Right?

I looked at my remaining stash of logs by the woodstove. It was nearly April, so I wasn't too concerned about the pipes freezing if the fire went out. Still, I'd need to venture outside eventually, if only to the screened porch for more firewood. I'd long ago finished all the perishables from the fridge, and the canned goods wouldn't last much longer.

I decided I'd give it two more days. If the power wasn't back on by then, I'd walk down to the highway and flag someone down for help. Unless everyone was still sheltering in place, then I'd walk the ten miles into town and find help there. I wished I could use my Jeep, but even though the ice was long gone, the oak tree crushing my car was still there. I supposed Mrs. Knudson's SUV was in her garage, but I didn't want to go over there and try to find her keys. What if they were in her pocket?

*

Friday, at least I think it was Friday, dawned bright and clear. This was the day. I was going outside.

I didn't have a choice. I was down to one milk jug filled with drinking water and just a few cans of soup. But I delayed. What if I died as soon as I went outside? Should I leave a note for my parents? Should I leave a note for Tyler, trying to explain? And *what* would I explain? Why wasn't I a normal seventeen-year-old?

I thought of my laptop in my bedroom and the disc still in the drive.

I could try watching it again. Dispassionately this time, without the pressure of Tyler lying next to me, excited, urging me to get into it. Maybe if I could figure out why it made me so anxious, I could get beyond that and respond the way I'm supposed to, the way everybody else does.

I brought the laptop into the living room and turned it on. I knew it was pointless, but I checked for available Wi-Fi connections. There were none.

I set the laptop on the low table in front of the couch, pressed Play, and leaned back to watch. The video picked up right where we had stopped it—the point where Tyler had decided it wasn't worth trying to make this work for me. There were two young guys on a couch, naked, sitting next to each other. Their knees were touching, and an off-screen voice was giving them instructions. Tyler had said, "The one on the left looks like you."

Did he? I studied him now. He was stocky, sort of a football player's build. We were similar that way. He also had black hair, but his was straight and short while mine was curly and, as Tyler had observed, getting way too long. He had a heavy pelt of black hair on his belly and legs. I wasn't nearly as hairy as he was. My skin was more pasty white, but that could just be winter in Maine. The biggest difference was the eyes. His were a very dark brown; mine are a bright blue.

"We could do this, don't you think? If we made a lot of money?" Tyler had asked then. No, I didn't think so, especially considering my obvious lack of arousal. It was working for Tyler, though. "Is something wrong?" he'd asked.

Everything, I'd thought.

Watching the video now, I tried to imagine what Tyler thought when he watched porn. What about this got him so excited? The guys on screen were clearly into it, or good at pretending anyway, and readily complied when the voice said, "Bobby, I'll give you another fifty dollars if you reach over and start stroking Kyle." I remembered Tyler's face as he watched the guys on-screen.

Now I closed my eyes, listening to the men on the screen as I thought of Tyler. Tyler's smile, the way his eyes lit up when he told a joke, the careful way he held a sandwich but the sloppy way he shoveled in his food. Tyler in his manual transmission pickup truck, his hand working the gear shift.

A loud knock sounded at the door. Twice, in rapid succession.

I nearly jumped out of my skin as I sprang from the couch. My first thought was that Mrs. Knudson had come back to life and was here to demand answers from me. Why hadn't I saved her?

I hurried to the front door, my heart pounding, and stood in front of its glass window. A tall guy, early twenties, maybe, stood on the other side, looking in at me. We blinked at each other.

"You're outside..." I began to say through the glass, at the same time he said, "You're alive!"

"Yes," we both replied at the same time.

He had a huge grin on his face. "I can't believe this!" he said. "You're the first one I've found. This means there's bound to be others."

"The first what?" I asked.

"What?" he shouted. "I can't hear you through the door." He cupped his palm behind his ear.

"I'm the first what?" I asked more loudly, mouthing my words broadly.

"The first one alive," he mouthed back.

I didn't let that sink in. "Mrs. Knudson is dead," I said, jerking my head in a direction behind him, toward where Mrs. Knudson's body had, at some point during the night, been dragged farther down her front steps.

"I know. I saw her right away—"

"What?" I leaned closer to the window.

"I said I saw her right away." He'd raised his voice again to be heard. "I thought maybe it was her fire still burning somehow. I was so disappointed. But then I saw the smoke coming from here. And here you are!"

We looked at each other through the glass.

"Can I come in?"

Oh. "Is the shelter in place order over?"

"What? Oh, that. No, that was a mistake! They rescinded it right away. Turns out it was already too late by then."

"A *mistake*?" I squeaked. I was pretty sure I did, anyway.

"Yeah. You must have lost power at the beginning of the storm if that's the last news you had. But yeah...it didn't matter, inside, outside. Too late for everybody."

"Too late," what did that mean? "So, I can go outside...?" Stupid question, but that's where my head was.

"Yes, or, if you invited me, I could come inside... where it's warm?" He rubbed his arms briskly and peered around me into my house. Behind him, a motorcycle leaned on its kickstand next to my ruined Jeep.

"Oh, right, yes, of course. Come in." I opened the door and was struck by how fresh the air smelled. He stepped inside and wrinkled his nose. I guess it was a little ripe in here after being closed up for so long.

"I have plenty of masks. Are we supposed to be wearing masks, or social distancing?" I asked as he walked past me and into the living room.

"Masks? No, it's not like that." He peered about the room, then turned back to me. "I still can't believe you're alive!" He couldn't stop grinning as he removed his coat. Now that he was inside, I noticed he was much taller than me. He took off his orange knitted cap, revealing thick, copper-colored hair, longer even than mine.

"Dude, I am so excited to have found you!" he said, bouncing up and down on his toes.

I left the door open for some fresh air.

In the middle of the room, just beyond the couch, a disembodied voice said, "Kyle, I'll pay you another hundred dollars if you stroke Bobby just like that too." On screen, Kyle did.

"Oh my god!" I exclaimed, spinning about and lunging for my laptop. I tripped over the edge of the couch and landed on the floor.

I managed to reach my laptop and fold the screen down as I turned it away from us. I started to explain about the video, but he waved me off. "No worries, man. End of the world and all that. I'm not judging."

My heart was racing as I went back to the couch; my legs wobbled as I sat. He stood over me, scanning the room once again. He placed a hand on my shoulder. "Steady there. You okay? You're not going to faint or anything?" I jerked at his unexpected touch, and he quickly removed his hand.

"I'm okay. It's just so much. I need to catch my breath for a minute—"

"Oh, yeah, that's nice, Kyle. Fifty more dollars if you kiss him while he's doing that to you."

"Goddamn it!" I yelled, scrambling off the couch and grabbing the laptop. I hit the eject button this time and, remembering the dwindling battery, went through the powering down sequence. "Let me just..." I hit the wrong button. "Take care of this..." I began again, face burning as I wrestled with the laptop.

"Take your time, man," he said, as he began wandering about the room, noting the stack of neatly folded, empty boxes of food, and the pile of flattened bags next to them on the floor, kept in place by a heavy stew pot on top. Empty juice and water bottles, and empty cans of soup and beans, were carefully lined up by the porch door, waiting to be removed to the recycling bins in the garage. "You did all right for yourself. Nobody's here?" I replayed his question in my head and thought he might have asked "No bodies here?" but I wasn't sure, and the answer was the same either way.

"Nope. Just me." I waited for the computer's red power light to fade to black. I considered removing the disc from the open tray but didn't want to draw any further attention to it. I turned back to my visitor. I wondered what his name was.

Before I could ask, he said, "And that lady across the street?"

"Yeah. Mrs. Knudson."

"How long has she been there?"

"A couple weeks, I guess," I replied. "I've sort of lost track of time, a bit."

"I get that, sure." He walked into the kitchen and picked up the open jug of water sitting on the counter. He took a sniff, frowned, and put it back down. "And you haven't been outside at all?"

"No. Just...in here." Something occurred to me. "But hey, now that I know the shelter in place order isn't a real thing, can we get an ambulance, or the police or something, to take care of Mrs. Knudson's body? Does your phone work? Mine still can't get a signal."

"Uh, right. No, no phone." He stopped smiling, and his face scrunched up. I wasn't good at reading expressions, but I thought this one meant he was uncomfortable. He rubbed his fingertips against his thumbs. "So...you don't know what it's like? Out there, I mean?"

"No."

"Wow. Okay. Where to start? Can I sit down, man?"

"Sure. I'm Franklin, by the way. Franklin Marshall." I mentally prepared myself for a handshake.

"I'm Patrick," he said, taking my hand and shaking it as he lowered himself to the couch next to me. "Patrick Larson." The DVD case with its lurid photos of naked young men sat in front of us. I leaned forward and picked it up, slipping it behind me on the couch. I glanced at the exposed disc in the laptop's tray, an explicit image of Bobby, or maybe Kyle, printed on the surface. I didn't want to bring further attention to it, so I pretended not to see it.

"So, okay. Here's the thing, should I lead up to it or just come right out with it?" He didn't wait for an answer. Maybe he wasn't expecting one. "This is hard, man."

"Lead up to what?" I was losing patience.

"To what happened," he replied.

"*What* happened?" I demanded.

"Dude, everybody's dead."

I just sat there. That didn't make any sense at all. I wasn't dead. Patrick wasn't dead. I'm sure my parents weren't dead, or Tyler. Mrs. Knudson was dead though. I must have sat there staring blankly for a while.

Patrick said, "Um, I guess I should have led up to it?"

I rallied to state the obvious. "Everybody is not dead, Patrick. You and I are having this conversation, right?"

"Right. Right, right, right," said Patrick, rubbing his hands together vigorously. "Point. But, well, most everybody is, anyway. I mean, there's no ambulance coming for your neighbor. No police or anything."

"Seriously? Well, *how* many people are dead? Where is everybody else? Is there a shelter or something we're supposed to go to?"

"Well," said Patrick. He reached forward and lightly tapped my shoulder. "There's you"—he touched his chest—"and me."

I waited.

"And that's about it. So far."

"*What?*" I jumped up from the couch. So did he. Maybe he thought I was going to freak out. Maybe I was. I paced around the room. "That can't be." I turned back to him. "There's twelve thousand three hundred people in Northwood."

"What?"

"People. That live in Northwood. According to the census, anyway, which they do every ten years, so it's probably a little less now."

"Wow," said Patrick. "I didn't know that. I was wondering about it, too, because I was trying to figure out what the survival rate is for...whatever this is. You know, when I thought I was the only one."

"And actually, it's closer to thirty thousand if you include the outlying villages."

"Right, okay, man, good to know. Uh...but, no...far as I know, everybody's dead."

I was staring at him blankly. I can't say I was thinking or processing. Just...sitting. *Everyone* was dead? Surely this hadn't happened in Puerto Rico.

Patrick walked back to me and reached a tentative hand toward my shoulder. I leaned away from him. "The good news," he said, "is that the survival rate just went up a lot."

"But...but there must be other people. They're probably sheltering somewhere. Maybe the high school? Did they announce a shelter location? We need to go into town. That's where everyone will be. At the police station maybe or town hall or the church."

"Franklin, I'm sorry, dude. But I live in town. I've been there most of the last few weeks, looking for other survivors. There's no one. A couple days ago, I started scouting around the outlying areas. And now I've found you! I'm sure there will be others now too. But, you know, no police or ambulance, no. And no shelter location either. I've been to all the schools; they're empty."

I collapsed back onto the sofa. I sat on the DVD case. "Ouch. Fuck!" I reached behind me and pulled the case out. "This wasn't mine." That was a stupid thing to say. I knew that. Nothing made sense right then. I felt myself slipping deep into my head, withdrawing, which I do sometimes. It's called a shutdown, and it's only triggered when I'm really stressed, but I hate it when it happens. It makes me feel so out of control.

I also realized I was rocking back and forth a little, which I hated even more. At least I wasn't making "the sound." Patrick started crying. He turned toward me and opened his arms.

"No," I said, sinking back into the sofa, as far from him as possible, chin tucked tightly against my chest. "No, no, no."

"Okay, right. Got it, dude. No touching. That's cool."

Chapter Four

"You got a helmet?"

"A helmet?" I asked, trying to make sense of the question. I think I'd shut down for a few minutes, but it hadn't been a long shutdown, because Patrick didn't look like anything seriously off had happened. Still, I knew I hadn't been paying attention and was only slowly returning to what was happening around me in the room. Patrick had gotten up and walked to the picture window. Was he looking at Mrs. Knudson or just thinking? He suddenly tapped his knuckle against the glass, twice, and then turned to look at me.

He took a few steps toward me and bent over to stare intently into my eyes. "Right. Okay. You look better now. So, you should have a helmet if you're going to ride on the back of my bike. We're heading into town."

Oh. I hadn't considered what would happen next. I thought once someone showed up, everything would get back to normal. But, from what Patrick was telling me, that wasn't going to happen, at least not anytime soon. And I couldn't stay here forever. I had to resupply. I was down to just a few cans of beans and the soups I didn't like. Why had my parents bought cream of asparagus soup, anyway?

But still, going outside with Patrick? Riding on a motorcycle? No. "You said so yourself, there's no place to go. And I can't just leave. I want to be here when my parents get back."

He was quiet for a moment, thinking. "I didn't say there's no place to go. I have a nice setup at the library. You should come with me." He waited for me to respond. I frowned, considering.

"I don't think so. I think I'll just get some more food and come back here."

"There's plenty to read at the library," Patrick offered. "It'd be something to do." When I didn't react, he sighed, turned back toward the window, and began drumming his fingers against the glass. I was sure he was leaving smudges. He didn't turn to look at me when he said, "She's not the only one, you know."

"The only one who died? I know; you said that."

"No. She's not the only body." Patrick turned, putting Mrs. Knudson behind him, and looked at me. "The only dead body, I mean, just lying out in the open. There's a lot of them." He held my gaze intently, waiting for me to say something. For the first time, I noticed his rich, amber-colored eyes.

"Still. I think I just want to come back after I stock up on food."

"Okay. We can come back if you want to. Just come into town with me."

"Can't we drive? My Jeep's destroyed, but I know Mrs. Knudson has an SUV in her garage. We could probably find the keys."

"No. The roads aren't clear."

"Oh. From the ice storm?"

"Yes...and other things."

Right. "It's only ten miles. I could walk and meet you there."

Patrick let out a frustrated grunt. "Franklin, you don't want to walk through all that."

All that? I hesitated. I didn't really know him; plus, I was nervous about motorcycles.

He grinned. "Tell you what...I'll give you ten dollars if you come with me into town."

"Ten dollars? What...?"

"I thought you'd like that sort of thing. Older men offering to pay younger men to...*do things*." He winked.

Ugh. I didn't respond to his comment. Instead, I realized I could take my bike, and I told him that. But I hadn't used it since last summer, so I'd probably have to put air in the tires and find the chain oil.

Patrick just looked at me, waiting.

"Fine," I said. "We'll go together on your motorcycle. I have a bicycle helmet in the garage."

"Great! Go get it."

*

I practiced sitting on the back of the motorcycle, parked, as Patrick wobbled back and forth, just to give me the feel of it. We made our way very slowly down the dirt road to the state highway, where we stopped. Patrick cut the engine.

"Hop off for a minute," he said.

I did, and Patrick pointed down the road, toward town. I looked where he indicated and suddenly understood why we couldn't drive. A big pileup blocked both lanes, and many cars had been abandoned behind it and on the shoulders too.

"It's the same mess on the other side. I almost couldn't get my bike through the gaps." He was looking at me intently, assessing my reaction. "It must have happened just as everybody was getting sick at the same time. There doesn't seem to be any evidence of an attempt to clear the wreck."

The last hour had been information overload for me, and I don't think I'd let much of it sink in. Seeing this began to make it real though. The pieces were coming together for me now.

"There are dead bodies in there, aren't there?"

He was still looking me in the eyes, ready, I think, to grab hold of me if necessary. "Yes. Quite a few."

"And that's why I wouldn't want to walk into town, right?"

"One of the reasons, yes." He was squinting into the sun, and the light picked out golden highlights in his deep-red hair.

I thought for a moment and looked back up the dirt road to my house. Only one way forward, I guess.

"You good?" he asked.

I nodded to him. My bicycle helmet wobbled awkwardly on my head.

"Okay. If you need me to stop, or if you feel like you're going to get sick or faint or something, just tell me. Punch my arm or something if I can't hear you over the engine. I recommend you just keep your eyes closed as we go through that section. Okay?"

I nodded again and swung back onto the bike. I settled in behind him, feeling uncomfortable with my legs wrapped around him and my crotch pressed into his ass.

He slid the visor of his helmet down and turned his head partway around so I could hear him. "One more thing," he said. "We'll be going a little faster now that we're on the highway." I could hear the laughter in his voice as he followed that with "I'll pay you twenty-five dollars if you wrap your arms around my chest and hold on." Before I could respond, he started the engine and we were off.

He was right about the accident scene. I closed my eyes and leaned my head sideways against his shoulder, my arms wrapped tightly around his chest. Given the circumstances, I didn't mind the physical contact too much. We wove slowly back and forth as he picked his way through the wreckage. I tried not to think about it.

Eventually, we picked up some speed and steadied out. He nudged me with an elbow. I took that as an "all clear" sign and opened my eyes again. There were still abandoned cars and trucks here and there, and plenty of downed limbs from the ice storm that had never been cleared. Fifteen minutes later, we reached the Highway 6 intersection, the retail center of Northwood and the surrounding towns. It's where the big box shops were and a few chain restaurants too. Home Depot, Staples, Pets World, McDonalds, Denny's. Wait! Pets World.

We were through the intersection and continuing on Highway 27 into town. I nudged Patrick's side. When he didn't respond, I risked unlinking my arms and punched him lightly in the bicep. After another minute I knocked forcefully on his helmet. He raised his arm in acknowledgement and slowly brought the bike to a stop. He cut the engine and removed his helmet. We both got off.

We'd stopped right next to an urgent care clinic, and there were several bodies sprawled across the parking lot. I looked away from them as I confronted Patrick. "What the hell? You said you'd stop when I signaled."

He got off the bike and took off his helmet. "What?"

"Why didn't you stop when I asked you to?"

"Because I was hoping you wouldn't do this." He placed the helmet on the bike's seat and crossed his arms.

"Do what?" I asked.

"What you're about to do. Go ahead; tell me why you wanted to stop."

"We need to go back. We passed a Pets World back there."

"Yep." He rubbed his face with one hand, then tilted his chin up. "Shit. Go on. What about it?"

"Well, people board dogs there when they go away. There could be abandoned pets there."

"And...?"

"What do you mean 'and'? We need to go back and rescue them." I thought that would be obvious. Why was Patrick taking so long to figure this out?

"No one's been in that store for over two weeks."

"You don't know that; a staff member could have survived. Like we did. They could be in there now even."

"Then we don't have anything to worry about, right?"

Why was he fighting me on this? It's just so obvious. "Okay, look. Even if there is no one there, they might have put down plenty of food and water when they realized what was happening. They would have assumed *someone* would be back eventually."

"Dammit. You *would* come up with that, wouldn't you?" He leaned back against the bike, as if settling in for a while. "Go on. Play it out."

Play it out? What the hell? "We go in the store, and we rescue the dogs." I felt like I was talking to a five-year-old.

Patrick sighed. "How do we get in the store?"

"Maybe it's open." Before he could counter that, I rushed on, "Or maybe we break in."

"How?"

"Smash out a glass door with rocks, maybe? Or ram a car into it?"

"Okay. Now we're getting somewhere." Patrick pointed back toward the intersection. "There were a lot of cars in those lots. A few of them might have keys in them."

"Right!" I said, relieved to see him coming around.

"Of course, the ones with keys probably have a passenger too. Plan on taking them for a ride or are we... excuse me...*you*, removing the body first?"

Oh. Well, still. "We'll see when we get there. We'd... *I'd*...only be in the car for a minute. I could probably stand it if I had to."

"So, okay, Franklin, keep going." Patrick was staring at me with a challenge in his eyes now. "You've buckled up the corpse so body parts don't go flying around when you ram the door, and you've managed to break in. Now what?"

"Uh...go unlock the cages and rescue the dogs." It was beginning to sound weak even to me.

"Are the lights on?" I looked at him blankly when he asked this.

"Lights?" I repeated.

"Yes, Franklin, *lights*. You know...so you can *see*?" He was getting angry now, and I was beginning to get an idea where this was going. "There's no windows or anything; it'll be pitch black in there. How are you going to find the dogs, and the keys to their cages, assuming they're not electric?"

"Okay, I get it." I said, starting to get angry myself. "But help me out here. Help me plan. Maybe we break into Home Depot first and grab a flashlight or something. Why are you being such a dick about this?"

Patrick reached forward and grabbed me by the shoulders, almost, but not quite, painfully. "Franklin," he said, exasperation clear in his voice. His eyes were damp. "They're *dead*. No one has been in there for weeks. Nothing can survive without water that long." He paused and took two deep breaths. "Please, let's just go."

"But..." I began, and Patrick interrupted me with a rough shake. "Don't...don't touch me."

He dropped his hands quickly.

"Fuck!" said Patrick. "I didn't want to do this. Not yet. Jesus. Do you think I haven't thought of this already? I've been out in this mess for almost three weeks. Listen. Let's say, by some miracle, a staff member herded all the dogs into a big area and put down plenty of water and food."

Yes, of course, they could have done that. Someone would have known what was happening and done something like that. They wouldn't have known no one would be coming back. But, if Patrick had already figured that out, why was he fighting me on this? I had that sinking feeling that I was missing something important. It happens to me pretty often.

"And let's say you managed to get in there, find your way to the dogs, and unlock the cage. Then what?" Patrick wiped his face with his arm and sniffed noisily. He was crying again now, but trying to hide it. I was getting confused and scared.

I knew what I was supposed to do in these situations. Dr. Levy said I should slow down and focus on my breath. Once I was calm, I should pay attention to what the other person is saying, and see if there are "context clues" I might be missing. "Stop, breathe, and think," he called it.

But I couldn't bring myself to do any of that.

"We'd just let them go." I said, although that seemed kind of cruel in its own way, now that I thought about it. Many house pets wouldn't last long on their own, and they'd already be weakened after a week or more in the darkness, surrounded by their own filth, little or no food or water left.

Through his tears, Patrick asked, "What will they eat, Franklin?"

I hadn't really gotten that far. Maybe I could open some of the bags of dog food, put them on the ground. But they'd need water, too, which I guess they could find outside.

"I...I'm not sure..." I began, feeling overwhelmed and afraid of shutting down out in the open.

Patrick moved to grab my shoulders but stopped when he saw me flinch. "Turn around!" he commanded, and I did, which forced me to confront the dead bodies in the parking lot of the urgent care office. I thought of Mrs. Knudson and the way she'd been dragged down her porch steps.

"What will they eat, Franklin?!"

Oh. With a dizzying rush it all fell into place. The finality of the situation. Its irreversibility. No one was going to turn the power back on, or the lights. The water would stop flowing from the taps. And no one was coming to remove the dead bodies. No. They will be food for animals, wild...or domestic.

I sank to the side of the road. Bits of gravel and stone dug into my wrist.

Patrick knelt in front me. His hands fumbled as he unhooked my helmet's chin strap. He lifted it carefully off my head and placed it on the ground. He smoothed my hair, and I pulled away.

"I'm sorry, Franklin," he whispered into my ear, again and again, not quite touching me, as I rocked gently back and forth.

*

I don't know how long we were sitting on the edge of the highway, me rocking back and forth.

Eventually, Patrick's murmurings turned into actual words. "Are you okay?" he asked, looking into my eyes, searching for a sign from me that I understood him. I thought maybe he'd done this a few times already.

"It's a lot, I know," he continued, after I'd blinked at him and nodded. "I mean, I saw everything unfold in real time. You're just kind of getting hit with it all at once." He looked back toward the intersection with the Pets World. "I'm not a monster though, you know? I mean, I did think about the options too. It's hard, but I can't stand to think about packs of dogs, pets really, going around eating the bodies." He stared at me intently with a questioning look in his eyes. "And, honestly, three weeks with no water? Nothing's been alive in that building for a while."

I took a deep, cleansing breath and nodded. I believed him. Or at least I chose to.

Then he said, "Well, maybe the turtles."

I froze for a second. He sat perfectly still, looking at me expectantly, cautiously. I couldn't help it; I laughed. Not that there's anything funny about dead and dying turtles. I know it was adrenaline and nerves and shock and emotional exhaustion. But I laughed, and it felt good to do it too. Patrick smiled, relieved.

"Good. Good," he said, reaching to rub my shoulder, then catching himself and stopping before I had to object. Patrick was a toucher. I'd have to remember that and learn to accept it when I could. "We're going to be okay, Franklin. We are." He stood and reached a hand out to help me up. I let him, feeling only somewhat uncomfortable at the touch. I brushed the grit off my legs and winced at the abrasion on my wrist.

"It's just a couple more miles into town," he said. "There's nothing too gruesome between here and there. Why don't we walk the rest of the way? It'll help you work

off some of the adrenaline, and it'll be good to talk more."
I thought walking sounded like an excellent idea and
agreed.

"But what about your motorcycle?" I asked.

"It's not really 'mine,'" he replied, making air quotes
with his fingers. "I can always come back for it, or just pick
up another one. There's plenty around." We shouldered
our backpacks and picked up our helmets. "Maybe we can
find you a bright-green Vespa," he said, nudging my
shoulder with his as we set off.

It felt good to walk. We set a leisurely pace. The sun
warmed my back, and it had been dry enough lately that
mud season was behind us. It was shockingly quiet, except
for the birds. I'd never noticed the variety and complexity
of birdsong before.

"It's April already, you know." Patrick said.

I hadn't been paying attention to the calendar, but as
I looked around I saw little shoots of green.

"Listen," Patrick said. "I know this a lot to take in all
at once, and I hate to say it, but there's more to come. Just
different things that will suddenly strike you. And it's okay
to be overwhelmed when that happens." He paused so he
could look at me, and I stopped walking and turned to face
him, listening.

"But I just want to say I'm really glad I found you. I
was afraid I was the only one, you know? You don't know
what that's like. Walking through a totally empty world,
thinking you might be the last person alive. So, what I
mean is, don't leave me, okay? Whatever happens, we'll
make it work, you know?"

"Okay. Sure." Where was I going to go anyway? I didn't know what would happen, and now I wasn't even sure I wanted to simply go back home. Why stay there? Except that's where my parents will go if...*when*...they make it back.

"Puerto Rico's an island. It's possible this didn't happen there, right?" I asked.

"I don't know. Why?"

"That's where my parents are."

"Oh. Well, I don't know, Franklin, but before everything stopped for good, the news was pretty grim. I hope they're okay though. Maybe if nobody infected got to the island...?" he trailed off and wouldn't look at me as he said this. He began rubbing his fingertips against each other. I suspected this was important body language for him, but had no way of understanding what it meant.

We continued walking, then stopped at a drug store just as we entered town. "Come on. This one's open. I've been inside already, and there's no bodies." He opened the door and motioned for me to wait. Immediately inside the doorway, he stooped and picked up a flashlight. "I left this here. It's a lot darker toward the back. Come on." He held the door open for me and stepped inside. "Don't worry. It won't lock," he said, as the door closed behind us.

He turned his light on and shined it down a long hallway as we began to head in that direction. "What are we doing?" I asked in a whisper.

He laughed. "I understand the urge—" He chuckled. "—really I do, but there's no need to whisper."

Of course not. Still, it felt like we were committing a crime, sneaking around in a dark, closed store. It was hard for me to speak at a normal volume, but I tried. "Why are we here?"

"Two reasons," he said as he passed his beam across the overhead signs indicating what products were in each aisle. He paused on aisle ten—first aid—and led us that way. "First, we need to clean up your wrist. After we do that, I'm going to lecture you on never allowing yourself to get cut or scraped again. It's dangerous, although I guess we can figure out which antibiotics to use if we had to. Best to be avoided though."

We stopped midway down the aisle. He played the light beam across the shelves for a minute before he found what he was looking for. He picked up a small bottle of rubbing alcohol and uncapped it, then removed the safety seal. "Do you mind if I hold your wrist for a second?" I was pleased he thought to ask. I held my hand out to him, and he turned my arm so my palm was facing up. With his other hand, he shined the light on my abrasion, lightly blowing on my skin to remove tiny pieces of dirt. "Not too bad," he said. He gripped my arm tight, tilted the bottle, and said, "This is going to hurt," at the same time as he poured the alcohol over my wrist.

"Jesus!" I exclaimed. That *did* hurt. Christ. "How about a little warning next time?"

"Why? Do you enjoy anticipating pain?"

He peered closely at the wound with the flashlight, turning my wrist side to side. It still stung something fierce, but the immediate shock was fading. "Good," he concluded after his inspection. "Now we'll spray some Bactine on it and get it bandaged." We proceeded down the aisle, found the antiseptic spray and bandages, and he finished fixing me up.

We made our way back to the front of the store. Patrick grabbed something small off a shelf in the party supplies aisle. I grabbed a large bottle of water from a darkened refrigerator case. He pointed to the shelves below the register. "Those candy bars aren't going to keep forever, you know." I stocked up on Skittles while he grabbed a few chocolate bars.

"You said there were two reasons we came in here. Other than doctoring me, what's the other one?"

"I'm glad you asked," he replied, smiling broadly now. He leaned in close and looped an arm across my shoulder.

"No. No, too much," I said, and he immediately removed his arm.

But he kept his head right next to mine and whispered, "See that magazine rack back there? I'll give you twenty dollars if you go steal a porn mag for me."

"Asshole," I said. "This is going to be a thing, isn't it?"

"This is *totally* going to be a thing, yes," he replied, grinning happily, bobbing his head up and down. "In fact, it already is. Nothing you can do about it now. And hey, like I said, I'm not judging. You be you, dude. What goes on at the end of the world stays at the end of the world."

Before leaving the store, he turned off the flashlight and left it on the floor just inside the door, which he closed behind us, giving it a good tug. "To make sure animals don't get in," he explained.

We made our way down Main Street to the library, the *scritch* of dead leaves blowing along the sidewalk the only sound.

Chapter Five

The Northwood Public Library was an elegant redbrick Victorian structure, with decorative white stone molding draped over the windows and large granite blocks lining the corners. I'd spent a lot of time here as a kid and knew a little bit about its history. It had been expanded several times, including an ugly glass and concrete addition built in the 1970s that connected it to the town hall next door. Sometime in the early 1900s, a modest caretaker's cottage had been built onto the back.

As we got closer, I noticed that Patrick had set up a propane grill on the patio in front of the addition. I noticed something else too.

"What's that smell? It stinks." I wrinkled my nose.

"That, my friend, is the smell of decomposition. It's worse here by the police station, and it gets bad again down by the church. Seems like a lot of people ended up at those spots." He looked over at me as we hurried past the station. "At the end, I mean." As if that needed clarifying. "It's *really* bad by the hospital. But we don't need to go anywhere near there."

The stench began to fade as we got beyond the police station. The library was only a bit farther down the same block.

"Come on," Patrick said. "Let's hurry. The smell is hardly noticeable once we get inside. Plus, I have a surprise for you!"

We reached the library and climbed the wide marble steps to the entryway. After pushing open the door, Patrick bent and picked up a large battery-operated Coleman lantern and turned it on. He held the light up and motioned me in. Despite the oversized windows letting in ample sunlight, it was cold. *Cold as a morgue*, I thought and immediately shut that image down. But Patrick was right: I barely noticed the smell once inside.

"The library was closed the day everything started to fall apart, so no one was here," Patrick explained. "And unlike the hospital and the police station, nobody came here after they got sick. I lucked out—not having to deal with any bodies."

We were in the main reading room, with its mahogany tables and leather chairs. There were floor-to-ceiling bookshelves built into the walls. The white-painted ceiling was at least twenty feet overhead, and a catwalk circled the walls midway up, allowing access to the second level of books. An enormous 1800s fireplace dominated the far wall, and I could see glowing embers there. Off to the side of the main reading room was another large space, this one more modern and filled with stacks of bookshelves arranged in a dozen or so rows.

A wide area had been cleared in front of the fireplace, and Patrick had placed a mattress as well as a comfortable wing chair there. He'd managed to pull one of the large tables over next to it. "Let me get the fire going again," he said. "It warms the whole place up."

He led me across the room to the fireplace and placed the lantern on the table. "Drop your pack and make yourself at home. I'll just be a couple minutes." He began gathering kindling and small logs from a basket against the wall.

I'd often wondered what it would look like to have an actual blaze in that magnificent fireplace. I noticed with approval that he'd also found two fire extinguishers and had them at the ready, just in case.

I put my backpack on the floor and wandered over to the table to explore the small stack of books there. Patrick had selected an interesting collection of titles. There were academic studies, like *Ancient Burial Traditions* and *A History of Electricity*. But there was also fiction: *Into the Dark* was described as a postapocalyptic tale of survival after an EMP takes out the electric grid, and *Sister Wives* was billed as a fictional account of early Mormon settlers in Utah. I thought the cover illustration of two women in tight blouses working in a small kitchen, with a bedroom visible behind them, was a little cheesy. There was also a small booklet on wild edibles and a poster describing nonpoisonous mushrooms.

"That should do it," said Patrick, rising up from a crouch in front of the fire. He brushed his hands off on his pants and turned to me. Rekindled flames grew behind him, making his copper hair dance with subtle colors.

I held up *Sister Wives*. "Seriously?"

"Dude. I don't think you're in any position to criticize another guy's entertainment selections."

Ouch. This really *was* going to be a thing.

"This is a nice setup," I said. "I get why settling in at the library was a good idea."

"Yeah, I thought so. Plus, there's plenty to learn too."

He walked across the room and grabbed another wing chair, then dragged it over to the table. He opened a shallow drawer I hadn't noticed below the lip of the table and pulled out a couple of beef-jerky sticks and a bag of dried apple slices. "Here, have a snack. I'm going to make us a celebratory dinner later on. We'll start making plans after we eat."

I opened the apples and took one, letting it soften in my mouth before chewing. I hadn't had fruit for a while, and I savored the taste, tart and sweet at the same time. After a few more apple slices, I started in on a piece of salty jerky.

"Ready for your surprise?"

"Um...sure?"

"Cool! Come with me." He led us through the room with all the bookshelves. In the back corner of that room was a nondescript door painted to blend in with the white walls. It looked like it could conceal a janitor's closet or utility room. A No Entry sign was screwed into the top of the door frame. He opened the door and motioned me through. I was surprised to find myself in a tiny bedroom with two cots against the wall. One had a mattress and the other didn't.

"This is the caretaker's cottage. I don't think it's changed since it was built in the early 1900s. We're going through there." He indicated an open door across the room. "After you." He waved his arm to indicate I should go first.

I stepped into what looked like a museum reconstruction of a bathroom from a century ago. A toilet with a wooden seat sat underneath a wall-mounted tank with a pull chain. A tiny pedestal sink with two knobby faucets was squeezed into a corner, a rubber stopper dangling on a rusted metal chain over its edge. A small square table with shampoo and soap stood at the front of a clawfoot tub. An empty plastic bucket sat next to the table.

The tub dominated the room.

Patrick grinned so hard I thought his cheeks might break. "Here's the best part!" he exclaimed and walked to the tub. He cranked the faucet, and water began pouring out. Within seconds steam started swirling into the cold air.

"Holy shit!" I exclaimed.

"I know!" Patrick was bouncing on his toes. "There's an old gas boiler in the basement with a continuous pilot light. As long as there's gas, and water in the municipal tank, we'll have hot baths."

We had propane heat at home, but the pump and hot water heater required electricity to work. I hadn't had a shower in weeks, and I know I smelled. "Boy, do I need this."

"Yeah, you sort of do." He smiled to take the sting out of it. "Enjoy. Feel free to refill it as often as you like; I imagine the first tubful will get dirty fast. I need to take care of a few things, but I'll be back with a towel in a few. Oh, and make sure you clean your wrist; we'll rebandage it later." He left and shut the door behind him.

As the bathtub filled, I peeled out of my dirty clothes. For the last week, I'd been hesitant to use any water for washing myself. I was saving the bathtub water for flushing the toilet when it *absolutely* needed it, and the jugged water for drinking. I'd quickly run out of clean clothes the first week, and began cycling through my dad's clean underwear and shirts too. The last few days I'd resorted to reusing my least dirty shorts.

So, yeah, I needed this.

I tested the water temp, turned off the hot water, and added some cold. It felt strange being totally naked after so long, and in an unfamiliar room. I lifted one leg over the edge of the tub and stood, half in, half out, getting a sense of the temperature. It was maybe a little too hot, but the rim of the iron tub was still cold to the touch, so I decided not to wait.

I stepped all the way in and sank down, then lowered myself deeper so that only my head and knees were above the water. The heat seeped into me, and I could feel my muscles clenching, then relaxing.

I closed my eyes and leaned my head back against the high curve of the tub. The cold on my neck and shoulders was bracing. In less than a minute, the water turned a murky gray, little bits and pieces of stuff floated on the surface. Gross. I stretched my toes about until I found the rubber drain stopper and kicked it out of place, listening to the water gurgle down the old drainpipe.

After the tub was mostly empty, the last of the dirty water, more brown than gray, spiraling down the drain, I was shivering and couldn't wait any longer. I re-stopped the drain, turned on the hot water, and added bath gel.

The strong scent of—I checked the label: citrus and ginger—rose with the steam.

I lay back again, relaxed and relatively clean, and let my mind drift. Was it only this morning I had thought I might die if I stepped outside? I wasn't sure any longer if I wanted to go back to the house. It would be a lot of work to get food and water back there, especially considering the road conditions. Plus, Patrick had a nice setup here, what with the reading material, hot water, and food, and he didn't want to separate from me any more than I wanted to go back to being alone. Much easier to plan our next steps here at the library.

Our next steps. How quickly I'd begun to think of us a team.

After about twenty minutes, there was a knock on the door. "You still alive in there? Oh, sorry. That didn't sound right." Before I could respond, Patrick opened the door and stuck his head in. "I brought some stuff." Arms full, he pushed through the doorway and stepped into the small bathroom.

He was carrying folded towels and packages of clothes. "So, I have underwear, socks, sweats, a couple shirts, and a pair of jeans. I guessed at sizes. Jarret's is just down the block and has plenty of options. We can go back tomorrow and get you some proper clothing." He paused and seemed embarrassed. "Um...that is, assuming you're staying? Tonight, I mean. You did say you just wanted to stock up and head back—and we can still do that if you want. I just thought, tonight, you could have a nice meal and a bath and think about what you want to do in the morning."

He shifted back and forth, nervously gripping his packages.

"Yes, I'd like to stay tonight," I said. "Thanks. You have a nice setup here."

Patrick grinned and relaxed. "Excellent." He put the things down. "It's impossible to get your head low enough to rinse under the spigot. I know; I tried. So, we'll use the bucket." He picked up a bottle of shampoo from the floor and handed it to me. "Here, soap up your hair, and I'll help rinse."

I slipped low into tub to dunk my hair under the water, then took the shampoo and began lathering. "You can do the same for me when you're finished," Patrick said.

"I wasn't sure if you were a boxers or briefs guy," Patrick said, as he eyed my pile of dirty clothes on the floor. He poked at my discarded boxer shorts with his foot and grimaced. "Dude, we need to burn these! The good news is I guessed right."

He set everything down and picked up the bucket, then knelt at the front of the tub and started filling it. He added some hot water and then some cold, until he was satisfied with the temperature. "Ready?"

I leaned forward and bent my head, as Patrick began slowly pouring from the bucket while I massaged away the soap. "One more rinse," he said, and we repeated the process.

What a relief it was to have clean hair again. "Thanks," I said.

"No problem! Had enough? Ready to switch?"

I thought he'd leave me alone to dry off and dress, but instead he reached into the tub, unplugged the drain, and placed a towel on the edge for me. *Uh, no, too close.* I shrank back in the tub.

As the water was draining, he began to undress. He pulled off his hoodie and the black T-shirt underneath. He was more toned than I thought he'd be, and I'd expected tattoos but didn't see any. Although the hair on his head was dark auburn, his chest and belly were covered in a light golden fur. It reminded me of Tyler.

There was nothing left for me to do but to stand and begin drying off. I was vigorously rubbing my hair dry, head covered with the towel, when I heard Patrick say, "You clean up nice." I was used to being naked around other guys from gym class, but this was making me uncomfortable, like I was under inspection.

I carefully stepped out of the bath, using one hand on the high rim of the tub for balance, when Patrick bent and removed his white briefs. He turned, and I noticed the hair around his crotch was a shiny bright-copper color, wildly thick and curling. I found myself staring. "What?" Patrick asked. "You've never seen fiery orange pubes before?" He laughed, and added, "It's kind of weird, I know. I thought about dying it once, or even shaving it off, but that seems kind of...I don't know...gay." He paused, then added, "No offense."

No offense? What is that supposed to mean?

Tyler had carefully trimmed his pubic hair very short. He said it made his dick look bigger. An image of Tyler on that last night flashed into my mind, excited and ready, trying to get me to that same place.

"Hey, I was kidding. What's with the frown?"

I shook my head. "Sorry, I was distracted."

"It is pretty big, isn't it?" He winked and bent over to remove his socks. When I didn't respond, he said, "Okay, fine. Maybe not so much. But don't mock me, dude. It's cold in here."

As I finished drying, Patrick picked up a package of boxers and opened it. "Here," he said, selecting a pair of shorts from the assorted colors. "I think you should go with the blue and white checks. It'll bring out your eyes." He smiled. I really wasn't following what was going on here.

I felt myself begin to panic as I tended to do in situations I didn't understand.

I took the boxers from him and slipped them on.

"You're in good shape," he said. "What do you play? Football? Or maybe you're a wrestler?" I wanted to reply "gymnastics," because it was the truth, but I was already too uncomfortable with him being naked and commenting on my body.

"No. No sports." I reached for the sweatpants. Patrick had already removed the plastic tags. "How about you?" I asked, both to change the focus of this discussion, and because Dr. Levy always said asking about the other person was a good way forward if I was stuck.

He stepped into the tub, even though it wasn't even a third full yet, and sat. "Well, I'm six two, so I've always been pretty good at basketball." He leaned back and rested his head on the curved wall. The water was slowly rising up the sides of his body. No, this was too much. Everything was running together in my head. The porn, Tyler, now this.

"Okay...well...um...I'm heading back to the fireplace now." I quickly gathered up the rest of my new clothes and hurried out. On my way, I remembered that I was supposed to help Patrick wash his hair, but I kept going.

Chapter Six

After our baths, Patrick prepared a meal for us. He hadn't mentioned anything about my awkward departure from the bathroom or asked why I hadn't gone back to help him wash his hair.

"Why don't we just have chips and salsa or something? There's so much food around. Why bother going through the effort to cook?" I wasn't being critical. I was honestly curious.

"Well, nutrition, for one thing. We need to remain healthy and strong for whatever's ahead. A junk food diet would make us sick soon enough."

I didn't have any thoughts about the future, which was odd, because I usually planned out *everything*. It was beginning to sink in for me that things wouldn't be going back to normal. But beyond that, I had no vision about what might happen next. How would I be reunited with my parents? How could we learn where we should go—someplace where the power was still on and people hadn't died? How would we travel there once we knew where to go?

"And for another thing, dentists," Patrick added.

I pulled my attention back to our conversation. "Dentists?" I repeated.

"Yes. There aren't any. So we have to be careful about our teeth. All those starchy, processed foods are sticky and cause cavities." I thought about the packets of Skittles I'd picked up at the drug store. "If you haven't learned how to floss yet, now's the time." Patrick looked at me. "You don't want me having to pull your teeth out, man."

That made sense, but it was concerning that he was thinking in such, I don't know, *long-term* ways. I mean, I didn't know how this was all going to end. But it *would* pass eventually. It had to. We'd find our way back to dentists and electricity and other people. Somehow.

"But hey, let's have dinner first; then we can talk about what to do next. Sound good?"

Dinner was chicken vegetable soup made from freeze-dried chicken. Patrick had prepared it in a pot on the grill out front. It didn't taste at all artificial, like the canned stuff sometimes does. The broth was rich and not too salty, and the vegetables were crisp and flavorful. "How did you do this?" I asked. "It's delicious."

"Plenty more where that came from. And it'll keep forever. You know that camping supply store just north of town?" Patrick asked.

"You mean the one where rich people from Boston come up to spend a thousand dollars on supplies for a weekend in the woods?"

He laughed. "Yes! Exactly. That one. They have all sorts of useful things: gas stoves, waterproof gear, fishing equipment, tents of course. And food. Lots and lots of prepackaged dried food. Organic, vegan, gluten free—you name it. And they just stocked up ahead of the summer season. So eat up!"

I did. I went back for seconds, and then thirds. We also had wheat crackers and blocks of sliced cheese. Patrick said it had been cold enough on the north patio of the library to keep the cheese fresh in a big cooler, and he thought it might last for a couple more weeks. There were eggs in there, too, and bacon.

"One more surprise?" he asked, after we'd finished eating and pushed our plates to the side.

I was full and content, basking in the warmth of the fire. "Go for it," I said.

He went outside and a minute later came back in with two plates. "This has been in the cooler box too. It's gone stale, but it still tastes good." He placed the plates on the table in front of us. On each plate was an enormous slice of a dark chocolate cake, covered in a thick raspberry glaze.

Mine had a lit candle in it.

"Happy birthday," he said.

Was it my birthday? I hadn't been paying attention. But now that I thought about it, it seemed right. "But, how...?"

"It was on your refrigerator calendar. Go ahead." He nodded at the candle. "Make a wish."

I hated this part. We didn't do it anymore at my house. What was a *wish* anyway? A hope that things would be different somehow? Why make one? It made no sense; I can't change how the world is.

Patrick must have sensed my confusion. He licked two fingers and reached forward, and pinched out the flame. "A silly tradition anyway, and, well, considering the circumstances…" he said.

"But take a bite," he urged, handing me a fork. "You won't have anything like this again for a while. Tell me what you think."

I broke a piece off with my fork and tasted it. "Wow" was all I could say.

We spent a few minutes absorbed in the cake.

"But what about our teeth?" I asked, licking velvety raspberry heaven off the back of my fork.

"Dude, we're celebrating tonight. It's not every day you go from being the last person on earth to finding a new friend."

I'm not sure why, but I blushed.

*

After dinner, we settled into the armchairs by the fire.

"Before we start talking about what's next. I wanted you to know…well, total honesty here…I'm hoping you don't *really* want to go back to your house." Before I could respond, he rushed on. "We can absolutely do that if you want. Tomorrow even, first thing, if you still want to." He stopped, looking down at his hands as he twisted them in his lap.

"To be honest," I said, "I don't feel as strongly about it as I did this morning. But now I wish I'd brought a few things with me…"

Patrick let out a breath he'd been holding. "Okay, good. Good. Then I hope you don't mind, but I thought, well, I'd *hoped* you might feel that way once you got here.

So, when you went off to find your bicycle helmet, I grabbed a few things I thought you might want, if, you know, you didn't end up going back there."

Hmm. That sounded...what? Presumptuous, I guess. Maybe a little creepy.

"Oh?" I asked.

"Hold on, hold on. Stay right there." He hurried to his pack on the other side of the room. "And don't be angry," he called to me over his shoulder as he stooped to pick it up and then headed back. "I promise, I'll take them all back tomorrow if this turns out to be a mistake."

I waited expectantly as he sat down again and opened his bag. He pulled out a framed picture. I recognized it right away. It normally sat on the mantel over our woodstove. Me, Mom, and Dad the summer before last on the Freedom Trail in Boston, the Paul Revere House behind us. My dad was wearing a Red Sox cap, and my mom had a bright-pink hat with LOBSTAH written on it over a cartoon picture of a smiling crustacean. I looked mildly embarrassed.

"You look very preppy in your button-down shirt and chinos," Patrick said.

"It was warm that day," I mumbled. I'd been sixteen and just started getting into gymnastics in a big way. I'd been building muscle fast and proud of my new body.

Patrick placed the picture on the table. "I just thought it would be nice for you to have this, in case...you know...you decide to stay here." It was...thoughtful?...I guess, but still a little odd that he had rummaged around my house going through my stuff. He leaned over his bag again. "And this one too," he said, pulling out another picture.

Oh. Me and Tyler. I was younger here, thirteen maybe, and Tyler and I were wading in a shallow, rock-strewn river in New Hampshire. We were both in our swim trunks, not boys any longer, but not yet the young men we would become. Tyler was smiling in a goofy way, and his blond hair was soaked, plastered to his head, looking almost brown and hanging down into his eyes. I was frowning slightly, looking at Tyler, not at the camera. I looked puzzled, as if I was trying to figure us out, even back then.

"Is this your brother?"

"No. No, he's my...friend."

"Boyfriend?"

I was silent. I wasn't ready to give up thinking of him in that way, even though we hadn't actually ever gotten to the boyfriend stage.

Patrick must have been troubled by the look on my face. "Well," he said, picking up the picture of me and Tyler, "let's just put this one away for now."

He put it back in the bag. "Just one more," he said, pulling something else from the bag. "Although we have a lot of DVDs here at the library, there's nothing quite like...this!" he exclaimed, lifting Tyler's porn DVD and waving it about. "I mean, I know it's important to you, since you chose to spend the last of your battery power watching it, rather than, say, going through your photos or something like that." He lowered the case and studied the cover. "I have to say, not my scene at all, you know? But, again, not judging here."

I felt my face heating, as much from anger as from embarrassment. I grabbed the DVD and threw it across the room. Distantly, I heard Doctor Levy's voice in my mind—"Try to catch the emotion before it catches you, Franklin"—but I wasn't willing to listen to him.

"Stop." My voice was loud, quivering. "I told you; it wasn't mine. It was—" I nodded to the backpack on the floor. "—his." I blew out a deep breath. "We were watching it the night...the night everything...fell apart. And it didn't go well, and I'm still trying to figure out what the hell is wrong with me...and what the hell is happening with...*everything*..." I was getting more upset now.

"I just don't want...I don't want"—I wasn't sure how to finish the thought. But I heard myself say—"to be made fun of." That was pathetic. I could feel my face pulsing with emotion. And I realized I was rocking slightly.

Oh no. This would be a horrible time to lose control, to shut down, or worse, *melt* down.

Don't; don't. Please. It had been years since I'd had a bad one. I thought they were behind me. But this was the third time since I'd met Patrick that I could feel myself beginning to lose control. I sat there, breathing heavily, concentrating on my control. Patrick looked stunned.

"I'm sorry, Franklin. Really. I was trying...well, I thought...shit. I don't know. I'm an asshole."

"Yeah," I said. But after a minute or two the moment passed, and I'd gotten through it, more in less in control, still aware of my actions. I was getting better at this, but it had been a close call.

"I need to be alone right now," I said.

We didn't get to do any planning that night. We were both a little thrown by my reaction, I think. We were cautious with each other. I browsed the bookshelves and settled into my chair with a short mystery novel. Patrick spent some time writing in a journal. "Do you want to play cards?" he asked.

"No," I replied and, to take some of the sting out the rejection, "I'm exhausted. As you saw. I think I just need to go to sleep."

"Yeah, Good. That's good, man. I'll go get the other mattress and pull it in here where it's warm. There's a new toothbrush for you in the bathroom."

*

Much later, sometime in the middle of the night, Patrick got up to tend to the fire. He poked the embers about, then slipped a new log on top of the coals. He stood there, silhouetted by the orange glow, waiting until the wood caught; then he slid back onto his mattress. I listened to the hissing and popping for a few moments.

"Patrick?" I whispered.

"Yeah?"

"Thank you," I said. "For everything. For finding me, for helping me through all this."

"Sure," he replied. "Thanks for being alive."

I was quiet for a minute. "It's a lot, you know, all of this," I continued. "And you were right; taking it in all at once was overwhelming. I'm sorry I freaked out about the porn thing."

Patrick rolled onto his side and looked at me for a moment. Then he stood and walked over to my mattress. He knelt next to me and put a hand on my shoulder. "Is this okay?" he asked, indicating his hand. He was learning how to deal with me. We were each learning, I think.

"Yes, thanks for asking. I'm getting better with you. About touching, I mean. You're not a complete stranger anymore."

It was dark, but I could feel his body relax, and his hand rested more comfortably on me. "And, Franklin, no. That's all my fault. I'm the one who should apologize. I just... I was so *afraid*, you know? Of being completely alone. Forever." I couldn't see his face clearly with the fire behind him. But his voice broke a little, and he wiped at his eyes. "And then I found you, and I was so...*happy*. I know, weird, right? How could I be happy in the middle of all this? But I was and relieved. And I wanted—no—I *needed* you to like me and to want to stick with me because I was terrified of being alone again." He sniffed loudly. "Still am. Jesus, I'm a mess."

"Patrick..." I began, but he cut me off.

"No. Wait. I need to say this. The thing is, when I found you and you were so embarrassed about the stupid porn, I just wanted to make sure you knew it was all okay with me, you know? That your being gay is fine. But then I blew it by trying to make a big joke about it even after I saw it was making you uncomfortable. I'm sorry, man. I really am.

"The thing is," Patrick continued, "you're doing something weird to my head that just doesn't happen to me. I don't respond to people like this. I mean, I'm ace. Gray ace, I'm pretty sure, but still..." He trailed off, wiping at his eyes.

I tried to follow what he was saying, but I couldn't. None of what he'd said made any sense. Plus, the crying needed to stop.

"It's very confusing," he said. "Sorry. I'm not making sense. I'll explain it when I figure it out myself. I just want you to know I'm grateful you're here...with me. I feel like we've bonded somehow. I didn't mean to freak you out."

Even I could see how upset he was, and I felt bad for him.

I sat up and—*You can do this; come on, Franklin*—touched him on his shoulder. "It's okay, Patrick, honestly. I don't care about the porn jokes. It was just...everything all at once, you know?" He nodded, and I went on. "I'm glad you found me too. We'll get through this together." I felt him let out a quiet sob. I'd been alone, too, but I hadn't known everyone else had died. I couldn't imagine what those weeks must have been like for him, watching it happen, all the while not knowing *why*. Why had he been spared when everyone around him had died? He stayed on my mattress, sitting cross-legged, our knees touching. "Can I tell you something...personal?" I asked.

"You can tell me *anything*, Franklin."

I took a deep breath and let it out slowly. I wanted to explain to him about the porn. "The thing is," I began, "it really *wasn't* my porn."

"Oh, but I'd never..."

I raised a hand. "Shut up, Patrick. It's my turn now."

"Right. Right. Sorry." He mimed locking his lips.

"Anyway, Tyler—he's the boy in the picture—wanted to watch it because he wanted the two of us to do stuff together on camera for that guy. His cousin told him the guy pays lots of money to film other guys...um...young guys, doing things with each other."

"Gross," said Patrick before he remembered he'd promised not to speak and clamped his hand over his mouth.

I smiled. "I know, right? The thing is...well, I always thought Tyler and I might become boyfriends someday, and I was ready to see if it might be able to happen. That night, I mean." Patrick reached his hand toward me. I thought he was going to touch me on the shoulder, but he pulled back.

I took another breath. "But then he wanted to watch porn, and he was"—I could feel myself blushing in the darkness—"really...um...*excited*, you know? And into it? And, crap, this is the hard part...or, I guess, *not* the hard part." I giggled nervously, then stopped abruptly. I was starting to lose it. *Focus, Franklin; finish this.* "Anyway, I just didn't get it, the porn part, you know? No, you probably don't. Everyone else seems into it, but...there's something wrong with me." My words were coming faster now, spilling out of me in a rush. "And I don't know what it is, and I've been trying to figure it out, and..." I was interrupted by two fingers placed against my lips.

"Shh. It's okay. You're fine. Perfect." He leaned forward and placed a slow, chaste kiss on my lips. "Go to sleep now. You have nothing to worry about." He stood and walked back to his mattress.

I was suddenly exhausted. I closed my eyes and realized, right before drifting off, I'd had my first kiss from a boy.

Chapter Seven

The next morning, things were good between us. Patrick made bacon with eggs fried in lots of butter. "Won't keep forever," he'd said. I agreed we'd stick together, for now, at least, until we could think through a plan on what to do next.

"First things first, though," Patrick said after we'd finished eating. "Let's get you some new clothes and good walking shoes."

I wasn't looking forward to going outside. Every time Patrick opened the door to the patio while making breakfast, a reminder of the stink waiting for us came drifting in.

"The good news is it's sort of warm out there today," he said. "You've probably figured out from the smell what the bad news is. But here." He handed me a small round jar. "Put a thick swipe of this under your nose."

I looked at the jar and saw it was a petroleum vapor rub.

"It'll help mask the odor," he said. "And put this on too," he instructed, handing me a blue surgical mask. After we both had our masks on, we headed out the door.

Once we were on the porch, Patrick turned back and stooped to place a lantern just inside the doorway on the floor. He stood and was closing the door behind us when we heard a woman calling out from across the street. "Franklin? Franklin Marshall?"

The voice sounded familiar, but it wasn't until I turned and saw the slight Japanese American woman that I recognized her. "Mrs. Nakamura?" I called. She was our high school's counselor; I'd spent many hours over the last few years in her office, working with her on my coping mechanisms and social skills. She wore jeans and a heavy waterproof jacket. She wore a surgical mask, too, and...was that...? Yes, she held a gun in her right hand, hanging in a nonthreatening way at her side, but still.

Patrick and I both froze in shock. At seeing another survivor, yes, but at the gun too.

Patrick recovered first. "Hello, Mrs. Nakamura," he called out. "I don't know if you remember me. I'm—"

She cut him off. "I remember you, Mr. Larson."

"Franklin," she called, "can you come over and have a word with me for a minute, please?"

Patrick gripped my bicep and tightened his fingers, holding me in place. This was not good touching. I tried to tug my arm away from him, but he held on.

"Why are you carrying a gun, Mrs. Nakamura?" he asked, pitching his voice too loud, as if she were a block away rather than just across the street.

"You can't be too careful," she responded. "I saw a team of coyotes eating bodies north of town a couple of days ago. They'll start getting bolder soon enough. Plus—" She paused, as if considering whether to continue, and decided not to. "—just, can't be too careful."

"No," Patrick said, "you can't. I was excited to find Franklin yesterday. You know each other from school, I guess?"

"Yes, that's right. Franklin, come over here a minute, dear."

Patrick released his grip on my arm, which I took as permission. Not that I needed it, but I found this entire interaction very confusing. I looked at his face but could see nothing there explaining what was going on.

I crossed the street, stepping carefully around small piles of debris, and walked to Mrs. Nakamura.

"Can I hug you?" she asked.

She knew to ask, of course, and I was pretty good with her. But I didn't want anyone touching me. I was already upset. "Not now, please."

If I disappointed her, she didn't show it, or at least I wasn't able to see it. Instead, she leaned in, lightly resting a hand on my arm, and said, "I'm so very glad you're alive, dear. Have you been with Patrick long?"

"No, just since yesterday. He found me at my house. I didn't know what had happened until he showed up. I thought we were still sheltering in place. My parents left for Puerto Rico the morning everything started. I don't know when they'll get back now."

She didn't respond. Instead, she glanced across the street to where Patrick still stood, waiting for me. "Did Patrick tell you what happened? I mean, how extensive it is?"

"He said no one really knows."

She frowned, then let her hand drift back to her side. "And how *are* you, dear? How are you handling...

everything?" Mrs. Nakamura knew I saw Dr. Levy regularly, and I think they sort of worked together to help me perform at school.

"I'm doing fine. In fact, Dr. Levy even suggested we cut back on our appointments. You don't need to worry about me. Besides," I continued, gesturing to the scene around us, "it hardly matters what's 'normal' and what's not anymore, right?"

"That's right, dear." She lowered her voice to a whisper. "And that young man over there, Patrick Larson, he hasn't...hurt you...has he? He's not forcing you to stay with him?" She looked into my eyes, as if I might lie to her.

"What? No. No, of course not. He's been really kind. He's taking care of me." I glanced over at Patrick. He was frozen in place, but leaning forward, toward us. He clearly didn't like not being able to hear what we were talking about.

"Everything okay, Franklin?" he called.

"Yes," I said, at the same time Mrs. Nakamura did too.

"Do you want to come with me?" she asked, quickly. "I've found a nice spot outside of town with solar power. I don't like being around all these bodies."

Patrick's patience had run out, and he was coming across the street now at a fast walk.

"No, thank you. I want to stay with Patrick, but you'd be welcome to join us?" This last I asked as a question since Patrick had arrived at my side.

"Of course, she's welcome," Patrick said as he casually draped an arm across my shoulder. I shrugged it off. "Sorry," Patrick whispered to me, removing his arm. "Can you at least stay for a meal, Mrs. Nakamura?"

"I'm afraid I can't." She frowned at him. "I've got more work to do." She removed a can of red spray paint from a pouch in the tool belt snapped around her waist. "I'm leaving signs for others directing them to the farmhouse that I found. Hopefully, more people will make their way there."

"Have you seen anyone else?" asked Patrick.

"I thought I saw a motorcycle far off on the highway, last week. Different than yours."

Patrick looked at me, then turned to her and said, "So you've known I was alive for a while now?"

She looked embarrassed. "Well, I saw you pass by a few days ago, north of town where I'm staying. I don't come into the center much; everything I need is at the camping store."

"Uh-huh." Patrick paused. "It wasn't like they said, you know. I mean, I did it, but not like how it was portrayed. I didn't do all those other things they said."

Mrs. Nakamura didn't change her expression at all. "I know what you said at the hearing. I followed it very closely."

"But you didn't believe me? *Don't* believe me even now?"

"I have no way of knowing the truth, Patrick. I only know what the State said, and the girl's testimony, and what social services said."

"And what I said too," he pointed out.

"Yes, I read your testimony too."

"What Alyssa said wasn't true. Plus, I'm not that boy anymore."

"Patrick, I understand people change—" she began.

I couldn't take it anymore. "Wait. What's going on?"

Patrick squeezed my shoulder. Why did everyone want to touch me? "Nothing. We're done here. Come on, Franklin."

*

Patrick set off at a quick pace toward Jarret's, and I struggled to keep up.

"I know you want to ask, but I don't feel like talking about it right now," he said.

"Okay." I was concentrating on breathing through my nose, letting the vapor rub fumes mask some of the stench, so it was easier not to talk anyway. Plus, there were lots of times I didn't want to talk about things, so I understood completely why Patrick felt that way.

The air was better inside of Jarret's, so I lowered my mask, and I took my time stocking up on essentials. Patrick was calming down, and he began pointing out things I'd need. Sturdy, comfortable boots topped the list, as well as rainwear and padded pants for the motorcycle. "Here," he said, handing me a pair of jeans and a shirt after searching through the racks. "Try these on."

I took the clothes he handed me, and was struck by how lightweight they felt. They didn't seem like practical outdoor clothing.

"Why?" I asked.

"Dude! Lighten up a little. I think you'll look good in them. You should have something nice in case we go out clubbing or something."

Right. That was ridiculous, of course, and probably a joke, but it still didn't answer the question. I took the lantern Patrick had pre-positioned by the front door, as well as the clothes, and began heading toward the changing rooms in the back of the store.

"Seriously?" Patrick asked. "I've washed your head while you were naked in a bathtub, and now you're getting all shy on me?"

I knew it was stupid, but I couldn't help it. "I feel weird stripping down in public."

Patrick laughed. "It's not *public* when everyone's dead. But go ahead, take the lantern. There's enough light by the front windows for me to see. I'll get you some waterproof socks." As I disappeared into the changing room, he called out, "I want to see how those look on you, though."

Again, why?

Once I got into the hallway with the changing booths, I decided I didn't want to go into one. It was dark back there, and something about all those dangling black curtains was creepy. I set the lantern down on the floor and quickly took off the clothes I was wearing and changed into the ones Patrick had given me. The jeans were odd—stretchy, but far too tight at the same time. Still, once I'd struggled into them they seemed to fit. The shirt was equally tight but incredibly smooth, like slick paint.

I left the lantern on the floor and went back into the store. Patrick was waiting for me by the windows in the front. As I walked toward him, he stared at me intently, slowly lowering the pack of socks he'd been holding. I thought something might be wrong. These clothes were making me feel exposed and uncomfortable. Naked almost. Like they were there and not there at the same time.

"Uh...wow," Patrick whispered when I stood in front of him. "Have you *seen* yourself?"

"No. It's dark back there and kind of scary."

Patrick put one finger on my shoulder—a light touch: he was getting better—and encouraged me to turn and face the full-length mirror against the wall between the windows.

Oh. With the outdoor light reflected in the mirror, I saw the shirt was a shimmering deep blue, almost purple, with a scoop neck and tight short sleeves caught high up on my biceps. The jeans were black and, although comfortable now that I had them on, skintight. I looked... I looked like someone you'd see on TV. Sleek and muscled at the same time. My ice-blue eyes sparkled in shock as I looked in the mirror. Patrick smiled behind my reflection.

"Man, you look...hot."

I guess. But why were we doing this? Dr. Levy's advice came back to me: "If you're confused, ask."

"Sometimes I have difficulty following what people are thinking. I don't understand what is happening now. Could you explain it to me?"

"Oh," said Patrick. "Well, I just thought... I mean, I wanted to...ugh. I don't know what's happening to me, why I'm behaving so weird. I guess everything is just getting to me..." He trailed off, took a deep breath, and continued in a different tone. "I thought it might be nice for you to dress up a little, just to see how attractive you are. Not worry so much about that other stuff with Tyler and all. Maybe make you feel good about yourself? It's been a hard couple of weeks."

That was true. But *why* was he doing this? I remembered one awkward session I'd had with Mrs. Nakamura a few years ago about dating. "It'll be hard for you, Franklin. Boys and girls send very subtle signals that are easy to miss and can be confusing. Even people who are good at reading others get it wrong. You'll just have to speak up and ask about how they feel."

I thought about the bathtub and the blue boxer shorts, his comments about my eyes, and my body. These were all signs, right? And the kiss, or sort of kiss, I wasn't sure anymore. And now these clothes.

"Is this you flirting with me?"

Patrick blushed and looked away.

"I…well…I… Do you *want* me to flirt with you? Would that be a good thing?"

Would it? I didn't think so. Flirting was hard to read and made me uncomfortable. Plus, it was supposed to lead to sex, which I didn't want. And after what happened with Tyler, I wasn't even sure I wanted kissing anymore, although Patrick was kind, and he seemed patient and looked at me in a way that made me think kissing him could be…good, maybe? Yes, maybe. But not now, no.

Plus, he was straight, right? All those comments about the gay porn not being his thing.

"No, I don't want that. I don't think it would be a good thing."

"Oh, well, okay," Patrick said. His face changed in a way I didn't understand, but probably communicated something, if I'd been good at reading those sorts of things. But he'd asked a straightforward question, and I had managed a direct answer. This was really good! I liked that he and I were developing this type of relationship. Patrick sighed, then smiled at me. "That's cool. Whatever you want, Franklin. Go get rid of those party clothes, and we'll get going."

*

We left the store, slipping our masks back on. Patrick stashed the lantern inside on the floor for next time and piled all our new things into a shopping cart. We made it less than a block back toward the library when a sudden explosion ripped through the air. Buildings shook and I heard glass breaking somewhere. Patrick ducked behind a pickup truck and pulled me down with him, covering my head with his arms. After a moment, silence returned and our hearing recovered. Patrick stood and helped me to my feet.

"Holy shit," he said. Thick coils of black smoke were billowing above a searing yellow blaze about a mile away. "Let's go see what's going on. Stick close to me and watch out for debris."

We left our carts and set off in the direction of the explosion, up a sloping hill through a residential neighborhood, into the east side of town. Here the small wooden houses were set closely together and became less and less well maintained as we headed up the hill. Some of the houses were boarded up, and a few had small trailers squeezed into their front and side yards.

There was a lot of wood and shattered glass scattered about the street, and I felt the heat of the blaze on my face as we neared the house engulfed in flames. The fire was close to the end of the road on the right, just where the street widened into a weed-filled dead end. Already a fire had broken out on the roof of a neighboring house, and smoke was rising from the attic window of another directly across the street. The fire was roaring, bright hot jets of orange and gold shooting into the sky, black clouds forming above.

"Stop," Patrick said. "We shouldn't go any farther. It must have been a gas explosion." He looked back down the street toward the center of town. "We should get to the hardware store and get a wrench to turn off the gas valves on this street." The smoke was getting so thick it was difficult to take a deep breath, especially through the mask. I was happy to turn around and head back.

"Can't we just let it burn?" I asked as we walked briskly downhill.

"Maybe, but we don't want to risk it reaching the library or taking out the downtown stores. I think if we can shut off the gas, it'll just burn this section."

The roaring of the fire began to fade after a block, and we were nearly back to Main Street when I heard it. A dog barking.

The noise was coming from a side street off to our left and sounded very close. I stopped and looked at Patrick. Based on the panicked look on his face, he'd heard it too. "Franklin—" he started.

I interrupted him. "No. I *have* to." I headed around the corner without waiting for a response. Patrick followed.

It was only three houses in, a ramshackle gray wooden home with a small unpainted picket fence collapsing around the perimeter. The front door was open, and a warped screen door hung loosely in the frame. A small dog with wiry black-and-brown fur—a terrier of some type, I thought—barked at us from behind the fence's gate, then turned and ran to the screen door, nudged it open with its snout, and disappeared inside. I went up to the gate, unlatched it, and stepped into the yard.

"Franklin...wait."

The door burst open, and the dog came scrambling back outside, tail wagging furiously, a bright-pink stuffed toy clasped in its jaw. *Squeak, squeak, squeak.* I stepped through the gate, and the dog jumped up onto my legs, pawing at my shins, squeaking its toy, then flopped on its belly at my feet, before jumping up again and rushing toward Patrick, who'd followed me through the gate.

Even Patrick seemed momentarily taken with the little thing, squatting down and scratching behind its ears. He read the tag on the collar. "Prissy," he said. "She seems healthy enough. Let's see if someone is in there who's been caring for her." We walked to the door, Prissy dancing circles around us. I noticed the yard was littered with piles of dog poop.

Patrick knocked on the screen door. He needed to hold it in place with one hand to keep it from falling from its frame while tapping on it with his other. "Hello? Is anyone there?" Prissy darted between his feet into the house. No one called out, so we followed her in. I cautiously lowered my mask.

"It doesn't smell like anyone's here," I said. But there was a different smell, thick and musty. The carpet squished when we walked on it. I followed the wet floor into the kitchen, where water was coming out of a burst pipe under the sink. The leak trickled at a steady rate, pooling on the blue-and-yellow linoleum floor, then seeping into the living room, soaking into the gold shag carpeting. The lower kitchen cabinets did not have doors, but were covered by curtains on tension rods. In one cabinet a large bag of dry dog food had a hole chewed out of the corner, and a smattering of wet, swollen kibble was strewn about the floor.

"That explains that," I said. "I guess she's been alone the whole time. She's lucky."

"We need to get the wrenches, Franklin."

I looked down at Prissy, sitting alertly on the damp floor, her stumpy little tail making splashing noises as she eagerly swept it back and forth. Her oversized pointy ears faced forward, her soft brown eyes locked on mine. "I know," I said. "Let's go."

Patrick looked at me like he'd been expecting resistance but didn't say anything as we both headed to the door. We slipped our masks back on and walked through the yard, Prissy at our feet.

"Stay," Patrick said to the dog as we stepped through the gate. He closed it behind us and latched it tightly. Prissy barked once, then ran back into the house. I opened the gate and leaned it all the way against the fence, so it couldn't close on its own.

"Franklin..." Patrick began, but I cut him off.

"Oh come on, we at least need to give her a fighting chance. She's got plenty of food here, and I really can't see her turning into a man-eating menace. She can't be more than fifteen pounds! And what if the fire spreads down the street this far? I'd feel horrible knowing we locked her in."

Patrick looked like he wanted to argue, but he didn't.

We headed down the street, back toward town and the hardware store on Main Street, where we could find the wrenches we'd need. We'd gone less than a block when I heard, from behind us, *squeak, squeak, squeak*; then Prissy shot in front us, pink fluffy toy in her mouth. I didn't look at Patrick but couldn't hide my smile. He didn't look at me but shook his head.

*

At the hardware store, we found thick leather tool belts with multiple pockets and loops, allowing us to stock up on flashlights, the special gas valve wrenches, and in my case, vacuum-sealed packets of dog food and jerky treats. Prissy stayed with us the entire time, and any attempts to go sniff at something she shouldn't were immediately corrected with a quick "No."

We worked our way back up the street, using our wrenches to shut off the gas at each house as we went. Prissy looked confused when we passed her street, but I managed to distract her with a treat. By the time we reached the top of the hill, five houses were fully engulfed in flames. Hopefully, they would burn themselves out and that would be the end of it.

"Come on," said Patrick. "I think we're done. Let's go get our carts from Jarret's and head back to the library." That sounded like a fantastic idea, I was exhausted. I gave Patrick a thumbs-up. "And we'll show this little lady her new home," he added. I smiled behind my mask and gave his arm a squeeze.

It was raining by the time we got to our cart outside of Jarret's. Stupidly, I said, "I didn't know it was supposed to rain today."

Patrick snorted. "The days of weather forecasts are long gone, my friend."

Mrs. Nakamura was waiting for us at the library. She was standing under the porch roof, out of the rain. Patrick stiffened when he saw her.

"I'm glad you're both all right," she called to us as we got closer. "I heard the explosion and was worried when I didn't find you here."

We joined her on the porch, and Patrick told her about what we'd seen and how we'd turned off the gas to all the houses there.

"That was a smart idea. I wonder, though, about the gas pressure throughout the rest of town." She looked down at her feet when Prissy approached to sniff her. "Oh! It seems you've found a friend. How did she manage?"

I relayed the story as Mrs. Nakamura stooped down to say hello. After giving Prissy a good long scratching behind the ears, she stood and faced Patrick.

"I owe you an apology. I've been on edge, of course, and I overreacted. I also feel...protective...of Franklin, and I was worried about him when I saw you together." Patrick was touching my arm again.

"Anyway," Mrs. Nakamura continued, "this morning, after you left, I did something I'm not supposed to do." She looked uncomfortable; even I could pick up on that. I was glad to see she'd tucked her gun into its holster. "I broke into your therapist's office and found your file. From when she testified at your hearing." Patrick stiffened and he gripped me even harder.

"I don't know what's in that," he said.

"I'm sorry. It was a gross invasion of your privacy, what I did, and a total violation of my profession's ethical standards. But now I know the truth. All the facts that didn't come out at the hearing, and the truth about Alyssa lying about the attack. And about...your mother."

Patrick didn't respond, but a quick glance showed me his eyes were bright and shiny.

"So, I want to say I'm glad you found Franklin, and I'm glad you two are helping each other through this. I *am* sorry, Patrick. I was wrong to react the way I did. Wrong then and wrong now."

No one said anything for a moment. After a moment, Patrick reached his hand out to Mrs. Nakamura and said, "Thank you for your apology." As they shook, he continued. "I'm becoming protective of Franklin too."

"I'm glad, and please, call me Sara. Both of you."

They seemed changed after that, easier somehow, like how people are after a violent storm passes.

"Let's go in and get away from this smell," I suggested. "Why is it worse now that it's raining? Shouldn't the rain make it better?"

"It's probably worse because it's just getting worse. Timing wise," Patrick said. "From what I've read, it'll keep getting worse, too, for about another month; then the worst of the stench should start slowly going away."

"I wish there was something we could do," Mrs. Nakamura—no, Sara—said, looking at the bodies down by the police station. "In any event, I can't come in. I have to get back. I'm hoping someone would have found my signs and headed to the farmhouse. It's got a nice solar setup, so there's enough power for lights, most of the time, and the water pump. If you get tired of the smell and the bodies, you can come stay there with me. There's quite a bit of space."

She walked to the other end of the porch where her bicycle was propped against the railing. She took her helmet from the handlebars. "It's a few miles north of town on Marsh Road. You can't miss the place. I've put up huge red signs to let people know where it is." Prissy cocked her head suddenly. "I'm still hoping whoever was riding that motorcycle last week—"

She was interrupted by another explosion. This one very far off in the distance, but much larger than the first, based on the low rumble and shaking. A bright glow filled the southern sky as if a bomb had detonated.

"Shit," said Patrick. "I think that might have been a compressor station. I've been reading up on how all of this works. They build them every fifty miles or so along the pipelines to keep the gas pressurized. I wasn't sure how to find out where the nearest one is."

"I hope that's the last of them," Sara said, looking toward the billowing smoke. "The explosions, I mean." She shifted her gaze to the clouds overhead. "It looks like this rain is going to stick around. I'm heading back while I still can. If there's more explosions, you boys come and find me. And thank you for accepting my apology, Patrick."

*

Patrick must have been right about the latest explosion because we discovered we no longer had gas in the library. "Okay, Franklin, time for the last hot...well, hopefully at least warm...bath. You go first."

I hurried through washing, glad to get the lingering smell of smoke out of my hair. Patrick rinsed the shampoo from my head with the bucket again, but this time there were no comments about my body and no jokes about his when we switched roles. I enjoyed the methodical scrubbing and rinsing, and Patrick sighed in satisfaction as I massaged his scalp.

Afterward I changed into my jeans, comfortable, heavy denim—not clubbing pants—and a sweatshirt. Patrick put on sweats.

Back by the fireplace, I opened a pouch of dog food and placed it in the shallow bowl I'd picked up in the pet section of the hardware store. *Good Girl* was printed in pink letters around the rim. The food bowl and the matching water bowl sat on a rubber mat by the fireplace. Patrick was in his wing chair engrossed in a magazine called *Wilderness Survival*. Prissy finished her dinner, lapped up some water, then leaped effortlessly into Patrick's lap. She squeezed between his thigh and the side of the chair, and wriggled tightly into place. She let out a contented yawn.

Patrick lowered the magazine and looked at me. "Seriously?"

"She likes you," I said.

"I did *not* agree to this." But he was scratching her head as he said it.

Chapter Eight

It rained heavily for several days, drumming loudly on the roof. Out on Main Street, the gutters were raging torrents. I hoped the deluge was washing away some of the stink.

Patrick and I got to know each other, or more accurately, he got to know me. I told him about my family, about my diagnosis, about growing up different than other kids, and about all the coping strategies I'd learned from both Dr. Levy and Mrs. Nakamura. He was a good listener and asked lots of questions, almost as if he was learning the coping strategies too.

I asked him about his family, and rather than answer he said, "Are you asking me about them because you were told that's what you're supposed to do?" That was an interesting question, and an honest one. I had to think about it, and it took me a while to get to the answer. Patrick waited patiently.

"Both," I said, finally. Which was the truth, of course. I *always* told the truth. I wasn't able to lie and didn't understand how other people could make things up and pretend they were real.

I understood about white lies and could even tell one when I thought about it in advance and planned for it carefully. I told Patrick about how my parents had taught me to lie when it was polite. Mrs. Knudson was coming for Christmas dinner one year, and she'd promised to bring cookies. "No matter what they taste like, Franklin, tell Mrs. Knudson they're delicious," my mother had said. We spent half an hour preparing for her visit, even practicing my response, with my mother insisting on the need for small untruths in order to be polite.

After dinner, Mrs. Knudson passed around her cookies, which looked very dry and had little green and red flecks in them. I didn't want to eat them. Still, I did what I'd been told and politely ate a cookie. It was horrible.

"Do you like them?" she'd asked me, even as I was still forcing the cookie down.

I dutifully repeated my lines. "They're delicious, Mrs. Knudson. Thank you so much for making them."

"Oh, I'm so pleased. I wondered if I should have added more sugar?"

"Yes, definitely. That would probably have helped a lot," I'd replied. "And these green and red things are weird. They don't belong in food."

Patrick couldn't stop laughing after I recounted this story, and I did, too, because I was capable of seeing the humor in it now, though I couldn't at the time, especially considering the frantic but indecipherable signals my mother had been sending me behind Mrs. Knudson's back. Still, I noticed he hadn't answered my question about his family. After a few minutes, he said, "So, you mean you really do want to know about my family?"

"Yes," I said. "I'm curious about you."

He seemed pleased, grinning broadly and bobbing his head up and down. "Excellent! I like that, and I'll tell you about them. But not right now. It's hard for me to talk about, and I'd rather wait until it seems like a good time. Is that all right?"

That was more than all right. I knew what it was like to not want to talk about something.

*

As the heavy rains continued outside, we gathered together a collection of reading materials to help us plan our next steps. Late one afternoon, Patrick was making his way through *A History of Sanitation* when he suddenly looked up at me, frowning. "We can't stay here," he said. "It's too dangerous."

"Because of the gas?"

"No, or at least not just that. I don't imagine there's much gas left in the pipes. But I don't know what the risks are of low pressure, either." He looked back at his book. "But it's not that. All of these bodies are the big risk. It says here that dead bodies spread disease, and there's no way we can bury them all or burn them or anything."

"So, where should we go?"

"Maybe Sara has the right idea. She said she's outside of town, right? I'll try to figure out how far away we need to go in order to be safe."

I reached down next to me in my chair and scratched Prissy's head while I thought about what Patrick had said. "But if we're outside of town, we'd still have to come in to get food and water, right? Would that be safe?"

"We'd have to, I guess," he said. "If we were quick about it and wore masks, it might be okay. Plus, Sara said the farmhouse had a solar water pump, so maybe we wouldn't need bottled water. Oh, but wait..." He turned back to the book and began flipping through the pages. "Here it is...dysentery, cholera." He scanned the page and closed the book, turning to me. "It might not even be safe where Sara is," he said. "See, it's all about contaminated water supplies. We'd need to know there aren't dead bodies near her water source."

"Would we be able to find out?" I asked.

"I don't know. It might be obvious, but if it's from a lake or river, we'd need to know what's going on upstream." He looked around the room. "But in any event, we can't stay here. Fleas and mosquitos will be spreading disease, too, as soon as it warms up."

I'd come to like our arrangement here, even without the hot water. Patrick and I were getting along well, and the more I got to know him, the more I liked him. He was good for me. Nonetheless, if he was right, and I had no reason to doubt him, we'd have to get away from all the bodies.

We agreed we'd spend another day researching our options, then gather what we could use and head to Sara's first. Maybe she'd have some ideas.

"You're going to have to ride your own motorcycle. We'll both want large storage compartments to take supplies with us." It was a measure of how much I'd come to trust Patrick that I didn't panic at the idea of his teaching me how to ride.

"Can I get a handlebar basket for Prissy?" I asked.

"Maybe a sidecar," he suggested. "She could wear a bright-pink scarf and goggles."

*

The next day, the rain began tapering off. Patrick and I rode to the motorcycle dealership a few miles out of town, only needing to pick our way through one pileup.

Marty's Motorcycles was a small operation and filled a space that looked like it had once been a dry cleaner's store. Patrick parked his bike, and we removed our helmets and headed for the showroom. He held up a hand when he noticed three motorcycles parked by the door. "Someone's been here," he said. "These bikes weren't here when I left last week."

"Hello?" he called out loudly, but there was no response.

All three of the bikes had large storage compartments attached to them and keys in their ignitions. "These are good selections given the road conditions and the need to carry gear." He opened up the compartments. They were all empty. "I just want to make sure no one is using these or coming back for them. Hello?" he called out again, louder this time. "Let's look inside."

We entered the small building. Patrick went to the far corner of the room toward the end of a row of motorcycles. A large open spot looked like it may have held a parked bike recently. "Huh," he said. "Whoever he was knew what he was doing. He took the one I had my eye on in case I needed to do any long-distance traveling."

"Maybe it's the person Sara saw last week," I suggested.

"Maybe," Patrick agreed. "In any event, the other three bikes he left by the front door will work well too. Let's go and pick one out for you."

I sat on each of the three options, and they all felt the same. There was a bright-green one with gold flecks in the paint that I liked, with slightly larger dials than the others, which I thought could come in handy for a first-time rider, so I picked that one. "Good choice," Patrick said, and we headed back into the store.

I was looking through the selection of helmets, much bigger and cooler than my bicycle helmet, when Patrick said, "Over here, Franklin. Check these out." He was standing next to a display of various bags and satchels that could be attached to the motorcycles in a variety of ways. Some had very large openings and areas covered in mesh. "This one's pretty cool. Black leather, little iron spikes..."

"For what?" I asked.

"Prissy, of course," he said. "They're pet carriers, and our dog needs to ride in style!"

Our dog. This man was really beginning to grow on me.

"Let's take the back roads home. We'll go slow, give you a chance to learn how to ride."

It took me a while to get comfortable using the hand clutch, but I'm good with mechanical things and caught on sooner than Patrick had thought I would. The most difficult part was getting used to the bulky helmet pulling my head side to side, but Patrick helped me fit it properly and eventually I got the hang of it. We were about halfway back into town when we came across a culvert that had washed out in the rain, making the road impassable. We were forced to backtrack all the way to Marty's again, so we ended up picking our way through the highway pileup on the way home once more.

This time, since I was riding my own bike, I couldn't close my eyes. I was relieved to think we might be heading somewhere without so many bodies lying around.

Chapter Nine

That night, after we'd packed—"Only one dog toy, Franklin. I'm serious"—we were sitting on our mattresses, Prissy wandering back and forth between us for belly rubs.

"What was it like?" I asked, as I massaged Prissy's shoulder. "Those first few days?"

Patrick took a swig of water from the bottle on the floor next to him. He looked at me and said, "I can't talk about that now, Franklin. I'm sorry. Maybe not ever."

"Okay."

"Can I tell you something else though? Something personal I want you to know. About me, I mean?"

"Sure. Is this about what Sara said to you?"

"Yes. I want you to know what happened." Patrick stood from his mattress and came over to mine. He dropped down beside me and crossed his legs. Prissy rolled away from me and leaned against him, positioning her head so he could rub behind her ears.

"I was fifteen," Patrick began. "Six years ago now. Mrs. Nakamura—Sara—was new at the school. I think I was her first *really* challenging problem." Patrick was looking down at Prissy as he began this story, but he glanced up at me quickly and gave me an uncharacteristically shy smile.

"You see, I had gone through a real mess at home. My mother, well, she couldn't handle...everything...and I was placed in foster care." Prissy yawned, stretched, then curled into a ball between us. "I guess I was a bit notorious at the time, and Sara had every reason to be cautious around me.

"Anyway, I was as surprised as anyone when Alyssa Curtain started showing an interest in me. She was a popular girl, you know? Cheerleader type and all that. We began dating."

The discussion immediately made me uncomfortable. I didn't understand dating much to begin with. I knew I'd wanted it with Tyler, even though I didn't have a solid idea of what would be involved. But I also knew a lot of people meant "having sex" when they said dating, and it wasn't always clear to me what they really meant. I didn't know if Patrick meant they were having sex or just spending time together. Was that important?

And I was surprised to feel upset by the idea he might have been having sex with this girl. I began to rock gently back and forth.

Patrick paused, then reached for my hand. "Are you okay? I want to tell you this because I want you to trust me, and you should know what happened. But I'm beginning to realize this sort of thing is...harder...for you. I'll stop if you want?" That last was more a question than a statement.

I wanted to trust Patrick, too, and I wanted us to be friends. "I'm okay," I said. "Go on. Tell me what happened."

Patrick squeezed my hand, but didn't let go. I was okay with his touching me too. Another surprise.

He took a deep breath and began again. "Well, it turns out she was just interested in me for all the drama she heard I'd been through, with my family and stuff, before I went into foster care." He was looking down at our linked hands. "If you had been just a couple of years older, you probably would have heard about all of this. I was all over the news for a while."

"Anyway, one day we were in the park, making out... sort of," he continued, and there was that uncomfortable feeling in my stomach again. "But I wasn't really...into it...you know? Like, she could see? I wasn't...you know, responding?"

Maya. Tyler. Yes, I knew. A dream I'd had danced right on the edge of recollection. Something about stones? Patrick was gripping my hand hard now. It even hurt a little, but that was okay. "Yes," I said.

"We were by the rock ledges, where it's private, and she kept kissing me, but really in, like, a mean way, you know?"

No, I didn't.

"Then she bit my lip on purpose, so it started bleeding. And she started groping at my crotch—maybe she thought this would all turn me on, but it didn't. I was actually disgusted by the whole thing, and I told her to stop and tried to push her away."

Patrick took a deep breath and studied my face.

When I didn't say anything, he continued. "She had this crazy grin on her face and her eyes were shining, and she started taunting me, cursing at me, saying, 'What's wrong with you, faggot?' Then she started slapping at my face and...and I pushed her...just lightly to get her away."

I could tell he was holding back tears.

"You don't need to do this," I said. Was I concerned for him or me? I wasn't sure.

"I do," he said. "But when I pushed her, she fell. Backward. And hit her head on something. A rock, probably. She was unconscious and bleeding, and I...I ran."

He started crying, and I was really uncomfortable. I could picture it, though, this girl lying there, Patrick's mouth bleeding. Him running away.

"I *know* I shouldn't have done that. Hell, I knew it *then*, but I panicked. I don't know how long she was there, but when she came to, she went to the police and told them I'd attacked her, tried to rape her. They came and picked me up right away. Somebody took a bunch of cell phone photos of me, and the next day my picture was all over the internet. Me with a big swollen, bloody lip, like I'd been in a fight or something."

He paused to take a few deep breaths. I wanted to help, I did, but I also wanted to run away myself, be alone and away from all this emotion. I tried to pull together everything I'd ever learned about being the person I wanted to be. I heard Dr. Levy and Mrs. Nakamura reminding me about being a friend, about putting others first. About really *trying*, not just knowing. I recalled how my dad made me feel better when I was upset, and what he would do. "Patrick," I said softly, "can I hug you?"

He let out a sob I don't think he realized he'd been holding in and then wrapped me in his arms, burying his head in my hair. "Thank you, Franklin." After a moment, he sniffed loudly and leaned back to look at me. "This is hard, I know."

Did he mean for him or for me? Both, I guessed.

"There was a hearing. An administrative thing, not a real trial. We were both juveniles, and thank god they examined her at the hospital right away after the alleged attack. So, it was clear she hadn't been raped. But everyone believed I tried to. Because of my...family situation. I think that's why she picked me."

I replayed the first part of the story in my head. I knew he'd been in foster care and that his mother hadn't been able to handle him. What did that mean? I didn't think I knew everything yet. I was supposed to ask, right?

"What do you mean by family situation?"

He eyed me. I was pretty sure he was checking to see if I really wanted to know. "Tell me, please," I offered.

"I mean," he answered, "everyone knew I killed my father."

Oh. Patrick was looking at me cautiously. Maybe he thought I would get up and walk away. I wanted to, but probably not for the reason he was thinking. "You mean, like, you killed him by accident?"

Patrick released my hand and sat back on his heels. Prissy stretched and stood.

"No. I mean I took an iron skillet off the stove and hit him in the head."

"Why?" Maybe it helped that I simply asked the question. Maybe it was good I lacked the so-called normal ability to react with some expected emotion. But whatever it was caused a change in Patrick's demeanor. He leaned back more and tilted his head at me.

"Why?" he repeated.

"Yes. Why? Is that a bad question?" What other question should I have asked? I was starting to get anxious again.

"No! It's the perfect question." He smiled softly at me. "Other people who've heard this have recoiled from me in horror. Nobody ever wants to know what I was thinking."

"So...?" I prompted.

"Because he was about to kill my mom. He'd been beating on her for years; me, too, actually. But that morning it was worse than I'd seen it before. She'd broken the yolk in an egg she was frying for him. It was always something stupid, something inconsequential to anyone else. But the broken yolk put him into a rage, and he threw a whole pot of hot coffee in her face. I'd covered my own face, but when she screamed I looked up, and he was about to bring the heavy glass carafe down on her head. So I grabbed the first thing I saw—the iron skillet with the eggs in it—and swung it at him.

"I don't know if I meant to kill him or not. But I did. Burnt my hands something fierce too.

"The authorities didn't think I'd done anything wrong, but Mom...well, she sort of had a breakdown, and I ended up in foster care. And then Alyssa came along, and after what had happened with my dad, everyone was ready to believe I tried to rape her. That's when they sent me away."

"Sent you away where?" I asked.

"To a residential facility for troubled boys—better than juvie prison, I guess. I spent two years there, then came back here a couple of months ago to take care of my mother. She has cancer...had cancer."

I thought about what it took for him to come back to care for his mother after...everything. I don't know why I was focusing on it, but I kept thinking about Patrick's lack of interest, sexually, in Alyssa.

As if he was reading my mind, he said, "It was hard coming back, you know? I mean, I wasn't convicted of anything, but it's a small town. People talk. And you heard Sara. I just wished more people had been able to learn the truth, about my mom's breakdown and the real reason I was sent off. That I *hadn't* attacked Alyssa. Maybe it would have been easier." He paused and took my hand again. "But probably not." We sat there on my mattress, holding hands. "Are you okay? With all this?"

One of my coping mechanisms in times of stress is to begin with an inventory of my feelings. What am I feeling and why? I thought about it. I didn't feel okay, no. But what *did* I feel? Sadness, I think, but for Patrick, not for me. That was good, right? What Patrick went through was really bad, and none of it was his fault. In fact, he probably saved his mother's life, coming back to care for her after everything that had happened, even though she hadn't been able to take care of him.

I also felt, well, excited, somehow. Pleased that Patrick wanted to tell me all of this. I usually didn't like learning about emotional things, or trying to figure out other people's feelings. This had been hard, but I was happy Patrick wanted me to know him.

And, yes, relieved, a little, to know he didn't like Alyssa that way.

Okay. I thought I understood now, as everything finally began coming together in my head. I *liked* Patrick, the way I liked Tyler. Maybe even more, because Patrick was being good to me and so patient. I felt myself beginning to rock again. This was all a little too much. "No, I'm not okay," I answered honestly.

Patrick's face did one of those things people do when they are feeling something strong but they try to hide it. "Of course, I understand," he said as he turned and began to pull away.

I increased the pressure on his hand. "Would you stay over here with me tonight?"

Patrick's smile was the biggest, brightest smile I've ever seen. "Oh man, you bet," he said, sliding down onto the mattress and pulling me into a hug.

Chapter Ten

A few hours later, Prissy, who had snuggled between us and was providing a steady warmth against my stomach, startled herself awake with a low growl. I lifted my head and felt Patrick next to me doing the same. Ugh. What was that *smell*?

"Was that *you*?" Patrick mumbled, groggily, pulling the cover up over his nose.

Gross. "No," I protested. "Prissy, did you poop in the bed?" I slid gingerly out from under the cover and began to cautiously peel the blanket off the mattress, just in case it was soiled. The sight of Patrick in my bed distracted me for a moment, as I considered what that meant, but a loud gurgling sound from deep in the library, followed by another wave of overwhelming stench, brought me back into the moment.

"What *is* that?" we both exclaimed in unison, as we stumbled toward the source of the sound and the smell. Patrick had grabbed the lantern, and we followed its light toward the attached caretaker's cottage and bathroom beyond. We hadn't even gotten all the way through the modern addition, with its rows of bookcases, when the lantern picked out a dark rippling sheen on the floor. Like a tide rising on the beach, slow, tiny ripples of oily sludge made their way closer to us, as we headed to the door.

"Don't step in it," Patrick called out as I neared the door. "And don't open the door!"

I gagged and put my hand to my face, wishing I had the vapor rub. "What the hell?"

Patrick grabbed my arm and began pulling me back toward the reading room. "Come on, we gotta get out of here. Prissy, get away from there. Come!"

"We're leaving now," Patrick said, picking up the bags we'd packed yesterday and heading to the door. "Let's get all this outside. Put Prissy in her carry pack so she's out of the way."

He picked up the dog and handed her to me. I was happy to get outside and out of the stench, but when I went through the library's front door, I realized it smelled just as bad out here. Mixing with the rotting stench, it was just too much. Still gripping Prissy with one arm, I leaned over the porch railing and vomited into the bushes.

Patrick was on his way out with his own handful of packages. He stopped next to me, put his things on the ground, and gently took Prissy from me. With his other hand, he rubbed my back as my heaving subsided. "It'll be okay," he whispered softly. "We'll be out of here soon."

With the vomiting out of my system, it got easier. I was glad we'd packed already, and in less than ten minutes Patrick was tightening my helmet for me. He made sure Prissy was secure in her bag and fastened the luggage straps on both bikes. He didn't need to say anything. He just nodded at me and we headed out.

It was still dark, so we took it slow, eager to get away from the smell but cautious with only our headlamps to reveal obstacles on the road. After about twenty minutes, we'd passed the last of the commercial district and had entered the northern outskirts of town. We passed a few final pawn shops and gun stores, and then were on a relatively open road. Patrick pulled into the parking lot of an old, abandoned church, a Jesus Saves sign barely visible in the dark above the door.

I pulled in next to him, and we cut our engines. I peeked in through the mesh at Prissy. She blinked back at me and wiggled some, enjoying the adventure. We took off our helmets, but stayed on our bikes.

"You okay?" Patrick asked.

Was I? No. I wasn't sure what was happening and didn't know what we should do next. There was no control or order in my life at all.

"No," I said.

Patrick chuckled. "I'm getting used to your blunt honesty." At my frown he quickly added, "It's good, man. I like it! I guess what I meant was can we keep going, or do you want to stop and think about things?"

Stop and think about things! No one had ever put it that way before, but yes, that's exactly what I wanted. Usually when people asked, "Are you okay?" they meant "What do you want right now?" even when I hadn't figured the answer out yet. I hated that. What I needed was just some time to understand what was happening, organize it in my mind, figure out how I fit into it, before deciding what came next. That's exactly what Patrick was offering.

"Yes, thank you. Let's think about things for a minute."

"Sure," said Patrick. "We'll just think for a bit. Let me know if you have any questions or anything." We settled into a comfortable silence.

I started with doing an inventory of my feelings. I was scared, mostly, which made me anxious. When I thought about it, though, I decided it was okay to be scared. Being nervous about what was happening was a proper response under the circumstances. I didn't know for sure where we were going or why we had to leave. I should start there.

"We're going to Sara's place, right? She has solar power."

"Right," said Patrick. "We told her we'd let her know if we were thinking about leaving."

Okay, that made sense and reduced my anxiety a little.

"Are we leaving? The area, I mean? Where would we go?"

"We should discuss that with Sara before we make any decisions." Patrick waited for me to think, then said, "Does that help? To know we'll be making a decision about our next steps later with Sara?"

Did that help? Yes. It would be better to already know what we were doing next, but it was almost as good to have a clear plan on how we'd get to that point.

"Yes," I said, sounding a little surprised. But it did help, and I was grateful Patrick thought to put it that way. Like we were solving a puzzle together.

"Good. What else?"

I was also upset about leaving so suddenly, and so soon after having to leave my house too. Too many changes happening all at once.

"What happened back at the library?" I asked.

"That was sewage," answered Patrick. "Disgusting, I know. I think all the recent rain overwhelmed the system, and without power to keep the pumps going, it just backed everything up. It's probably happening all over town, which is why it smelled so bad everywhere. It won't be safe there at all now with raw sewage everywhere."

That made sense too. It didn't make it better that we had to abandon our space like we did, but at least it was understandable. I felt my anxiety beginning to fade.

"Won't it be bad at Sara's too?"

"No, she's too far out of town to be part of the sewer system. There'll be a septic system there. But even that will need pumping out every few years."

All right. Now I understood what had happened, where we were going, and what was going to happen next. "Ask me again," I said.

Patrick looked confused, but only for a moment. Then he smiled and asked, "Are you okay?"

"Yep, I'm good. Thanks for stopping to think about things with me. Let's go."

Chapter Eleven

Dawn hadn't yet arrived when we reached Sara's, but the huge red sign—Survivors Here—Sara had put up at the side of the road wasn't easy to miss. She'd illuminated it with lanterns.

The house was dark, but the sound of two motorcycles pulling into the drive woke her. A lantern appeared in the front window. Patrick and I got off our bikes and were removing our helmets when Sara opened the front door and stepped onto the porch.

"Boys," she called. "Come in. Are you both okay?"

"Yes," said Patrick. "But there's a problem. A new one, I mean." He explained about the sewage as we unpacked.

"Are we still welcome to stay here for a few days?" I asked. "Just until we can figure out what to do next?"

"Of course, dear, stay as long as you like." She stepped aside and ushered us through the door. "It's great to see you, but I'll admit I was hoping you'd be other survivors when I heard you. Despite all my highway signs, no one has shown up."

We put our things down, and Sara told us to head into the kitchen. We sat at the table, and she began putting out crackers, cheese spread, and strawberry preserves. "I'd like to offer you something hot, but all the rain lately has left the solar panels with nothing to do, and the batteries are drained. I haven't bothered with boiling water by the fire for a while, but I can get some started." She bent down and placed a bowl of water on the floor for Prissy. "But it's bottled water for all of us until the well pump is back online."

Patrick and I exchanged looks. Bottled water might be best anyway.

After we'd eaten, Prissy went off to explore, and the three of us went into Sara's living room to talk about what to do next. I noticed several photograph frames lying facedown on the tables and on the mantel. "It's silly, I know," Sara said when she noticed where I was looking. "They seemed like a nice young family. I don't know where they ended up, but they weren't here, thankfully. It just feels weird to have their pictures out, but disrespectful somehow to put them away."

We talked about what we should do. Finding other survivors would be a priority, but we also had to start thinking longer term. The canned goods wouldn't keep forever. And the bottled water supplies would go eventually too. We didn't know enough about the diseases associated with all the dead bodies, but we agreed we needed to avoid developed areas for the short term. Leaking oil tanks and gas stations, pipeline explosions, sewer system failures—there was just too much risk in towns and cities.

Sara left for a moment and returned with a large framed map of the State of Maine. "It was hanging upstairs in the hallway," she told us. The map was a topographical one and had all the national and state parks identified. Several pushpins had been placed in the map, presumably places the family had already visited or were intending to.

"Maybe this is a place to start considering options?" Sara asked. "They shouldn't be contaminated, and they might have some simple facilities operating off the power grid."

"And I guess if we focused on places along the coast or rivers, there would be good fishing options," added Patrick.

I thought they were being too pessimistic. "I don't know," I said. "I think we should focus on finding out where all of this *didn't* happen. There must still be places that are relatively intact, right? Places where people were able to quarantine themselves before the virus got there."

Patrick stood suddenly. "I'm going to go see where Prissy got to." That was...odd.

After he left the room, Sara turned to me. "He hasn't told you about those last days, has he?"

"No."

Sara sighed and leaned back in her chair. "Well, I can't say I blame him. It was awful, Franklin. Of course, we all thought we were going to die. The first day it was a few dozen people dying around us, then hundreds the next day; day three was worse, and by day four everyone was gone. I imagine anyone who lived through it felt the same way. 'Why me?' Right? 'Why am I still alive?' But, Franklin, the thing is before the news went dark the virus was reported everywhere.

"It made no sense, but scientists were starting to figure it out. The last I heard was the North Koreans probably engineered the virus to circulate for about a month, spreading rapidly, until it ultimately 'activated' and killed its host. They said it was something about shortening telomeres on the engineered gene, so each time the virus reproduced, it passed on a slightly shorter...fuse, I guess...for lack of a better word."

I knew something about telomeres because I'd studied genetics in school. Scientists thought they might be the secret toward extending human life, maybe for centuries. Last year I had decided I wanted to study biotechnology in college.

Sara continued her explanation, and I turned my attention back to her. "Anyone who'd been in contact with anyone already exposed over the last month was infected by the time the virus eventually...*activated*, I guess is the best word. That's why everyone started dying at the same time. And when you think about it, just about everyone on the planet came in contact with *someone* over the course of a month, and even just being in the same room was enough to spread the virus. So, for a whole month the virus spread everywhere there were people. Anyone who went through an airport and then went home, or went to work, or whose kids went to school, or who went shopping, they were all spreading the virus, and no one even knew it until it was too late."

I thought about that. I played out the math and transmission trajectories in my head. That *couldn't* be right, could it? It would mean *everyone* had been infected, unless they were truly a hermit, and had been completely isolated for an entire month.

"Then why are we alive?" I asked.

Sara sighed. "No one knows, dear. No one even knew if anyone would survive, once they got sick. But no one recovered from it. If they got it, they died."

My mind was spinning. Where could we go to find survivors?

"So, what Patrick didn't tell you, Franklin, is that there *is* no safe place. It really happened everywhere. By the time the last telomeres on the last gene ticked away to nothing, the virus...exploded...in every person at just about the same time. It was over within just a few days."

"So...Puerto Rico too?"

"Yes, Puerto Rico too. Why?"

"My parents are there."

"Oh, honey, I'm sorry. But, yes, I think it's the same there. I know how you must feel. My husband was in France on a business trip."

For the first time, it felt real for me. My parents, I mean. Probably being dead.

I felt overwhelmed and knew I wouldn't be able to control this one.

"I'm going away for a while," I barely managed to get out.

I rushed outside and went to the barn I'd seen when we pulled up. It was starting to get light, but I still stumbled twice as I made my way through the yard. As soon as I was inside the barn, I pressed myself against the wall next to the entrance and then slid to a sitting position on the straw-covered floor.

I don't know how long I was there. My head hurt, I think because I'd been softly knocking it against the wall, over and over, as I rocked back and forth, knees wrapped in my arms. I heard the noise I was making, a repetitive moaning sound. *Uhn, uhn, uhn.* I *hated* this about myself.

A thick pillow appeared behind my head, floating there against the wall. I could feel it each time my head went back, and after a while I slowed down, wondering about it, curious as to how it got there.

I was rocking a little slower, and maybe I was doing it more quietly. I wasn't sure. Patrick squatted next to me, not looking at me, not touching me. Just there, his shoulder keeping the pillow in place. I was beginning to come back to myself, and I didn't want him to see me like this.

I heard Sara's voice. "Give him this jacket. It's cold out here."

"Okay, thanks. I'll stay here and make sure he doesn't hurt himself. He'll come out of it when he's ready."

That was nice. Patrick.

For the first time ever, as I was returning to normal, it didn't bother me someone else was nearby. He was just there. Not trying to talk to me, or touch me, or calm me. It was good.

Eventually, I stopped moving. Patrick scooted closer but still didn't touch me or say anything. By then, sunlight was streaming into the barn's windows, and I noticed chickens rummaging about in the straw, kicking up dust.

"That happens to me sometimes."

"Okay."

More time passed. That was a particularly bad shutdown, and it always took me a long time, sometimes hours, to recover enough to move on. Patrick waited until I made the first move to stand, and then he offered his hand to me. I let him pull me up.

"Ouch," I said, reaching for the back of my head. The pillow dropped to the floor behind me. Blood spotted its cover.

"Leave it. We need to get you cleaned up." He waited until I was steady on my feet; then he helped me into the house. We went into the kitchen where Sara had already warmed water over the fire and filled a bucket with it, leaving bandages and towels.

"That was a bad one, wasn't it, dear?" she asked, more I think to just acknowledge it and get over the awkwardness. I didn't bother answering. "I'll leave you two to wash up. Join me in the living room for hot chocolate when you're done."

I took off my shirt, and Patrick pulled a chair up to the kitchen sink. He guided me to sit and helped me lean over the sink, my arms resting on the edge. Patrick poured warm cups of water over my head, gently washing the blood from my hair. "We have to stop meeting like this," he whispered.

I groaned. Patrick startled. "Did I hurt you?"

"No, your joke deserved a groan though."

Patrick continued his work; when he finished, he patted my head carefully with a clean towel. "I'm sorry I ran off. I shouldn't have left it to Sara to explain things to you."

"It's okay."

"No, it's not. I knew you'd be upset, and rather than staying to help you through it, I ran away." I was still in the chair, facing the sink, but I held my head up now, cool drops of water trickling down my back.

Patrick was standing behind me, hands on my shoulders. I couldn't see his face, but I could hear the emotion in his voice. He sniffed back tears. "I just didn't want to watch you get hurt. That's really weak of me, I know. You deserve better." He stopped speaking, and I didn't know if he knew he was massaging my shoulders or if it was just nervous energy, something he could do with his hands. In a whisper, right into my ear, he added, "You're becoming very import to me, Franklin Marshall."

I smiled. He was important to me, too, I realized. Probably in the same way.

"Do you remember in the clothing store, when you asked if I wanted you to flirt with me, and I told you I didn't?"

Patrick froze. His hands disappeared from my shoulders. "Right, right, of course," he said quickly. "I'm sorry. *God*, I just don't *think* sometimes, and after what you just went through. I'm sorry, I—"

"Patrick," I interrupted him. "I just want to know if I can change my mind now."

Chapter Twelve

After Patrick helped me clean up in the kitchen, we rejoined Sara in the living room. We didn't actually pretend nothing had happened to me, but we didn't dwell on it either.

"So, where were we?" Patrick asked. He had a goofy grin on his face even I had no trouble reading. It was exciting for both of us to acknowledge we liked each other, that way.

"We were going to consider national parks as an option, maybe look into which ones had facilities that we could use somehow."

Prissy lifted her head from my feet and perked her ears forward. "Did you hear something?" I asked.

"I didn't hear anything," said Sara.

"Me either, but my mind was on something else," Patrick added, blushing.

"Well, let's try to pay attention, shall we?" began Sara, but then we all heard it. A horn.

"That was a horn," I said. We froze for a minute. The sound came again, louder and closer. The kind of horn you'd hear from the stands at a sports game. We all moved at once and rushed out the door.

Patrick got to his bike first and blasted its horn. We only waited a couple of seconds before two quick blasts from the approaching air horn responded, and before much longer, a woman on a bicycle appeared around the curve.

She looked about thirty. Her skin was very pale, and she had bright white hair with a yellowish tinge to it, tightly curled and cropped close to her head. When she hopped off her bike, I realized she was very tall, easily over six feet. She was also very rounded, in a way I knew a lot of guys would find attractive. "Curvy" my father would have said. "Heavyset" my mother would have offered, judgmentally.

"Fat," Maya would have said with a sneer. Not that I wished her dead, but I'm glad she's out of my life.

The newcomer wore black cargo pants and a thick, short, green jacket. She was crying, and saying "Oh my god, oh my god" over and over again. Sara was closest, and the woman immediately enveloped her in a tight hug. Then she moved on to hug Patrick.

She let go of Patrick and turned to me. "Don't touch him!" Sara and Patrick both called at the same time.

Seriously, people? I'm not *that* fragile. Mostly.

I approached her with my hand extended. "They're a little overprotective," I said to her. "My name is Franklin Marshall." Then I remembered the basic instructions I'd been given about being sure everyone is introduced. "And this Sara Nakamura and Patrick Larson."

"I am so, so happy to see you," she replied, shaking my hand, maybe a little too vigorously. "And strong young men too! Exactly what I was looking for." She smiled, Sara frowned, Patrick raised his eyebrows, and I, well, I just stood there trying to make sense of her comment.

Sara spoke up first. "And your name is...?"

"Oh! Loris. I'm Loris. Loris Beauchamp." She looked at each of us in turn, taking us in. "I've only met two others, but I was afraid I was the only one left under eighty."

"There's others?" Patrick asked, at the same time Sara said, "Where?"

Loris looked between them. "Yes," she said to Patrick, and "I'm not sure," to Sara. "And I know Grace isn't going anywhere, and I have my doubts about Stan and whether he'll ever make it to Paradise." She looked to me and Patrick. "But you two are perfect. Oh, thank god. You might even be able to make it by the end of the day."

She looked about the yard and spotted our motorcycles. "Even better! You'll definitely get there before dark."

Sara interjected, "Let's not get ahead of ourselves. We'll go inside and have a cup of tea and a bite to eat, and we can update each other on what we know."

"Right," said Loris. "I'm probably not making any sense. I've been traveling for three days." She turned her attention back to me for an uncomfortable moment, her pale blue eyes studying me.

"You're right," I said. "You're not making any sense."

*

Patrick sat right next to me on the couch, our knees touching, bringing to mind the confusing memory of Kyle and Bobby. Confusing because although it was uncomfortable to watch Kyle and Bobby perform for the camera, I was sort of enjoying feeling Patrick's knee against mine. He knew it, too, and he kept adjusting the pressure so I was constantly aware of the contact, once even reaching down to scratch his knee, then letting his fingers trail lightly along my thigh where it pressed against his.

Loris was talking about Paradise Shaker Village, a self-sufficient community from the 1800s, just fifty miles north of here. It had been restored to its former, pre-industrial-age glory and was now a living history museum, complete with livestock, crops, food production, and craftworking facilities.

Loris worked at the museum as a modern-day blacksmith, demonstrating the trade to tourists.

Before Loris could go into too much detail about Paradise, Sara interrupted her. "But tell us about these other survivors. Grace and Stan, you said?"

"Yes. I need to get people to Paradise. Urgently. I can't manage the place alone, and I've spent the last three days looking for others. I put out food and water for the animals, but I'm not sure how long it will last. I was on my way to Northwood, figuring there must be some survivors here, you know? But I've been honking my horn every time I pass a house or small village and haven't found anyone yet. No one useful, anyway."

Sara drew in her breath, and I waited to see how she'd respond. This was a *huge* thing for her. "*Never* judge a person by their usefulness, Franklin," she had admonished me once a couple of years ago after I'd said the class bully, Brian Watkins, wasn't good for anything.

"People can be compassionate, honest, trustworthy, and helpful, or they can be mean and vindictive. But their *usefulness* isn't for you to decide." She was right, and I'd thought about her advice many times over the years since.

Patrick stretched out his left arm to rest it along the back of the sofa, his fingers briefly brushing my hair as he did.

"I met Grace first, poor thing," Loris continued. "She was sitting in an old beach chair in front of a gas station, eating from a bag of chips and drinking a warm Coke. She's at least in her eighties, and I don't think she knew what had happened or what was going on around her. I tried to explain about the Shaker village, and left her with a map on how to get there, but I think she'll be right where I left her when we head back. Or maybe she's passed on by now; she didn't look like she had much longer to go."

"But you two at least," she said, looking between me and Patrick, "you *must* go. Today."

Patrick stiffened. Before he could say anything, Sara jumped in with "Please, understand that we'll have to talk about what we plan to do next." She nodded to include me and Patrick on the couch.

"Oh, but you *have* to come," said Loris, her focus mostly on Patrick now as if she'd reached some sort of decision. "I put down feed, but I can't leave the animals alone too long. And the lambs will start giving birth soon. They might have started already! I *can't* do everything alone. I need young, strong people to help work the farm."

Sara looked over at us, then turned back to Loris. "Tell us about Stan."

"Stan was inside a small church I passed on the first day. I'd only gone about five miles before I found him.

He's eighty-two, but seems sharp as a tack. He understood about Paradise and the need to keep it going, but he's slow moving and can't ride a bike. He agreed to head there while I continued on, but I don't know if he'll be able to do much once he gets there. Assuming he does."

"How are the roads between here and there?" Sara asked.

"Not too bad. One major blockage about halfway up. An overturned tractor trailer. From the ice storm, I think. It's about fifty miles."

Sara turned to us. "That's not too far. You could go, check it out, come back if it doesn't make sense." Loris looked at us hopefully.

I wasn't comfortable with all these decisions being made so fast.

"I need to talk to Patrick," I said. Loris frowned and Patrick smiled.

"But, no—" Loris began. Before she could continue, Patrick interrupted.

"Let's go back out to the barn," he said as he stood and turned to me, waiting for me to join him.

"More tea, Loris?" I heard Sara ask as I followed Patrick through the kitchen and out the back door, Prissy trailing close behind us.

*

I hadn't noticed the inside of the barn the last time. It was a large space, twice as big as the house and half again as high. Dim light came through the milky windows, and also filtered between the clapboards on the upper level, where

I could just make out piles of hay and a rake propped against the wall.

A few animal pens, too small for horses, lined one wall, but the doors were each open and the floors clean, so I didn't think anything was living there currently. I noticed milking equipment next to the stalls, and stapled to the wall above, a poster displaying different breeds of goats.

Chickens scratched about. Some were speckled black and white, and others were a deep brick red, the same color as Patrick's hair in the filtered barn light. We listened to their soft clucking while our eyes adjusted.

I looked to my right and saw the pillow with the blood stains lying on the floor. Patrick followed my gaze. "Let's go up top," he suggested.

We climbed the open wooden stairway to the loft. Other than the rake and hay piles, there was nothing up here. A sharply peaked roof crowned the space, and the gable end had a large square window, open now, with a series of hooks and pulleys built into the wall above it. We made our way to the window and knelt in the soft hay, side by side, looking out the window, over the treetops to the woods beyond.

"It's pretty," said Patrick. We both took in the view for a minute, silently sitting with our own thoughts. "So...we need to think about things," he added.

Yes, we did. But it was distracting in a new way for me to have him so near, not touching, but almost. "We do," I agreed. I turned from the window and stole a quick glance at his face, my gaze dropping to his lips. What would it be like, I wondered, for him to kiss me? I don't know how he always seemed to know what I was thinking, but he curled his lips into a smile and turned to face me.

"You know what?" he asked. Before I could reply, he continued, "I should have kissed you in the kitchen, but I was too nervous. Would it be good if we kissed now, and then maybe we could think about things after?"

Yes, I may or may not have said out loud.

Moving very slowly, leaving me plenty of space to react, Patrick leaned forward and brought his mouth close to mine. "You have to say yes, Franklin," he whispered, his breath puffing on my lips. I guess I hadn't said it out loud earlier.

"Yes."

Patrick closed the distance and lightly placed his lips against mine. I surprised myself, and Patrick, too, I think, by increasing the pressure and moving my lips a little bit. I wasn't sure what I was doing.

Patrick knew what he was doing though, and he took my clumsy effort as a sign, and, so subtly it was almost like he *wasn't* doing it, he drew just the tip of his tongue softly along my own lips. Oh. I breathed out a sigh, and as I did, Patrick slipped his tongue *between* my lips, gently licking as he pushed just the slightest way into my mouth.

A flush of heat ran through my body, my ears were on fire, and I suddenly felt overwhelmed. Too much, too much. "Stop!" I managed.

Patrick pulled slowly away. "Wow," he said. His eyes, a bright sparkling jade in the light from the window, focused intently on me. "That was really something, Franklin. Did you like that?"

Hell, yeah! And I felt *relieved*, responding the way I did. Excitement and anticipation rolled inside me all at once. What else, I wondered? What more?

"Uh...you still in there?"

"Yes. I'm here. That was good." I paused and shifted to adjust myself in my pants. "I...uh...responded the way I'm supposed to. This time."

Patrick blushed and smiled. Then he turned so his back was against the wall and slid all the way to the floor, splaying his legs out in front of him. I did the same. "Yes, I see," he said, nodding toward my lap and grinning. "Me, too, obviously. Is that something that doesn't normally happen for you?"

"Not at the right times, no," I answered, thinking of Maya and Tyler.

"I hear you," he said. "It was the right time this time though, huh?"

Yes.

"Do you want us to do something about it?" He gave me an opening to say something. I didn't. "Or are we good for now, and it's time to do some thinking?"

I wondered what doing something about it might entail and was pretty sure I'd like to find out. But not now, no. This had been overwhelming. "I don't want anything else now. Let's think about what to do next."

We fell into what was becoming a familiar and comfortable pattern. Patrick silently waiting for me, unhurried and unhurrying, while I inventoried my feelings and tried to determine what I thought and what to say.

I didn't want to go to this Shaker village, this Paradise. But why? Was it just my reluctance to make one more move? We'd only just gotten to Sara's, after all; we hadn't even unpacked, and I was still reeling from my new understanding of the scope of...everything. But still.

We *were* looking for a better place to go, and the way Loris described it, Paradise seemed to check all the boxes. Clean water and air, sustainable food production, and buildings designed to operate without electricity. Maybe if we went there, we could settle in for a while. Plus, there were four of us now, maybe five if Stan made it. And it would be good to settle into a routine, make things work again.

"Do you have any questions?" asked Patrick. "Anything you want to talk through?"

"Not yet," I replied, still thinking.

"Okay," said Patrick, and he leaned his head against the wall and closed his eyes.

I thought about my parents. I'd sort of known, I guess, that all this meant I wouldn't see them again any time soon. Even if they were still alive in Puerto Rico, reuniting with them seemed impossible right now. I realized part of the reason I didn't want to go to Paradise was the farther away I went, the harder it would be to go home again, to leave a message for my parents if they did make it back.

But I wasn't the only one in that situation. Sara's husband is...was...in Europe; Loris probably had someone in her life too. And I had to face facts: their making it back any time soon was unlikely. Whether they were dead or alive, it didn't matter for deciding what I had to do right now. I wasn't ready to believe they were dead, so I made a decision.

I turned to Patrick, and he opened his eyes to look at me.

"I'm going to believe my parents are still alive."

A look passed quickly across Patrick's face, but I couldn't read it. Before I could study it and try to figure out what it might mean, his expression changed.

He reached over and took my hand. For just a second, I thought I understood something. Some confusing pieces of a puzzle falling into place. I thought Patrick might be comforting *himself* by doing this, not me. If that were true...but no, I couldn't follow it. Whatever I thought I had grasped was gone.

He let out a nearly silent sigh, a light puff of air. "Okay." His eyes became misty. Why?

"But I can't just wait for them," I continued. "It might be years before we're able to find each other. So I need to stop thinking in terms of when they'll get back and start thinking about what we should do in the meantime."

Patrick squeezed my hand. "Oh, Franklin, thank god." A tear slipped down his cheek.

"Why are you crying?"

"I was afraid. Afraid you'd be stuck. I mean, as much as I want to help you, I know I can't make you do anything. Or believe anything you don't want to."

"But...why are you crying?"

"I was afraid you'd want to stay here forever; I was afraid I was going to lose you."

"Well, stop. I don't like it when people cry, especially if I don't understand what's going on." *And I don't like it when you cry.* But that thought made me uncomfortable, too, and I didn't say it out loud.

He laughed and sniffed at the same time. He wiped his eyes and quickly transitioned the motion into pushing his unruly hair out of his face. He smiled at me. "Fine, man, I'll stop. But tell you what... We're going to need to work on your 'Patrick is crying' coping skills."

We sat quietly again, Patrick letting me proceed at my own pace.

I didn't get the sense he was pushing me, or trying to force a decision, but he said, "You know there's gonna be tiny little lambs there, right?"

I pictured Prissy sniffing at the lambs and running about the farm. "What are we waiting for?"

Chapter Thirteen

We agreed we'd leave for Paradise right away. Loris would ride with Patrick on his motorcycle, and Sara would stay behind to go back to each of her highway signs and redirect people to the Shaker village. Loris had had a plan to set off the Northwood firehouse siren, or failing that, the church bell, in order to draw out any survivors. I was embarrassed none of us had thought of that, and Sara agreed to do it before leaving to join us.

Sara said it'd be two, or at most three, days before she'd catch up with us.

Patrick set a slow pace, both to allow me to keep up, and to calm Loris's fear about riding on the back of a motorcycle. We occasionally had to weave our way around road debris—cars, tree limbs, bodies. Between the ice storm and people getting too sick to drive with little notice, there had been plenty of accidents during those first couple of days. As Loris had indicated earlier, there was one large pileup with an overturned truck in the center. We had to walk the bikes through that section.

Patrick had to refuel at one point, which meant getting out our handheld syphon pump and finding a car with an unlocked gas cap. Fuel was plentiful, but it wouldn't keep forever and we'd have to think about what to do once the gas sitting in tanks started deteriorating.

But mostly what I was thinking about on the ride to Paradise was the way Loris clasped Patrick's waist, and the way she leaned her head against his shoulders. At one point I was certain she widened her legs and squeezed in even tighter against his backside, and I nearly drove into a ditch.

I did *not* like seeing them like that.

It took us most of the remaining daylight hours to get to Paradise. We'd stopped only once along the way, to give everyone a chance to relieve themselves, and wasn't *that* awkward. I took Prissy quite a way off for privacy while we took care of business, but I was disappointed to see Patrick didn't make the same effort. Although he was at least modest enough to step behind a bush.

The Shaker village itself was located about five miles down a country road off the main highway. I could immediately see why the Shakers had chosen this location. It sprawled across a relatively flat plateau, set midway up a sloping hill.

From the entry to the wide drive, I could see a half dozen substantial timber and red brick buildings, as well as an enormous stone barn. Meadows, crop fields, and hayfields spread into the distance. Fruit tree orchards expanded downhill in a southerly direction, toward the river.

Two tall stone pillars stood about twenty feet apart to left of the drive's entrance. The sign between them read "Welcome to Paradise Shaker Village, a Living History Museum." A fence extended in both directions along the roadway a few feet into the woods.

Loris removed her right arm from Patrick's waist and pointed toward the barn. She returned her grip by sliding her hand slowly down his chest and tightening it once again across his waist. Stop! Surely, we could get off the motorcycles and walk from here, but I was too far behind them to offer the suggestion.

Eventually, we arrived at the barn, killed the engines, swung off the bikes, and removed our helmets. Loris wobbled a bit—unnecessarily, I thought—prompting Patrick to take her arm to steady her.

The barn itself was a huge, three-story stone building. It was round, and the granite blocks shone a bright white in the late afternoon sun. The third story was made from wood, but painted white, and was inset from the first two. The entire effect was of a wedding cake, with a cupula and weather vane on top.

We immediately heard loud bleating coming from the barn. I'm not an expert in the noises sheep make, but this sounded kind of frantic. I was still unzipping Prissy's carry case when she shot out of its opening and darted toward the barn, letting out a little snarling sound as she went.

"Shit," yelled Loris, following closely behind the dog.

Patrick and I looked at each other, and he cocked an eyebrow at me. "Maybe we should work on the 'stay' command," he suggested.

Before I could respond, Prissy's snarl turned into an awesome growl even a Doberman would be proud of. And then she was through the archway and into the barn. Loris picked up steam right behind her.

Patrick turned from me and took off at a quick sprint, and even as I shot forward to follow, I took a moment to enjoy the view of his athletic frame exploding into action, and I sent a mental note to Loris: *That's the last time you'll ever be squeezing yourself up against his backside.*

It was dim in the barn, with most of the light coming in through the numerous windows surrounding the third-floor cupula. I caught a glimpse of agitated sheep massing together, and Loris dropping to her knees near something bloody. But my eyes were following Prissy, already rushing out the far exit of the barn, a hundred feet away, still growling like a dog ten times her size.

I let Patrick and Loris deal with the sheep, and I raced across the barn in pursuit of our dog.

By the time I reached the exit, Prissy was already far into the empty field that stretched from the barn to the woods a few hundred yards in the distance, her excited barking echoing in the stillness. She was chasing something. Could that be...a coyote, maybe? Yes, but a big one, bigger than any I'd seen before. Something white and red dangled from its jaws. It was moving at a trot toward the tree line, but its calm pace was still enough to outdistance Prissy. Thank god.

"Prissy!" I yelled, setting a commanding tone and willing my voice to carry the distance. "Come!"

I prefer to think she didn't hear me as she continued her pursuit. But once the coyote slipped into the forest, Prissy slowed and eventually stopped. She momentarily distracted herself investigating a downed tree limb, then turned to look at me and sat, panting heavily, her tongue dangling out the side of her mouth.

I continued at a run across the long field, and I was panting, too, by the time I reached her. We both looked at each other, as if neither of us could believe what had just happened. I glanced nervously into the trees where the predator had disappeared.

Patrick must have seen at least part of the chase. "Franklin! Get back here," he called from just outside the barn.

I started back, but Prissy was spent, and I ended up having to carry her back to the barn.

Loris came up behind Patrick and rested a hand on his shoulder as they watched us close the distance. No. Not good. Stop touching him.

She beamed down at Prissy, who was still panting heavily in my arms. "That little dog is a hero! What's her name again?"

"Why do you keep touching him?"

"Franklin..." Patrick began.

Loris quickly removed her hand. "Oh," she said.

I continued into the barn, a little bit embarrassed and confused by what I was feeling. "She needs water," I said as I pushed past them through the dark enclosure and back to where we had come in, heading for our bikes and supplies.

The sheep still seemed agitated, but less so than before, and I noticed a small red-stained bundle had been wrapped in a towel and placed on a shelf above the pen. One of the sheep, off by herself in the corner of the pen, was nursing two newborns. Her lambs kept wobbling and repositioning themselves, apparently still trying to figure all this out.

Me too.

I got to my motorcycle and opened the bag with Prissy's things. I took out her water bowl, filled it, and put it on a level spot of ground, wiggling it back and forth to settle it into the dirt so it wouldn't tip. I sank down to sit cross-legged next to her as she drank. "Good girl, Prissy," I said to her softly as she lapped at her water, her flanks beginning to quiver. She paused briefly, shook her head, then went back in for more. "That was very brave. Foolish maybe, but brave."

She stopped drinking, and dropped flat onto the cool ground, her back legs splayed out behind her, still panting to cool herself. "I'm glad you found us," I whispered to her, massaging her shoulders.

"Franklin?" I looked up at Patrick and didn't say anything. He lowered himself to sit cross-legged beside me, pushing his shoulder up against mine. "She saved the day, you know. Whatever that was could have killed the entire flock. What was it anyway? Did you get a good look?"

I was beginning to rock back and forth. I willed myself to stop, and I did, which was progress.

"Why does she keep touching you?"

Patrick sighed, leaned into me harder, and let me support his weight. "I don't know. She's lonely, I guess. She was all alone too. You remember what that was like." He didn't sound right, and he was rubbing his fingertips together. Something about his voice was off, and I suspected this was one of those times when normal people claim to be able to hear meaning behind the actual spoken words. Like maybe Patrick was saying one thing but meaning something else.

I realized I was rocking again. Loris stepped out of the barn. *Uhn, uhn, uhn.* I heard myself, from a distance, making that noise.

As Loris started walking toward us, Patrick put up a hand to stop her. "Loris, we're going to stay out here for a while. Would you leave a lantern for us by the barn door?"

"Sure," she said, putting the flashlight from her belt down by the barn's entrance. "I'll just leave this here for you. The kitchen and bunk rooms are right there." She indicated the nearest two-story redbrick building. "I'll have a fire in the kitchen stove and leave some food out for you. When you're ready."

I felt Patrick nod and then she disappeared.

He wasn't stopping me from moving, but his weight made it difficult for me to continue rocking. That was good. He leaned in close to me and said, softly and calmly, "It's okay if you need to disappear into your head for a little while. But if you could, I'd prefer it if you stay here with me. Help me think about things a little bit."

Uhn, uhn, uhn.

"Either way it's okay. I'll wait right here with you."

I was on the edge, teetering on the brink. Still in my own head enough to know what *could* happen, but also that I didn't want it to. And Patrick said it was okay either way. I didn't have to fight it. And I didn't have to rush into it either. That was nice. What if I just floated here and let everything settle?

And that's what I did. I practiced my breathing until I settled. I don't know how much time passed, but when I realized I wasn't rocking or making that sound, it was nearly dark. The western sky glowed a bright orange and blue. Prissy lay stretched out against my right thigh, snoring, and Patrick still leaned against me on my left. He must have sensed the change in me.

"Listen," he said.

I turned my attention to sounds around us. A growing chorus filled the evening sky. *Peep, peep, peep.* "Spring peepers," I said, and smiled.

"Yep, must be wetlands nearby," he replied.

We sat and listened to the peepers for a while, watching the sky darken and the first stars come out. Patrick stood and told me he was going to get the flashlight while he could still see. He came back and sat again, but didn't turn the light on. Prissy still didn't stir.

After a few minutes, he asked, "What are you working on?"

Working on. I liked that. I knew he meant: What was I thinking about? But phrasing it the way he did made me feel productive. I didn't like it when people said I got lost in my thoughts. Like it was pointless to figure things out.

"I'm working on you," I replied.

"Excellent! I like that." I could sense his grin in the darkness. "I could probably help you with that too."

"You kissed me."

"Yep. Sure did. I liked it too. A lot! I want to do it again sometime, if you'd be okay with that." He paused, and when I didn't respond, he said, "And maybe a few more things too."

"Maybe," I said.

We were quiet again. I felt Patrick breathing evenly and slowly against my side.

"There's something else you're working on, Franklin. I can feel it. What would happen if you just asked me?" He reached across my thigh and took my hand in his.

What *would* happen? Even if I learned something I didn't like, it would still be more data to work with. That's always good, right? Okay then, here goes.

"So, you're gay, right? Like me?"

"Oh."

I felt Patrick stiffen, which is another thing I knew meant *something*, if only I knew how to read it.

"I didn't see that coming."

Chapter Fourteen

Why didn't he just say yes? I mean, *of course* he was gay. He wouldn't have kissed me otherwise. Or promised *more*. It wasn't even the real question I had. I was just building the case in my head. What I *really* wanted to get to, after we both agreed that, yes, he was gay, was to make sure he didn't like Loris too. That way.

"It's complicated," he said, finally.

I didn't want to hear about complicated. I rushed on. "I mean, you kissed me, which is gay, but then you also said you weren't into my porn—I mean Tyler's porn. So, you know, I wondered. But I was pretty sure you were gay because you said I looked really good in the clothes you made me try on. And you said I was becoming important to you, but then I saw Loris put her hands on you...that way...and you didn't push her away, so I...I..." I trailed off, not sure how to finish.

We were still sitting side by side on the ground, in the dark now, outside of the barn. The call of the peepers filled the air.

"I like you, Franklin. I *really* liked kissing you. I'm attracted to you." He gave my hand a tight squeeze.

So gay then, right? Right?

"Okay...?" I said, drawing it out. Making it a question.

"But I don't identify as gay, Franklin."

"You're...you mean, you...you're *not* gay?"

"That's right. I'm not gay. At least, not in the way you mean it."

He sounded so sure. Like this made sense somehow.

"But...what...what *are* you then?" I'd heard of bi, but I didn't completely understand it. Was that what he was saying? I hoped not, because wouldn't that mean he could like Loris too? That was the wrong answer. I scooted farther away from him, putting a couple of inches between us and waking Prissy in the process. She yawned loudly, then repositioned herself along my side.

Patrick sighed in a frustrated kind of way. "Why do we always have to *label* things?" he asked.

What? What a stupid question. Labels were great, and useful, and necessary. It's how we organize things and identify what's what. How could you even *live* without labeling things? I was missing something, again.

"Patrick, that makes no sense. Of *course* we label things. I mean, without labels you don't know what things *are*, or what they do, or...or..." I was getting upset now just thinking about the chaos of a world without labels. It would be like a world with no names.

Patrick threw up his hands. "Stop! Franklin, wait. Sorry. I forgot. You're more...literal...than I'm used to." He rubbed his hands through his hair. "Jesus, this is going to be hard with you."

That didn't make me feel any better.

"Okay, fine. Yes, I have a sexual orientation label. I'm ace. I told you already, back in the library. Remember?"

"No," I said. Patrick had said lots of things that didn't make sense.

"Well, gray ace, actually," he continued, as if he was clarifying something that made sense in the first place. "I'm demisexual," he added.

Huh?

"I have no idea what you're talking about."

"I'm the *A* in the LGBTQIA+ acronym. Way down there at the end?"

I'd heard of LGBT, but I didn't know anything about the rest of it. "I've never heard of that. You're the *A*? What does that mean? What's the *A* stand for?" I asked. I wasn't sure I was going to follow any of this, but I needed to understand this whole Patrick-is-not-gay thing.

"Asexual. Or ace, as we call it." He shifted closer to me so we were touching again. "It means I don't feel any sexual attraction normally, at least, not to a specific gender expression." He paused there to let that sink in, then continued. "But I'm gray ace which means it's not so black and white. Some of us are in a gray zone, where it's a little less clear."

I didn't understand *anything* about what he just said.

"*Less* clear?" I asked. Seriously? "Less clear than... than..." Once again, I was at a loss.

"Let me finish. I'm in the gray zone because I'm demisexual." Oh god, I was starting to rock again. But Patrick continued anyway. "What *that* means is I *do* experience sexual attraction, only I need to feel attracted to someone first as a person, you know? I need to get to know them, and like them, before I can become sexually attracted."

I was still stuck on all those letters. Did they *each* mean something? Was it like a code...or...maybe a puzzle? Yes, maybe Patrick was a puzzle, and I just had to figure him out. I liked puzzles. Not the tricky kinds; I hated those. But I liked the ones you just had to sit and think about.

"And I'm sexually attracted to *you*, Franklin," Patrick finished, pulling my mind back into the present. He settled into silence.

"I know it can be confusing at first. Some people say demisexuals shouldn't be part of the ace group at all, because we *do* feel sexual attraction, like me now, with you. But there's so many letters in the acronym already..." He trailed off.

I was rocking, yes, but pretty gently, and I wasn't making "the noise," which was good. I was thinking, but not getting anywhere. I didn't have a way of usefully organizing this information. I didn't know what to *do* with it. So I asked.

"What am I supposed to do with this?"

Patrick sighed again. He was doing that a lot tonight. "Nothing!" he said. "See, this is why I hate labels. I like you, and I think you like me. I know we both enjoyed kissing, and I'd like to go further with you. And I think you would like that too. It's all good. Let's just see where this goes."

I thought for a moment. "But you're not gay?"

"Nope. I'm ace."

"Which is the *A* in...all those letters."

"Asexual. Right. All the way at the end there. Although other people have said it could stand for other things, like ally, but I don't want to confuse you."

Way *too late for that.*

Chapter Fifteen

It had gotten cold. The chorus of peepers slowed to an occasional lone chirp.

"Let's go into the kitchen and get something warm to drink," Patrick said. "It's time for Prissy's dinner too. We should give her a little extra tonight after all her work."

When I nodded my agreement, he switched on the flashlight and helped me up from the ground. We'd been sitting for hours and I'd become quite stiff, so I needed his support. We walked our motorcycles to the building with the kitchen and the dorms and grabbed the bags we'd need for the night.

After the barn, this was the largest structure in the complex, a full two stories with many rectangular windows outlined in white trim running along the walls on both levels. It had a sharply peaked third floor attic with much smaller square windows set into dormers. The basement and foundation were made of large granite blocks, but the rest of the building was redbrick.

Loris had left a lantern for us at the door, and Patrick picked it up as we stepped inside. We entered into a long wood-paneled hallway extending the length of the building. Simple wooden pegs set above benches lined the interior wall. It was the biggest mudroom I'd ever seen.

We'd unpacked our lanterns from our bikes, so Patrick left the flashlight on the bench right next to the door, in case anyone needed to go out during the night. We set our bags on the floor and then walked through to the kitchen, an enormous room occupying the entire width of the building. There were several stoves and counters, plus one long wooden table in the middle of the room. There were cupboards on the walls wherever there weren't windows. Two wide, deep sinks were set into the counters.

The kitchen felt comfortably warm, and a fire burned in one of the stoves. A stew pot and water kettle sat on top, and whatever was in the pot filled the kitchen with smells of onions, garlic, and herbs. My stomach rumbled loudly. Patrick chuckled, then took my elbow and steered me to the table, which already had a half dozen narrow chairs surrounding it.

There was a note on the table from Loris, telling us how happy and relieved she was we were here. She said it had been a long few days for her and she was going to bed. The note had directions to the men's dormitory, through the dining room behind the kitchen and up a flight of stairs. She'd be across the hall in the women's dorm, and we should wake her if we needed anything.

"I'll feed Prissy and get us some tea," Patrick said, "and a couple bowls of whatever smells so good." He filled the dog's water bowl at the sink, saying, "I'll be curious to see how they keep the water running here." He brought it over and placed it on the floor, then filled the food bowl and put that down too. Prissy dug in.

I was still thinking about all those letters in Patrick's acronym. I could guess some, but I was stumped on *I*. There was an *I*, wasn't there? I thought so anyway. "Here." Patrick interrupted my thoughts by placing a mug of tea and a hot bowl of beef stew in front of me. "This smells absolutely incredible. Stop thinking so much and enjoy your dinner." He put his own bowl down and joined me.

We ate in silence, and I must have fallen deep into thought at some point, because I missed the part where Patrick cleared the dirty dishes and washed them in the sink. It was only after he was finished and had returned to the table to sit next to me again, freshening the hot water in our tea, that I realized I had lost track of time.

"Only cold water at the sink. So be prepared if you go to wash up," he said.

I turned and looked at him. He looked—oh, I was so bad at this—but he looked...unsettled, maybe. Nervous?

"Patrick," I began. "I'm still confused about what you are. I mean, how can..."

He cut me off with a finger to my lip, just like he had that first night in the library. "Shh," he said. "It's okay to be confused. It's a lot of new information. You don't need to figure it all out right now. This has been enough for one day, right?"

Yes, probably. But what am I supposed to do now?

"Look. Have you ever seen one of these?" he asked, placing a small white object about the size of an apple on the table in front of me. It had a flat bottom, so it sat without wobbling, but was otherwise mostly round, with a dial of some sort taking up the entire front surface. There were numbers on the dial.

"No. What is it?"

"It's a mechanical timer. They didn't bring electric wires to any of these buildings, but I guess the people who run the kitchens now needed to use a timer. I found it in the cupboard."

I picked it up and turned the dial. It started making a steady ticking sound.

"Huh. Clever," I said.

"Yes, and simple. You can set the time for anywhere up to an hour. It dings when the time is up."

Patrick reached over and took the timer from me, then put it back on the table. "Here, lift your feet a second," he said, as he reached over and took the sides of my seat and twisted it in his direction. He turned his own chair so we were both now seated facing each other, so close we had to move our legs out of each other's way. "I want to try something. Do you trust me, Franklin?"

I didn't have to think about that too long. I *did* trust Patrick. Even though he confused me with all this ace stuff, and him not being gay.

"Yes."

Patrick smiled, the big goofy one he uses sometimes. "Good! Good. That part was easier than I thought. We're going to be okay, Franklin. We really are." He reached over and took both my hands in his. I was becoming totally fine with Patrick touching me. In fact, I was beginning to like it.

"I don't want you becoming all uncomfortable trying to figure me out. I know you. You've been thinking about everything I said about ace and gray and demisexual. Running it through your head, tying to make sense of everything. And it's upsetting you that you can't figure it out."

Guilty as charged.

"But none of that matters. To us I mean," he said. "So here's what we're going to do. I'm going to set this timer for five minutes. And for exactly five minutes, no more, no less, we're going to kiss. Like we did in the barn at Sara's. You liked that right? I know I did."

I had liked that. A lot.

"Five minutes seems like a long time, though," I said.

"Maybe," Patrick responded. "But we can try, right? I mean, you'll know exactly how long it will be, so no surprises."

"Why though?"

"Franklin, dude, come on! Because we'll both enjoy it, that's why! And because it'll help you to stop worrying about what everything *means* and start enjoying what it *is*. I really want to kiss you again, Franklin. And maybe, later, you know, we can try doing more? We did both think doing more than kissing might be fun sometime, right? But for now, let's just kiss again."

Yes. I thought I'd like to do that again. See if it was as good as I remembered.

He pulled out a twenty-dollar bill and placed it on the table, then quirked a challenging eyebrow at me.

"Ugh," I said, and Patrick laughed. "This really *is* a thing with you. Okay," I said. "Let's."

"That's my man!" Patrick responded, his grin, unbelievably, widening even further. He picked up the timer and turned it so I could see him set it for exactly five minutes. He was careful about being precise, too, which I liked. He put it on the table, and it started ticking away.

He turned back to me and scooted his chair even closer, creating a loud scraping noise that almost put me off the entire idea again. But when he pushed my legs apart with his knees so he could squeeze between them, I was back in the game. He leaned forward and placed his hands on my hips, closed the gap, and kissed me.

It was as good as before, better even. Everything was new and a surprise, the searching tongues—not just his, but mine too!—the clashing teeth, our noses bumping at first, then simply finding their spaces together. Early on I thought, *No, too much*, but when Patrick felt me start to pull away, he slowed the pace and began stroking the side of my face with his hand while moving his mouth to my neck.

Oh. That was...that was...oh wow. I realized I was running my hand through his hair and couldn't even remember putting it there. He kissed my mouth again, and one of his hands massaged my thigh, up and down, up and down. I was aroused and excited, and it was too much and not enough. I was lost.

The ticking stopped. *Ding*.

We both froze. I pulled my mouth away from his. My lips were tingling and felt swollen.

"Fuck," Patrick said softly. "That thing must be broken, right? That couldn't have been five minutes."

It *had* seemed awfully fast. Patrick still had his hand on the top of my thigh, his fingers not *quite* touching the bulge at my crotch. My hand was still cupping the back of his head, and I gently let it go.

The light from the lantern turned Patrick's hair a deep fiery red, and his eyes were shining. "Franklin..." he said, letting out a soft breath.

Before he could continue, though, I said, "Um, about that idea of *more*?"

He squeezed my hand and said, "Let's go upstairs."

Chapter Sixteen

I stood and lit my flashlight. My shaking hand sent its beam bouncing off the kitchen walls. Patrick took my free hand as we left the kitchen and passed through the dining room.

It was a large room with several tables arranged in neat rows, but I didn't even bother sweeping my light over the space. My eyes were fixed on the stairway beyond, and what waited for us upstairs.

When we got to the back of the dining room and entered the small hallway there, I noticed there were actually two stairways leading to the second floor. An ancient wooden sign reading SISTERS hung above the stairs on the left, and a similar sign reading BROTHERS hung on the right. We took the stairway leading to the men's dorm. I was in front with my flashlight, Patrick behind me reaching up, not letting go of my hand.

At the second-floor landing, the sisters' stairway met ours once again. The hallway was wide and long, running the full length of the building. Doors along both sides opened into sleeping quarters.

We were in a hurry. We didn't pause to examine the hallway or our options.

Instead, I led Patrick into the first door on the right, shining my light above it quickly to verify the sign read BROTHERS. This would be a bad time to bump into Loris. Prissy padded in silently behind us, and Patrick let go of my hand to reach back and close the door. "No locks," he said. "We'll have to try to be quiet."

I swept the beam across the room. There were ten beds, five along each wall. I let out a shocked gasp when my light settled on the farthest bed in the corner.

There was a dead body in it. "Shit," I whispered.

"What?"

"A dead body!" I was still trying to whisper. "Right there in the bed. Gross."

"Goddammit. Loris said there weren't any bodies here." Patrick ran his hands through his hair.

"I guess she didn't check the men's dorms," I replied.

"Um, maybe we could check out the next room?" Patrick asked.

"No!" I said. "We can't go next door to have...to do... more...with a dead body right here."

Patrick muttered something that sounded like "cockblocker," but I didn't know what that was, and I wasn't sure I'd heard him correctly. I was carefully keeping the light beam away from the corpse. Patrick was pacing, thinking, Prissy at his heels. "Shine the light back over there again."

"Ugh," I said but did what he asked. The corpse looked more desiccated than rotted, with a few strands of wispy white hair, skin pulled taut over a white skull-like head. It looked like it had been there for years, rather than weeks.

"It doesn't smell *too* bad in here..." Patrick began, hopefully.

"Bad enough," I said.

"Maybe we could wrap it in a blanket and carry it outside," he suggested, "and come back and find a different room?"

I wasn't sure about that; the mood was kind of fading.

Prissy made her way to the far end of the room, toward the bed with the body in it.

"Prissy, no! Come away from there," I commanded, or tried to, anyway, as Prissy ignored me and trotted toward the bed.

"No!" Patrick and I yelled simultaneously as she jumped up onto the bed and started licking the side of the body's head.

"Oh, gross, stop!" Patrick rushed toward her to pull her off.

"I'm going to be sick," I whispered.

"What the hell?" mumbled the corpse, opening its eyes.

Patrick screamed like a little girl. He really did.

I thought, *Zombie!*

Prissy wagged her tail and squiggled like she'd just won a game of hide-and-seek.

The door burst open and Loris rushed in. "What? What is it? What's wrong?" Her own flashlight's beam swept the room and landed on the zombie. He was trying to gently push Prissy aside, sit up, and find his glasses on the bedside table, all at the same time.

Okay, maybe not a zombie.

"Stan?" Loris asked. "You made it! Oh, how exciting! When did you get here?"

"Loris?" the zombie—well, Stan I guess—asked. "What the hell's going on? Who are these people, and why are they screaming at me in the middle of night?"

"Franklin didn't *scream*," Patrick said.

Of course I didn't. That was you, you big sissy, but I didn't say that out loud.

"Okay, let's all take a deep breath," Loris said. She turned to me. "Franklin, since you have a flashlight already, would you run down to the kitchen and bring back a lantern? All of these flashlights bouncing around are giving me a headache."

I glanced at Patrick to make sure he had Prissy under control, then did as she asked. By the time I was back, Stan was sitting on the edge of his bed with his glasses on, and Loris was sitting next to him. Patrick sat across from them on a different bed, and Prissy stretched out on the floor between everyone's feet. I put the lantern on the table between the two beds and sat next to Patrick. Loris and I turned off our flashlights.

Loris started. "Stan, this is Patrick and Franklin. I met them down in Northwood. Boys, this is Stan, the man I told you about when we met at Sara's."

"Who's Sara?" Stan asked.

"She's from Northwood too. She'll be here in a day or two. When did you get here, Stan?"

"The day after we met on the road, so two days ago now, I guess. I've been feeding and watering the animals. I think the sheep are getting close to birthing."

"They've started already," Loris said. "Two of them gave birth this afternoon. I appreciate your help with them, but you've got to keep the barn gates closed. A coyote got in today and killed a lamb. It could have taken out the whole flock if it wasn't for our hero, Prissy, here." She reached down and scratched the dog between her ears.

"It was huge," I said. "It could have been a wolf, maybe. Much bigger than any coyote I've ever seen."

"Haven't been wolves in Maine for a hundred years," Stan said.

"There will be again soon enough," Patrick pointed out. "Maybe the one that took the lamb is just the first."

We spent a few more minutes talking; then Loris asked if we could try getting back to sleep. Patrick and I decided to simply bunk down in a couple of the cots across from Stan. We were tired and overexcited at the same time, and the moment had passed for us to explore what *more* might mean.

Although that was something I was very much looking forward to.

Chapter Seventeen

A faint silvery light came through the dorm's windows, and I woke up feeling energized.

I got out of bed quietly and looked down at Patrick in the cot next to me. He was still sound asleep, and his long hair was a tangled mess. I remembered running my hands through it last night and smiled. I felt excited and ready to see where this went. Maybe I even had a...a boyfriend? Maybe. We'd have to figure that out, but for the moment, it was good. But then I remembered his discussion about asexuals and gray colors and demi-somethings and frowned. Patrick had said he wasn't gay.

Prissy wasn't in my bed, or in Patrick's, and I looked across the room and saw her curled up with Stan. Huh. They were both sound asleep too.

I left the room quietly, pulling the door closed softly behind me, and headed to the steps and the small toilet off the first-floor hallway under the stairs. After I was finished, I pulled the chain dangling from the tank above the toilet and flushed it. It worked, but I realized I should have asked about the setup here first. I hoped I hadn't just wasted the last water in the tank.

Although the sky had begun to lighten outside, I still needed my flashlight to make my way around the dining room, taking it all in for the first time. There were four long tables, and dozens of simple chairs lining the walls. Framed oil portraits hung along all the walls, and based on dress and pose, I assumed they were paintings of the Shakers who'd built Paradise and made their lives here. There was as many women as men, but somehow the women looked more serious, frowning from the canvasses with their tight bonnets and sharp eyes.

The door between the kitchen and the dining room opened, spilling in a pool of lantern light. Loris leaned in the doorway. "I thought I heard someone in here." She left the door open and stepped into the dining room. She looked at the paintings. "I wonder about them whenever I'm in here. What was it like? I mean, we reenact their lives here every day—or we did—but what was it *really* like?"

I looked at the painting of the woman in front of me. Sister Elizabeth Johnson. She was older than many of the others when her portrait was painted. Probably in her eighties. Did she cook in this kitchen? Did she share secrets with any of her sisters? Did she worry about asexuality?

As if she were reading my mind, Loris said, "Did you know they were all celibate?"

I did not know that.

"They were very advanced for their time in some ways. Women were considered equal to men in all things, but there was no mixing of the sexes. No marriages, no children. No sex."

I thought about that. I hadn't had sex yet, but I wanted to someday, maybe with Patrick. As scary as it was, I couldn't imagine why you'd willingly give it up. But Patrick might, I thought. He'd said his normal state was not to be sexually attracted to anyone, no matter what sex they were. Or, he might have said gender. I'd have to ask him if there's a difference.

When she saw I wasn't going to comment on the celibacy issue, she said, "They danced a lot, though. Well, no explaining people, I guess." She sure was right about that.

"Ten new lambs last night," Loris told me. "And still more to come. I'm so thankful you guys agreed to come here. I couldn't possibly have handled all this alone." She was next to me now, both of us looking up at Sister Elizabeth.

"Well, the eggs aren't going to scramble themselves. Come help me."

We went into the kitchen. Loris had already prepared a bowl of fresh cracked eggs, and she'd been busy chopping onions and carrots. A flattened towel on the counter by the sink held a damp handful of herbs. "These are for the frittata. There's an amazing root cellar downstairs; there's still plenty of onions, potatoes and carrots, even after this long winter. We're out of milk, though, I'm afraid."

I knew you could get evaporated milk in a can that keeps a long time and was going to tell her that, but she kept talking. "Hopefully, someone will be able to figure out how to milk these sheep! There's a cheese-making workshop here, too, and once we have time, we'll figure that out. A hundred and fifty years ago these Shakers were famous for their sheep's milk cheese."

She talked a lot, which was another thing I didn't like about her. I mean, in addition to the "touching Patrick all the time" thing.

She sautéed the onions and carrots in an iron skillet for a few minutes, then removed it from the heat. She looked around the kitchen. "We'll put the eggs in once they wake up. Could you bring those potatoes over to the table? We'll dice them up for hash browns."

I collected the potatoes, and Loris brought two sharp knives, two cutting boards, and a ceramic bowl to the table. "You know how to do this? Safely I mean?"

"Yes."

We set to work. She was quiet, which was nice, and I enjoyed doing something useful. The bowl filled quickly with diced potatoes.

"I think we should all be honest with each other, don't you?" she asked.

I'm always honest, as I explained to Patrick earlier. Sometimes "to a fault" as my mother claimed. "Sure," I said.

"So, I'm just going to ask this straight out. I mean I'm not trying to be rude or anything, and it really doesn't matter either way..."

I hated when people did this. It usually meant they were going to ask something complicated or deeply emotional in a way I didn't understand.

"But...you guys are gay, right?"

Oh. Turned out to be an easy one.

"No."

"No? But I thought, you know, the way he is...with you...I mean..."

"No. Patrick isn't gay." Then I remembered she asked about both of us. "I am though."

"Oh. Well, that's surprising. Are you sure? About Patrick, I mean?"

"Yes. I asked him, and he told me he wasn't gay. Twice."

Loris sat up straighter at the table and rubbed her palms in small circles on its surface in front of her. She looked far into the dining room for a moment, or maybe she was looking someplace else entirely.

"Well! That's good," she said, finally.

"Is it?" I asked. I thought the whole thing was confusing, but not *good* particularly.

She turned back to me in a startled motion, and her face turned red. "Oh! No, of course not, I'm sorry. I wasn't thinking. *Of course* it's not good, for you, I mean. That must have been very hard for you."

Not really, no. The "I'm not gay part" was actually easy. The hard part was trying to follow along when he explained what he was.

"No. It wasn't. I thought he was gay, but I asked him, and he was very clear that he wasn't. And he told me that twice, so, no, that part wasn't hard at all."

She took my hand in hers. I didn't like her enough to permit the touching, but I did my best to sit still, willing her to stop.

"Well that's very brave of you. Even if you claim it was easy. I know it can be hard when your feelings aren't returned." She squeezed my hand, and now I *really* wanted her stop. I started inching my own hand out from under hers.

"Well, good for you for being so strong. Plenty of other fish in the sea and all that, I guess." She patted my retreating fingers and gave me a smile, then gasped as her eyes widened. "Oh my god! What a ridiculous thing to say! I just need to shut up today," she exclaimed.

That would be a good thing, yes.

I tried to replay what she had said and could only come up with "plenty of other fish in the sea" which I assumed was one of those expressions people used not because it made *actual* sense, but because it had a separate meaning that *did* make sense.

There were a lot of those kinds of sayings, and I'd memorized many of them. "It takes two to tango," "killing two birds with one stone," and my favorite, "There's more than one way to skin a cat." Honestly, sometimes I think it must be hard for ordinary people.

Chapter Eighteen

Our first breakfast at Paradise was...odd.

It was clear to me there was a lot going on just beneath the level of my understanding. Undertones, my mother had called them. The word made me think of undertow—the ocean current that can sweep you out to sea if you weren't aware of it. Both presented the same risk for me.

Stan still looked like a corpse. He had a bony head with just a few strands of silver hair. But he also had bright-blue eyes, crystal clear even after eighty years, and he smiled a lot, which was nice. And Prissy liked him.

Loris kept glancing at Patrick, smiling before looking down, then away. Weird. Once we'd poured our tea and coffee and gathered at the kitchen table, Loris put out plates and silverware. She brought the skillet with the frittata and the baking dish with the potatoes to the table, along with handful of nondairy creamers. She stood directly behind Patrick, lightly placed her hand on his shoulder, then said to the table, "And that's both the first time and the last time you're going to see me cooking up breakfast for the men." She smiled as she said it, which confused me even more.

Plus, I was distracted by her hand on Patrick.

She sat and served herself from the egg dish. "We have a lot to decide," she said, "but first I want to thank all of you for agreeing to come here. I know you each might decide not to stay on, but even being here for a few days to help me stabilize the situation is helpful. Especially with the animals. I'd hate to see more of them die."

We all nodded in agreement as we served ourselves from the platters.

"I also need to figure out what crops I should try to manage this year, either alone or with help. Clearly, I'll need to plant animal feed crops, but I'm also thinking vegetables and things for us too." She looked around the table. Stan was nodding thoughtfully. "It may seem silly to think about growing food," she continued, "with all of the canned goods and dried food available, but fresh vegetables are important. And, I'm trying to think long-term, you know, five or ten years down the road when the canned goods might have been used up or gone bad."

I still didn't like thinking that way. Surely we would find a way out of this mess and back to a normal world before then. But in the meantime, this did seem like a good place for us.

Stan spoke up. "Well, I'm not sure I'll be with you in five or ten years, but I want to do whatever I can to keep this operation up and running while I'm still alive and kicking. You're thinking about things the right way, Loris."

Loris nodded to him, then looked at Patrick, waiting. He said, "Franklin and I will talk about it, but I think we're both probably in. Before you showed up, we were talking with Sara about a place to settle for a while. This seems like a good choice."

Loris looked toward me and frowned, just for a moment. Then she turned back to Patrick, smiling again, and said, "Sure, you can talk to Franklin. Although, I mean, we all have to decide what's in our own best interests."

Stan looked between the three of us but said nothing. I felt the undertones pulling me out to sea.

We spent the next hour discussing immediate needs, such as looking after the sheep through the birthing process, stockpiling wood for the kitchen stove, and making sure we had enough animal feed on hand.

Once those things were taken care of, there were a number of short-term projects we'd need to tackle. The most pressing was bringing in food for the humans. It was about ten miles to the nearest small market. We'd be able to stock up on rice and flour, soups, canned goods, and other staples there. But we also had to find a better way to heat water for washing and bathing. Patrick said he'd research what would be necessary to install solar panels.

There was a separate laundry building in the complex, built during the early 1800s. It had three large tubs, two for clothes washing and rinsing and one for human bathing, but the water was heated in a separate wood-fired tank and manually poured by the bucketful into the tubs. Loris wanted to figure out a way to make the entire process less labor-intensive, and I suggested a syphoning hose, like how we got gas into our bikes, to move the water between the tubs.

I was thinking about the water problems we had back in Northwood. "How do you power the pumps to keep the water flowing?" I asked.

"We don't," replied Loris. "The Shakers were very smart when they chose this spot. Just at the top of the rise at the eastern end of the property there is an artesian well. There's a small stone waterworks building surrounding it, and a large holding tank they built inside. The water is stored there, then flows through wooden piping to the barn, the laundry, and here to the kitchen."

"What's an artisan well?" I asked.

"Not artisan. *Artesian,*" Stan said, pronouncing the word carefully. "It's a well that taps directly into an aquifer underground, and it's under so much pressure there that the water naturally forces its way up once an opening is provided. No need for pumping." Stan looked at Loris and said, "That *is* clever. So the water in the tank is always full?"

"Yes, we just need to heat it for washing and bathing."

"Speaking of washing," said Patrick, "why don't you go check on the lambs again and leave the cleaning to the men?"

Loris, who'd been sitting next to Patrick through breakfast, *right* next to Patrick, leaned into him, grabbed his bicep, and squeezed. "My hero," she said, batting her eyelashes at him in a way even I saw was intentionally exaggerated.

"*Uhn,*" I may have said out loud. I *really* didn't like her.

Patrick reddened, then turned to me. "After we clean up, let's go inventory the feed situation; see what we might need to get from a supply store."

"I only live—lived—about five miles from here. I can point you to the Agway," Stan said. "They'll have everything you need. Back when I was still driving, I was there most every weekend."

"Thanks, Stan," said Patrick. "Franklin and I will check out the Paradise garage too. See what we're dealing with by way of trucks and equipment. With any luck, we can all head over to Agway in a pickup."

"You boys go ahead and check it out," said Stan, rising from the table and carrying a load of plates over to the sink. "I think I can handle the cleanup." Patrick and I helped carry the remaining dishes to the sink, where I filled a fresh bowl of water for Prissy.

"Oh, wait!" said Stan, turning to us, cold water dripping from his hands. "I can't believe I forgot to mention this earlier. If you find a working truck or car with one of those plug-in cigarette lighters, bring it back. I want to try my radio."

Loris finished putting on her barn coat and pulling on her thick work boots in the entry hall but came back into the kitchen when Stan mentioned the radio. "Um, Stan," she said as she buttoned the jacket, "I don't think there's going to be any stations broadcasting anymore. Not that it wouldn't be nice to have some music, but I'm not sure we should waste the gas just for that even if we could find a station."

"No, no," said Stan. "Not that kind of radio. I have a ham radio. I've got a big setup at home, but I also have a portable field radio that fits in its own backpack. I brought it with me. But I need a DC power source."

"A ham radio?" asked Loris.

"Yes. It's a hobby of mine. You can talk to other operators all over the country. Even in other parts of the world. I figure there's got to be other ham operators out there too."

Chapter Nineteen

Patrick and I headed out to check on the animal feed situation. A heavy frost lay across the yard and fields, and farther away, the trees in the forest glistened in the soft amber light. The ground was hard underfoot as we made our way to the barn, Prissy darting about enthusiastically, tracking the scents left behind overnight.

As we approached the barn, I heard a soft murmuring of sheep, but nothing panicked liked they'd sounded yesterday during the coyote attack. Patrick didn't bother with the lantern by the arched gate, and instead, we stepped into the dark interior and let our eyes adjust for a moment.

The first five pens along the curved wall to the right each housed a new mom and one or two newborns. Loris was herding the remaining dozen or so sheep out another archway farther around the side of the barn to the left.

"Come on," said Patrick. "It looks like all the hay and storage and stuff is upstairs."

In the interior ring of the barn, a partially enclosed, narrow wooden stairway curved its way up to the second floor. Patrick led the way. Halfway up, on a landing tucked behind one of the structure's enormous supporting columns, Patrick paused. He turned to face me and said, "Come here." He held out a hand, and when I took it, he pulled me up the two steps to his level.

The landing was barely big enough for both of us to stand on. Patrick pulled me into an embrace and kissed me. It wasn't a deep, passionate kiss like the one we'd shared in the kitchen, but it was sweet and not at all rushed. "Good morning," he said after he pulled away.

It was thrilling to me to be held and kissed—and to like it! I wasn't even annoyed he touched me without asking first. In fact, I wanted him to do it again.

"We'll have to figure out a way to be alone more," he whispered, still holding my hands. Then he let out a soft laugh. "Who would have thought *that* would be a concern just a couple days ago." Without waiting for me to respond, he turned and continued up the steps.

On the second floor, we discovered a wide and open deck circling the entire barn. A third of the way around, to the right, was a doorway large enough to drive a truck through. This seemed odd, given that we were on the second floor, but when we walked over and opened the expansive doors, we saw the ground level was slightly higher here than in the front of the barn, and a massive earthen ramp had been built to lead up to this level.

Patrick stepped out into the sun and peered over the side of the ramp. "Nice job," he said. "It's only about twelve feet high, and the sides have granite blocks holding it together." He looked around the grounds, then came back in. "But why bother with all that? I mean, you could just drive your cart or whatever in on the ground floor."

I studied the wide ramp and sturdy decking running around the circumference of the interior. And then, just like that, I understood. "Oh," I said. "I get it. They drove their wagons up here from outside. They loaded them up with hay and feed and whatever else they needed first, and stored everything up here. Even a big wagon could fit, because you can drive it all the way around and back outside without having to turn it around."

I looked around a bit more, then studied the chutes and wide bins lining the side wall alongside the decking. "This must be where they would send the feed down to the animals." I was nodding to myself. "Yes. That way they kept the entire first floor open for housing the animals and working with them there, milking and stuff. This is really smart. I think I like these Shaker people."

Patrick was looking at me strangely. I sensed an undertow.

"Franklin, did you figure all that out by just looking around?"

"It's not that complicated," I said. Then something else occurred to me. "Oh! And those trap doors on the floor just beyond the pens..."

"What trap doors?"

"You didn't see them? Square doors set in the floor all along the perimeter of the inner ring? I'll bet that's where all the animal waste went, to be collected and removed later from the basement."

Patrick went to the edge of the deck and peered over the waist-high wall to the open area below. "Yes, I see them now. That makes sense." I walked over to join him. He turned to me and said, "You should tell Loris." At my frown he added, "You know, just in case she doesn't already know how the whole thing is supposed to work."

"Okay," I said. I didn't particularly want to talk to Loris, but I definitely didn't want Patrick seeking her out to explain it. We stood for a moment looking down at the center ring of the barn below, listening to the soft clucking of the dozen or so chickens making their way about the second level. They seemed to prefer it up here rather than down with the sheep.

Prissy hadn't been able to climb up the steep and narrow steps, and as we watched, we saw her dart across the barn and out of sight on the lower level.

"Looks like Stan already took care of the feed," Patrick said, nodding at the small bales of hay—the old-fashioned square kind—piled near the chutes, and bags of chicken pellets leaning against the wall. "Let's go check out the garage and see what kind of vehicles and farm equipment we have."

We headed back down, pausing again on the landing for a quick kiss. "Maybe this will become a tradition," Patrick murmured. I could support that. When we reached the open space of the barn's main ground level, Prissy appeared and dropped a dead mouse at our feet.

*

It was shockingly bright when we stepped outside the barn, and we had to stand for a moment, shielding our eyes. Wisps of moisture rose above the empty fields as the spring sun warmed the dirt. We began following the graveled road, making our way slightly uphill across the village grounds. At the top of the rise, we passed the small brick and granite water-works building housing the well and holding tank.

We continued following the road down the backside of the hill and through a lightly forested stretch of pine and oak until we reached the garage. It was a modern building, a large Quonset hut with room for several trucks. It had been cleverly sited in such a way to keep it from the visitor's view. One of its wide bay doors was open.

A paved work yard filled a broad space next to the garage, and beyond that a chain-link fence extended into the woods in both directions. A gate in the fence hung wide open, leading to an exterior gravel road.

"I wonder if the fence runs around the entire village?" Patrick asked. "I bet if we drove all the way around we'd end up back at the front entrance. The open gate might be how your coyote got in."

"Maybe," I said. "I think there was a fence on either side of the main gate we came through yesterday, but it was getting dark, and I can't be sure now." Plus, I'd been distracted by Loris clinging onto Patrick.

We walked into the garage through the open bay. In addition to two pickup trucks, there were a few pieces of modern farm equipment, plus a scattering of antique tractors and wagons. A corner of the garage was fitted out as an office of sorts, with a desk and computer. A pegboard beside the desk held several labeled keys dangling from hooks.

"It smells in here," I said.

"But not like bodies, though," said Patrick. "More like garbage."

We walked to the desk. Two paper coffee cups had been knocked over, and the spilled liquid, evaporated long ago, had left wide sticky stains covering the desk's surface. A donut box had been pulled to the floor and partially shredded. A small metal trash can, the kind with a foot pedal to operate the lid, had also been upended and had rolled to a stop against a chair leg. A dried puddle of— something—had seeped from the closed container.

"I bet that's where the smell is coming from," I said.

"Probably," said Patrick, surveying the scene. "Hey, look. There's a handwritten note on the desk."

Neither of us wanted to touch the paper, which had been under one of the coffee spills, and the smeared lettering was difficult to read, but I was nearest and it was facing me, so I read it out loud for Patrick. "Trev stopped by with his state plow rig. He's really sick..." Here I stopped reading from the note and looked at Patrick. "The word really is underlined twice," I said. Then I continued reading. "He says he can't even make it back to the depot. I think he's about to pass out. We're taking him down to the hospital in Northwood. Back this afternoon. Damn phones are still out. Tell Loris when she gets in."

We were both silent for a minute. I was imaging how the morning must have played out, with Trev getting sick so fast these other two didn't even grab their coffees before rushing him to the hospital. Did they make it, I wondered?

I looked at the pegboard on the wall and noticed the key labels had license numbers written on them. Patrick grabbed the key to the nearest truck, a dark green Silverado with the Paradise Shaker Village logo painted on the side, and opened the driver's door. "Let's see if we can move this out into the light," he said. Prissy scrambled to climb in but couldn't manage on her own, so after a quick check to confirm the truck was empty of bodies, I lifted her up.

I walked around to the passenger side, opened the door, and pulled myself up and in. I wasn't used to the idea of climbing into a vehicle. Tyler's battered black Tacoma was much easier to manage.

The Silverado had both kinds of outlets in the dash, the normal three prong I was used to, and two of the old round plug types Stan was interested in. Patrick turned the key in the ignition, and the engine started right away. The gas tank was full. "This should do the trick," Patrick said. "Let's bring it over to Stan. He can fiddle with his radio thingy, and then we can all head out to the Agway and stock up."

He backed out of the garage and pulled into the work yard. I lowered my window, and Prissy hung her head out, tail wagging vigorously. She'd obviously done this before. As he was changing gears to put the truck into drive, I noticed something else parked outside on the far end of the garage.

Trev's state plow rig.

It was an enormous truck, with actual steps leading up into the front cabin, and two steel scoop-shaped plows angled together on the front to form a triangle, like in the pictures of the old steam locomotives.

I thought about what it must have been like that day. The confusion, the fading hope, the slowly dawning horror. The panic. I'd missed it all, isolated from the world as I'd needlessly sheltered in place. But Patrick? He'd lived through this. What were his memories of that day?

I looked over at him now. He didn't meet my gaze, and his eyes were shiny. Dr. Levy told me that when I was feeling pretty good and ready to build on my skills, I should make an effort to ask people how they felt. He said I might not be able to fully understand their answers, but just the act of asking—showing empathy, he called it— would help me develop. My mom called it "Fake it till you make it."

"Patrick, I know you don't want to talk about what it was like, but I know it must have been hard. I know I might not be the *best* person for sharing things, but I'd like to be here for you if I can."

A tear slipped down Patrick's cheek, and then another, all the way to his chin. He didn't say anything but reached over and gripped my hand.

And I didn't need to fake it at all.

Chapter Twenty

We retraced our path, this time in the pickup. Through the woods, up the hill, past the waterworks, along the orchard, around the barn, and then back to the Shaker dwelling house. Patrick parked right in front of the door and turned off the engine.

We got out of the truck, and Prissy leapt down on her own. It was a steep drop, and she let out a soft yelp when she landed. She gave her head a shake, and I knelt to make sure she was okay. "We'll have to be more careful. Make sure we lift her in and out," I told Patrick.

I was struck once again by the silence. Or, rather, the uninterrupted sounds of nature and how everything is different without the background hum of the modern world. Even at this distance, I could hear the low murmuring of the sheep in the barn.

Stan must have heard the truck. He came out the door with a rectangular black piece of equipment in hand, about the size of a shoebox, as well as several dangling cords and wires. Loris followed behind him, a notepad and pencil in hand.

"Nice ride," she called to Patrick.

"You boys found me a winner," Stan said, as he came forward and leaned into the open cab. "Multiple power options too." He pulled himself back out and stood straight. "Good work," he said to me. Prissy wagged her tail, then stood up, placing her paws against his knee, giving herself a good stretch. Stan absently reached down and rubbed behind her ears. "Well, moment of truth. Let's see what happens."

Stan slid into the passenger seat with his radio where he'd have more space to maneuver without the steering wheel in the way. Patrick went to get in the driver's seat. "Should I start it?" he asked as he headed around the back of the truck.

"No need," replied Stan. "I'm just after the battery power. Franklin, can you sit up front with me? I want you to see how this works." I was curious about the radio and pleased Stan wanted me to learn. Patrick backed away from the door, and I went around the front of truck to the driver's side. I froze for a moment when I realized this meant Loris would be in the back with Patrick. Stan was watching me. "It's all right, son. Come on in here."

Stan and I settled into the front seats, while—dammit—Loris and Patrick slid into the back. Prissy awkwardly tried to pull herself in behind me so I reached down, picked her up, and immediately twisted around to hand her to Patrick in the back. I noticed a couple of small, pale drops of blood on my hand and made a mental note to check if she'd cut herself when she tried to scramble into the truck on her own.

Stan set the radio in his lap and reached forward, removing the plug on the round power supply port. "Glad we don't need the converter since I didn't think to bring that along," he said as much to himself as to me. "This one'll do the trick," he said, lifting a short cord with a long prong that would fit into the opening on the dash. "This end plugs into the back of the radio." He shifted the radio so I could see the back. "Right here, see?" It was an odd plug. It looked more like a collection of pins than anything else, and I watched carefully as Stan inserted the cord into the radio, then plugged the other end into the battery outlet.

He settled the radio on top of the wide dash and oriented it so its front was facing us. It had two large dials, a narrow horizontal screen across the top, and numerous other buttons crammed onto its small surface. "Here goes," he said and turned a dial, causing the screen to light up a pale yellow. A loud squealing sound filled the truck.

"Sorry, let me adjust the squelch," he said, reaching for a small knob and turning it slightly, first in one direction, then the other, until the sound quieted to something more manageable. In the back seat, Prissy cocked her head to the side, ears forward and twitching.

Stan adjusted a different knob, and suddenly we could hear a voice under the other sound. It was difficult to make out, and inconsistent, fading occasionally as the louder squeal rose and fell above it. A woman was speaking, but I couldn't quite hear what she was saying. Or, I could, but I couldn't make sense of it.

"French, I think," said Patrick from behind me. I turned my head to look at him and immediately turned back, upset by how close to him Loris was sitting.

"Anyone speak French?" Stan asked.

No one did, so we listened as the voice faded in and out. Then, during a brief pause, Stan brought the microphone to his mouth, pushed a button on its side, and said, "Kilo One Bravo Yankee Oscar." He released the button and waited a moment. We didn't hear anything so he repeated the process.

Then, fainter than before, a voice said, "Oui? Hello? English...go on."

Stan smiled and spoke into the microphone. "Hello, this is K1BYO calling from Maine. There are four of us here. Where are you?"

In the back seat, Loris leaned closer to Patrick and said to him, "I bet she's in Quebec. They speak French there. It's not far."

There was a slight pause, and we could hear at least two voices conferring in French. Then, in halting English, "My name—" I couldn't make out the next few words. "—very bad—Dunkirk—" The squealing sound filled the truck again, and Stan fiddled with the knobs.

"Lost them," he said after a while. "I'll scan for other stations." The numbers on the screen kept changing, pausing now and then as the radio tried to lock on to a transmission. At one point we heard music, a march of some kind, Russian maybe. Stan looked over his shoulder at Loris and said, "Write that number down. They're broadcasting to let others know it's a live channel; we'll keep checking back for them." But it too faded abruptly, and after several more minutes, Stan gave up on finding another station.

Without the engine running, the windows had steamed up, and I started to feel panicky. It smelled in the truck. *We* smelled. We hadn't been in such close quarters before. I tried to lower the window, but the button wouldn't operate without power.

"Right," said Stan, opening his door as Loris and Patrick quickly did the same. "We're going to have to work on a bathing solution." Stan unplugged the radio and carried it out of the truck. Loris headed back inside. Patrick told Stan about the perimeter fence and told him we wanted to check it the entire way around before the three of us headed to Agway, just in case we needed to pick up some fence repair items while we were there.

We agreed we'd meet back here and leave in an hour.

"Let's drive back to the garage on the exterior road and see if the fence goes all the way around," Patrick said to me. I bent to pick up Prissy. "Maybe leave her this trip," Patrick suggested. "She can stay here and catch a few more mice."

I was a little uncomfortable with that, but it made sense. If we were going to settle in here, and it seemed likely we were, Prissy would need to find her own way without being constantly attached to us. Luckily, she didn't seem too upset when Patrick and I climbed into the truck and shut the doors. She waited a moment, then turned and trotted off toward the barn.

Chapter Twenty-One

We left through the village's main entrance. Patrick was driving, and we had the front windows down to air out the cab. As soon as he was beyond the fence, he parked and turned off the engine. We hopped out and each grabbed an end of one of the double swing gates, bringing them together to latch closed in the middle of the drive.

"That should keep out the coyotes," he said.

We pulled onto the gravel road and turned right, driving slowly along the fenced grounds of the village. A thick, unbroken forest filled the landscape on our left. The fence continued along the road's edge to our right and seemed to be in good shape, occasionally running through light thickets of bushes, but more often simply defining the edge of the village's fields and pastures. After ten minutes, we came to the back edge of the property and the gate to the garage.

We pulled into the work yard, and Patrick drove up to the open bay of the garage. He turned off the engine.

"Aren't we going all the way around?" I asked.

"Yes," he said. "But now that I know we'll be using this truck to get around, I want to fit it out for hauling what we need. I noticed some cargo bed covers and blankets against the wall in there this morning." He nodded to the garage. "We should load a few of those into the back so we can carry things like camp stoves and lanterns."

He opened his door and jumped down. "You can stay here. I'll just be a sec."

I stepped out of the truck, too, and waited for him, turning my face to the strengthening sun and lifting my arms high above my head, locking my hands together and tilting from side to side in a good stretch. I let myself relax into the moment as my gaze drifted about the yard. Against the foundation of the building, next to where a drainpipe emptied into a gravel-filled hole, I noticed a bright flash of yellow. I walked to it and stooped for a better look. Coltsfoot. Always the first flower of spring here and a welcome sight.

"Hey! No sleeping on the job," Patrick called to me as he exited the garage, using both hands to balance a stack of blankets on top of his head. He'd taken off his flannel shirt and tied it about his waist, leaving him in a dingy white sleeveless T-shirt. He walked toward the truck, and I noticed his hair was looking even more shaggy, and his chin was covered in a dull copper fuzz. I reached up to touch my own hair, and it felt greasy too. I pulled out a piece of straw lodged in a curl.

"We need baths," I said.

"I know. We've got to get cleaned up," Patrick said as he reached the back of the truck. "Lower the gate for me, will you?"

I went to the gate and pulled the latch, lowering it flat. Patrick placed the bundle on the edge, then seamlessly leapt up into the cargo bed and began pulling the blankets forward toward the cab. When they were piled in the corner, he took the top one and began rolling it out across the bed, smoothing it down as he walked back to the gate. When he reached the edge, he lowered his hand to me. "Here. Come up and help me out."

I didn't see what else needed to be done, but I grasped his hand and allowed him to lift me into the cargo bed. Once he did, rather than letting go, he pulled me close and said, "Now, were you trying to say earlier that I *smelled*?" He tugged me tighter and lifted his right arm, guiding my head toward his armpit.

He *did* smell. "Gross! Yes, you stink!" He pushed my face closer. I let out a helpless laugh. This was funny and...something else too.

He dropped his left hand down to my butt and lowered his face into my hair. He took a deep breath and murmured, "You stink too, Franklin. And I *like* it!"

Yes. I liked it too. I don't know why, but something about Patrick's smell, even his sweat, appealed to me. I ran a hand through his greasy hair and felt the slickness stay on my fingers when I pulled back. He tilted my head up to kiss me, and I pushed him back. "Wait," I said. "I...I smell. Really bad."

"I know." He grinned and reached down for the hem of my sweatshirt and, before I could object, pulled it over my head. The blast of chilly air sent a shiver through me, but at the same time I could feel my entire body heating as a flush rose up my chest. "Um..." I managed. I was suddenly having a hard time thinking clearly. "Wait...I think..."

Patrick placed his right palm flat against my chest and dropped his left hand to the button on my jeans. "Shut up, Franklin. And stop thinking so much," he murmured into my mouth as he guided us both down onto the blanket.

*

A half hour later, we were side by side on our backs, the sun warming us as our breathing returned to normal. Our clothes were tossed in a pile in a corner of the cargo bed. We smelled even worse than we did before, only now with the added layer of spunk on top. Patrick lifted up on an elbow and used his discarded shorts to wipe us both down.

So now I knew what *more* was. Or at least one version of it. Patrick assured me there were many other things we could try, but this was plenty for me. For now.

It had been mind-blowingly awesome. For the first time in weeks, years maybe, I felt all was well with the world. I could lie here forever.

Patrick tossed the soiled boxers away and blinked down at me. "Well?"

"That was good," I replied.

He snorted and rolled on top of me, wedging his legs between mine and pinning me in place. "Just *good*?"

I snickered and lifted my head three inches to give him a quick kiss.

"Okay. Fine, better than good. But you still stink, and you're heavy. Get off me."

"I'm just trying to keep you warm." He smiled and ground into me but then rolled off. He stood, a little wobbly on his feet, and made his way to the corner of the cargo bed where he bent over and began sorting through our clothes pile. The bright sun revealed a soft cinnamon dusting of hair across his butt. I liked it.

"Here." He tossed me my shorts and socks. I slipped those on, still feeling sticky despite his efforts to clean us off. I picked up my jeans and sweatshirt and finished dressing, then slipped on my boots.

"Okay," I said. "Spectacular. Extraordinary. Life changing."

"Dude! Yes! That's what I wanted to hear," said Patrick as he stepped into his jeans and, very carefully, worked the zipper. "We should go back now, collect Stan, and head into Agway."

"Yes," I agreed. "But...can we do this again? Soon?"

Chapter Twenty-Two

We discovered that both the fence and the graveled road circled the entire village, and the fence was in fine shape all the way around. Both Loris and Stan had assessed the animal feed situation and determined there was no immediate need to head to Agway, so Stan proposed a different idea.

"Let's take the truck and head to my house. It's only a few miles from here, and we can dismantle my ham gig and set up a new radio shack here. It has much greater capacity to reach more stations, both local and international. And my deep cycle battery still has juice in it."

"Why don't we just use the radio there?" I asked.

"Well, you never know when someone is going to be broadcasting, so we should have ready access to the radio. Plus, my shack is set up in my basement, which flooded after my pipes burst in the ice storm. The equipment should all be fine because it's up on tables, but we'll have to wade through a few inches of water to get to it."

We were standing out front of the dwelling house, enjoying the spring sun. Prissy lay at our feet, no worse the wear for having been left alone. Stan looked off to the side and said, softly, more to himself than us, "I set that rig up twenty-five years ago—long before Nancy died." He looked back at us and brightened. "It sure will come in handy now, though, if we can get it here. You boys game?"

Patrick and I looked at each other and nodded. "Sure," I said.

Stan looked at me. "I've got a bunch of books about the radio hobby, too, Franklin. I think you'd enjoy learning the art." I had to admit I was curious about how it all worked. Stan headed around the back of the truck toward the passenger seat. If he noticed the wadded-up pair of checkered boxers in the corner of the truck's bed, he didn't say anything. After instructing Prissy to remain at the village on guard-dog duty, I hopped into the back seat.

We first drove back to the garage, where we found a few good pairs of barn boots we'd be able to use if there was still standing water in the basement. We also grabbed a couple of plastic bags and several cardboard boxes for carrying the radio equipment. When Stan saw the massive state plow on our way out the back gate, he gave a low whistle. "That's a beauty," he said. "I drove one like it years ago when I worked for Central Gravel."

An idea was beginning to form in my mind. I'd need to give it time to develop.

We drove ten minutes to Stan's place. He lived in a small, neatly kept, gray ranch house in a neighborhood of similar houses spaced far apart. Some had been updated and expanded, but not Stan's. Patrick backed into the driveway, in front of the attached garage, and cut the engine. We stepped out of the truck. I was struck once again by the eerie silence. Something rummaged through the leaf litter on the far side of a short picket fence.

"Oh no!" Stan said suddenly. "I don't have my keys."

Patrick began walking toward the front door. "Are you sure you locked it?" he asked.

"Probably. I've lived here fifty years. Even with everyone dead, I can't imagine thinking about it enough to *not* lock it." Patrick rattled the doorknob. Locked.

"You said the basement is flooded?" Patrick asked as he walked to the garage door. He tried to turn its metal handle, giving it a hard twist, but that was locked too. He wiped his hands on his jeans and looked back at Stan.

"Yes, at least a few inches."

"Couldn't we just break in?" I asked. Patrick shot me what was probably a meaningful look and discreetly waved his hand in a shushing motion to me. Stan looked...confused, maybe...as he peered at his house.

"Fifty years..." he murmured to himself.

"Stan, is there a back entrance? We could try there." Patrick was speaking slowly, in a gentle tone.

"Yes, a kitchen door," Stan said, blinking at us. Patrick walked around the garage and disappeared for a moment, then returned and told us that door was locked, too, as was the storm cellar bulkhead. He placed his hand on Stan's shoulder.

"Stan, I can break just one of the small panes of glass on the kitchen door and reach in to turn the latch. We can even tape cardboard over it after if you want."

Stan was silent for a minute and was still looking at his house when he responded. "It's not much, you know?

But I always did what I could. These last few years have been harder, though, alone here. But I never let it become an eyesore." He turned to face Patrick, as if he'd asked a question.

"I know. It's a well-maintained little house. You must have led a wonderful life here."

Stan sighed. "Yes." Then he pulled himself up straight. "Go ahead. But come through and let us in the front once you're in, okay?"

Patrick squeezed Stan's shoulder and turned to walk behind the garage again. He took his shirt off as he went, wrapping it around his right fist. A minute later we heard a muffled thud, followed by tinkling glass. Stan didn't move, but stared off into the distance.

Shortly afterward, the front door opened and Patrick waved us in. "Brace yourselves," he said. "It smells in here."

It really *did* smell in Stan's house.

"Oh," said Stan. "I remember. I had just stocked up on frozen fish."

It also smelled of mildew and mold too. I knew I wasn't going to get used to it. I looked out the window and tried not to gag.

"Which way to the basement?" Patrick asked.

"Through the kitchen, I'm afraid. Sorry."

"No worries, Stan. Franklin, you two stay here for a minute while I go and check out the situation and figure out what we'll need. Maybe open a couple windows, yeah? Back in a flash."

Stan opened the two living room windows and propped open the front door. A cool draft immediately started pulling air from the kitchen out through the living room. Stan walked to a corner bookshelf with several framed photos. He picked one up and handed it to me. "This is my Nancy on our wedding day."

They were both dressed in what I thought of as "hippie" style. She looked very young, with a garland of flowers woven loosely through her long, dark hair. She wore a gauzy white shift that bulged tellingly across her belly, and was barefoot in the grass. Stan was strikingly handsome and not as young. He wore white pants and a white blazer with no shirt underneath. He was also barefoot.

"What times those were," Stan said. "She was still a teenager, but kids got married early back then. I was already thirty though! Scandalously old." I stared at the photo and couldn't get beyond Stan's long, curly blond hair—longer than mine—and strangely thick sideburns. "We were in love though; that's for sure. Fifty years of marriage. Nancy passed a few years back."

He picked up another photo and turned it toward me. This one showed two young men, both in their twenties. One had dark, mahogany skin, with slicked black hair; the other looked like a mirror image of Stan in his wedding photo, except neater. Both men were wearing crisp gray suits with white ties, and they stood in a tropical garden. They had their arms around each other, and a small dog sat at their feet. "My grandson, Garrett, on *his* wedding day, and his husband, Ernesto. They live in Colombia now. I hope."

"My parents are in Puerto Rico."

"I hope they're safe, son."

I didn't reply; instead, I reached over and put Stan's wedding picture back on the shelf. "Garrett here," Stan continued, turning the picture of his grandson toward me once more. "Well, it came as a surprise when he told us about himself. Him and Ernesto that is. But we love him more than anything, and I was proud of how Nancy and I responded. His mother—our daughter—ran off when he was just a baby. Drugs." He shrugged. "Addiction is a horrible thing. Anyway, we're the only real family he's ever had, and I was glad to make this easier for him."

We both looked at the picture of Garrett's wedding. "If I'm right, I'm guessing you and Patrick might be the same way?"

He phrased it as a question, but I didn't answer. I wasn't sure what everything meant anymore. Would I marry Patrick some day? Stan accepted my silence. "Be careful with each other's hearts," he said. "They're fragile things."

Patrick came back through the kitchen. "Jesus, Stan, that's a lot of equipment down there."

"It's a hobby I've built up for decades."

"Well," Patrick said, "at least we came prepared. And most of the water is gone now, but I wouldn't want to breathe the air in the basement longer than necessary."

"We won't need all the stuff down there. The computer and monitors need the internet to work, so they can stay. But I want the VHF and UHF band capacities that the mobile unit back at the village doesn't have. And I'll need my books, especially the directory of repeaters. I hope it specifies which ones run on solar. Anyway, I'll go down with you and show what needs to be brought out."

I didn't understand anything that Stan had just said, but it was more intriguing than frustrating. It wasn't about emotion and undertones; it was about science and technology. I could learn all of that.

Stan led us downstairs and showed us what we needed to pack. He then went back up to collect a few things of his own.

Patrick and I made short work of the project and had everything safely stowed in the truck's cargo bed within half an hour. Stan had filled a cardboard box with a few things, mostly pictures and small items I assumed had some sentimental significance. I also noticed a clear plastic bag sitting on top of the box with half a dozen prescription pill bottles in it.

We were standing in the living room by the front door, Stan's box on an end table. Stan kept glancing toward the kitchen, then at Patrick, then at the floor. Patrick was a holding a box cutter and a roll of thick blue electric tape he'd carried up from the basement. "Let's fix that window," he said.

"I'd hate to ask you to do that…" Stan began.

"Not a problem. We *should* fix it. Can I use this cardboard box?" Patrick asked, indicating a smaller, empty box Stan had placed next to the one containing his things.

"Yes. Thank you."

Patrick took the box and tools into the kitchen, and we followed him to the door. He cut a piece of cardboard to fit the space in the broken windowpane, taped it securely around the interior frame, then went outside and did the same, covering the cardboard itself on the outside to protect it against the weather.

"There. That should hold it," he said.

"Thank you. It's silly…" Stan began.

"No, it isn't. It's your home," Patrick said. "We'll bring you back anytime you want—"

"We won't be coming back," Stan interrupted.

Chapter Twenty-Three

The following morning, we set up Stan's radio in the barn's loft. It wasn't an ideal location, but Stan wanted to get an antenna attached to the cupula on top of the building, and he only had enough wire to connect the radio if it was also in the barn.

I climbed up the outside of the barn, all the way to the top, screwed in the bracket, and attached the antenna and wires. The morning was cold, with a bright sun causing the overnight dampness to evaporate quickly, rising up in wispy streams far into the distance. After I'd finished with the antenna, I rested for a moment and enjoyed the expansive view.

This was the highest spot in Paradise, and I could see clear across the river to the low hills rising on the opposite side of the valley. Halfway up a steep hill, a mile or two beyond the lower ridge across the river, I noticed what looked like a castle, a large squarish gray-stone building complete with corner towers and narrow vertical openings in the walls. I did a double take when I thought I saw a thin tendril of smoke rising above the castle but concluded it was moisture evaporating from a nearby bog. I made a mental note to ask Loris about it.

The wire was just long enough to make it to the radio, and we added antenna wire to our growing shopping list of items for our next trip to Northwood. In addition to the wire, Stan wanted another couple of deep-cell batteries which we could probably find at Home Depot, although he said a boating supply store would be a better choice. But that would require heading all the way to the coast, maybe Bar Harbor, which is at least another fifty miles after Northwood. Loris wanted books, anything we could find on sustainable small-scale farming and animal husbandry.

We also needed lots more flashlights and batteries, as well as personal supplies—toothpaste, floss, soap and shampoo, deodorant, cleansing wipes, ibuprofen, vitamins—everything, really. But we were stuck with just our motorcycles for the shopping trip because the highway down to Northwood was blocked by that big traffic pileup.

We were all sitting at the kitchen table trying to prioritize what we should get first, given our limited carrying capacity, when the thought that had been floating around in my head, just out of reach since we'd been to the village's garage, finally landed in place.

"Wait a minute," I said. "Why don't we take the plow?"

Stan got it first. "Yes!" He stood from his chair and came to grip my shoulders. I leaned away, flinching. "Right, sorry." He stepped back, grinning at me. "You're a genius, young man!"

Patrick and Loris looked confused. "The plow," Stan said to them. "You could drive the plow all the way to Northwood. Clear the entire highway I would imagine."

"Oh," said Loris. "We could drive cars or pickups or anything else between here and there as often as we want. Carry as much as we need."

"As long as the gas holds out," I said.

Patrick, sitting next to me, reached over and squeezed my shoulder. Loris noticed and gave me a look that was hard to describe, sort of a soft half smile. I'm sure it was intended to mean something.

"Was there fuel in the truck? Did you see keys?" asked Stan. "It'll be harder to find diesel to syphon, and we'll need to keep the gasoline and diesel pumps separate." Stan was getting excited about the idea, and I was pleased I'd thought of it. "I could teach you how to drive it, too, Franklin!"

Much as I found the idea of driving the enormous truck exciting, I was a little unsettled at the thought of plowing a bunch of cars, maybe with bodies in them, off the side of the roadway. Could I do it with my eyes closed? Probably not.

"Come on," Stan said to me. "Let's go see if this will work."

And it *did* work. Our biggest concern had been that Trev may have still had the keys on him when he was taken to the hospital, but instead, they were still in the ignition. There was only about a quarter tank of fuel, though, so we'd need to be on the lookout for other diesel vehicles as we went along, but any autobody shop or garage would probably work too.

It only took Stan a few minutes to teach me the fundamentals of driving. I'm a fast learner with anything mechanical. The trickier part was understanding the electronics of the plow operation. Both plows would have to be raised and lowered repeatedly throughout the drive to Northwood, and the angle of the plows would have to be changed sometimes too.

The plan was for Patrick to come with me, and our goal was to simply clear the highway all the way to Northwood. If things were going well and we had fuel, we would continue on through the town to the Home Depot. Loris or Stan would then join us for supply runs in the pickup, always leaving at least one person at the village in case of any emergency with the animals.

Our trip started off easily enough. We came across an abandoned, and thankfully empty, Subaru that had been pulled to the shoulder, and I conducted a practice run, lowering the plow, adjusting its angle, and maneuvering the truck to push it down an embankment.

"That wasn't too bad," said Patrick, from the safety of the passenger seat.

I thought about the gasoline and motor oil I'd just sent leaking into the creek alongside the highway. I wondered where the driver of this car had gone. Had they become too sick to drive and wandered off somewhere? If we looked, would we find a body close by in the woods, or maybe lying on the highway farther ahead, where they'd gone to wait for help that never came?

I didn't express any of those thoughts. Instead, I said, "When we get there, I want to stop at the library."

"Okay. We can do that." Patrick was silent for a minute as I continued the slow drive south. We passed a number of abandoned vehicles, but if they'd been pulled far enough to the side, we let them be. "Looking for anything in particular?" Patrick asked.

I stole a quick glance to my side and saw Patrick was rubbing a finger along the tip of his right thumbnail. He was looking away from me, out the front window and to the side, so we weren't making eye contact. And that's when something important occurred to me.

Dr. Levy had told me that when I became very close to someone, I might develop the capacity to read their body language. It would be a way for me know what wasn't being said. He warned it might never happen, but it would be a huge breakthrough for me if it did. And it would allow me to have a much deeper relationship with that person. At the time, I hadn't understood what he meant by reading a person. People aren't books.

But now I knew. I could read Patrick! What he was doing with his finger and his thumb and not looking directly at me—it all meant something. And what it meant was he was hiding something. This was an exciting new development. I wondered, could I push this further? Could I figure out what he was avoiding or not saying? I began to puzzle through that.

"Uh...Franklin?"

What? Oh, I'd slowed the truck to a crawl without realizing it. And he'd asked me a question. What was it? Right. The library.

"Books on human sexuality. I want to understand about you. About us."

Patrick let out a long sigh; he twisted in his seat and turned to me. I stopped the truck because obviously I couldn't read Patrick and drive at the same time.

"I explained about myself already."

I began to interrupt him, but he held up a hand to hold me off.

"*And*," he continued, "I explained the label didn't mean anything. We have this great thing that doesn't need to be defined. You're the one who wanted the label."

"That's true, but...it's important I understand things...when I can. You know? I don't always understand why people do what they do. The more I understand, the less chance I'll...screw up." I looked down at Patrick's hands to make sure he wasn't rubbing his thumbnail. He wasn't. In fact, he reached out his right hand and brushed it through my hair.

"You won't screw up. Don't be afraid. Don't get too lost trying to define things."

He continued to run his hand through my hair, and his finger suddenly snagged uncomfortably on a thick, matted curl.

"Sorry." He untwisted his hand and freed my hair.

"Gross," I said, embarrassed. "We need to do something about ourselves."

Patrick leaned forward and buried his face in my hair, his mouth brushing my ear. "You know you turn me on when you're all sweaty and ripe," he whispered to me. "Turn off the truck."

"Why?" I could feel my body beginning to flame with heat.

"I want to show you something," he mumbled into my ear, gripping my head tightly with his left hand as he used his other to pop the button on my jeans and begin working the zipper.

"You know, for an asexual, you're really..." He stuck two fingers, still slick from my hair, into my mouth to silence me.

"Demisexual," he corrected. And then he showed me what it was he'd wanted to show me.

*

This time we used *my* shorts to clean up our mess afterward, and I wasn't too surprised when Patrick reached into his pack and brought out a fresh pair for me. Green boxer briefs this time. I eyed them suspiciously.

"I know, I know. You're a boxers guy. But it's good to switch things up occasionally. Try new things."

I didn't think so, and I told him that. He said I wouldn't know until I tried, and I said I knew what I liked, and I didn't want to change. He said it would be good to test limits, and I said I liked my limits where they were.

"Albert Einstein once said that the measure of intelligence is the ability to change," he quipped.

Seriously? And then I said—and honestly I don't know what made me think of it, I didn't even know what it meant, but Loris popped into my mind, and that whole confusing conversation about whether or not Patrick was gay, and for some reason it just triggered me to say—"Well, lots of other fish in the sea."

Patrick's eyes widened. "*Okay*, sure, okay, Franklin. No problem." He was holding his hands up in surrender. "I get it; boxers-only for you from now on." He took his own jeans back off, then slipped off the underwear he'd just put back on. "Here, take my boxers, and I'll wear those briefs." I handed them to him.

"But you know, not really, right? About the fish? I mean, it's a pretty empty sea, you know?" He looked a little bit angry, maybe, as he pulled his jeans back on. Yes,

I think that's right, about him looking angry. I was getting better about this, at least with Patrick. And so I knew I was missing something. Again. Probably about the fish.

"Uh, no," I said. "I don't know—about the fish, I mean. I don't even know what it means. I just heard Loris say it, and for some reason it came out now."

"Dude! Seriously? You just threatened to break up with me over *underwear,* and you don't even know you did it?"

"Break up with you? No...I...wait... Do you mean we're together? Like boyfriends?"

Patrick blushed. "Of course we're boyfriends! Franklin, you are *everything* to me, man." He paused and let me finish getting dressed. "I mean, you know, assuming you *want* to be boyfriends?" He was rubbing his thumb, waiting for me to respond.

"I've been waiting for you all my life," I said, because it was true.

Chapter Twenty-Four

We continued our drive and hit our first snag just a few miles farther along. A half dozen dead bodies, maybe more, mostly, but not entirely, intact blocked the roadway. They had been dragged about and, unfortunately, ended up sort of *strewn* across both the shoulder and the travel lane, leaving no room to go around.

I stopped the truck. I couldn't just run over them.

"You'll have to just run over them," Patrick said.

"Gross. No."

"Well, then we'll have to move them out of the way."

I couldn't imagine doing that, either. I didn't want to even *look* too closely at them. I thought for a few minutes. Patrick didn't push me. My boyfriend—boyfriend!—was very good about being patient with me.

"I could drive," he offered.

"No."

I could do this. It had to be done, and besides, there were bound to be bodies in the big pileup, once we got to it, and others along the way too. I needed to face facts and man up.

"Okay," I said. "Let's do this." I started the truck again. "Talk to me while we go, though, the whole way through, okay?"

"Sure," Patrick said. I made certain the plows were lifted; then I began to move the truck forward.

"You know, Franklin, I've never felt this way about anyone before."

I smiled. He'd picked a good topic.

"What's amazing to me is that I want to be intimate with you all the time. I've never been excited about the idea of sex before."

Squish. I *felt* the slipperiness of it, or maybe it was my imagination. *Don't look; don't look.*

"In fact, if I'd met you ten years ago, maybe I never would have learned to identify as ace. I mean, if I'd met you from the first, I probably would have just thought I was gay."

Wow. Really? I was looking ahead into the distance, but I still knew each time we drove across another obstacle. *Crunch. Squish.*

"Well, of course, ten years ago I would have been, like, eleven, so, that's not exactly right. But what I'm trying to say is let's just forget about the labels for now, okay?"

Crack. Crunch. Uhn.

"I don't think they mean anything anyway here at the end of the world."

And then we were through.

*

Patrick talking me through the experience had been great and just what I'd needed. Unfortunately, he'd *kept* talking. "Of course, I still think demisexual is the right label for me because I only feel this way about you. Have only felt this way about *you*, ever. I mean, I'm ace, obviously, because I've made it to twenty-one without ever feeling like this before. It just happened so fast—with you, I mean. It's surprising, you know?"

No, I didn't.

He reached over and put his hand on my knee. He looked away from me and out the window, and that part of me that was just beginning to understand the undertones, at least with Patrick, thought what he said next was more to himself than to me. "Still, it would be interesting to know if it *could* have happened with someone else, now that I know it's possible, hypothetically anyway."

I thought of Loris. Uh, no; that wouldn't be interesting to find out, hypothetically or otherwise. I wiggled my knee to let him know he should remove his hand. He did.

*

It was only a few miles further before we hit the big pileup, the one with the overturned tractor trailer at the center and dozens of cars stuck on both sides.

"Ready for this?" Patrick asked.

"Yes."

I stopped the truck and arranged the plows. I set them both so they oriented to the right, the idea being the first plow would dislodge the vehicles and the second would scoop them farther to the side. I figured a few runs would be necessary to clear the right lane and shoulder first; then I'd adjust the plows and repeat the process on the left.

It went pretty much as planned. I pretended I didn't see the occasional body in a car, and Patrick made a point of not commenting on them.

The worst part came as we neared the center of the pileup, and we noticed the dark-green Silverado with the Paradise Shaker Village logo on the door. We couldn't pretend not to see that. "I guess they didn't make it to the hospital," I said.

"No," Patrick agreed. The passenger door was open, and I didn't see any bodies in the front seats. I had to assume, though, that Trev was still in the back. He would have been too sick to walk after they got stuck here.

No way but forward. "Well, plenty of fish in the sea," I said and started the truck moving again. Patrick looked over at me and quirked an eyebrow. He had a slight smile on his face.

We made it the rest of the way through without incident. Even the overturned tractor trailer was easier than I thought it would be to push aside. After that, it was a quick ride all the way down to Northwood. We had three more smaller blockages to clear, and we stopped once to siphon fuel for the plow.

We reached the camping store on the northern part of town first.

"I know this isn't a shopping trip," I said. "But shouldn't we stop here anyway and at least stock up on lanterns and boots and things?"

"No, we still don't know what we have to deal with ahead. And if we can, I'd like to clear all the way through the town and then out to the Home Depot."

And the Pets World, I thought to myself, but didn't say out loud.

"Plus, now that we've made it this far, we can easily come here in less than two hours any time we want to. Let's keep going."

We did and soon found that Northwood was a horror show. There were large pools of dried sewage and decomposing remains of bodies everywhere. The stench was overwhelming, even in the plow truck with our windows closed. We'd suited up with masks and vapor rub, but still.

"Do you *really* need to stop at the library?" Patrick asked through his tightened mask.

Well, I knew it would be difficult, but "Yes."

"Okay." We made our way down Main Street, past Jarret's and then farther along, past the side street running up the hill toward where we'd found Prissy. I stopped the plow in the middle of the street in front of the library, and we got out.

In front of the town hall next to the library, Sara had hung a large red banner reading: Virus Survivors: Come to the Paradise Shaker Village—50 Miles North. And, she'd stapled many pieces of paper with directions to the bottom of the banner. It looked like none had been removed yet.

"Where is Sara?" I wondered.

"She's probably been making lots of stops along the way, looking for others. Maybe she's even taking the back roads. She'll make it." Patrick looked toward the library. "Let's get this over with," he said.

We walked up to the porch, and I avoided looking over the edge of the railing where I'd spewed my guts out just, what—two? three?—days ago. We stepped through the front door. We'd rushed off in such a hurry that morning; I couldn't remember if Patrick had left a lantern there, but he had, and he picked it up and turned it on. I took my flashlight out of my tool belt, turned it on, and looked at Patrick. I knew he wasn't happy about the books I wanted to find.

"You go do what you need to do," he said. "I'm going to hunt down books on farming and sheep." He headed off into the stacks.

I went to the card catalog—thankfully they hadn't moved exclusively to digital yet—and looked up sexuality. There were a lot of entries, and I used the tiny pencil and scrap paper next to the catalog cabinet to jot down the numbers for the ones I thought I'd be most interested in. The books I wanted were clustered together in the textbook and research section of the newer part of the library.

I found what I was looking for and made my way back to the main reading room in the library with a heavy armload of books with titles like *Human Sexuality* and *The Science of Sexual Attraction*. They were mostly published by professional organizations. I had two from the American Medical Association and one from the American Psychological Association. I also found a book titled *Abnormal Sexuality*, which I tried to hide at the bottom of the pile.

I glanced over at the mattresses next to the fireplace, and at the plates from our last meal still sitting on the table. It seemed like so long ago.

Patrick returned with his own load of books and went right for the door. "Got everything you need?" I nodded. "Let's get out of here," he said.

Chapter Twenty-Five

There was plenty of room in the cab of the truck for all the books, and Patrick piled his in first, then turned to me and reached his arms out for my books. I took a step to the side and went to bend around him to put the books in myself, but he stepped smoothly in front of me, deliberately blocking my path. He looked me straight in the eyes, lifted his chin slightly, and said, "Give me your books, Franklin."

What could I do? I carefully handed over my stack of books.

He shook his head sadly as, one by one, he read each title and placed them on the floor next to *So You Want to Live off the Grid?* and *The World of Sheep's Milk Cheeses.* When he got to *Abnormal Sexuality*, he stopped. He'd been leaning over into the cab, but he stood and turned to me, holding out the book. "Seriously?"

"Uhm…"

"Come on! You're not going to learn anything about me, or *us*, by reading this crap, Franklin!" Patrick dropped *Abnormal Sexuality* onto the ground. I walked over and picked it up.

"I just want to learn as much as I can. I know it won't all be true."

Patrick stood in front of the truck door, flexing his hands, eyeing the book I was holding.

"Fuck," he said. "Fine. But we're going to Carole's Reading Room right now."

"The little bookstore? But they won't have more books than the library," I said, as I threw *Abnormal Sexuality* into the cab with the other books. Patrick's gaze followed the toss, but he said nothing. Instead, he turned, stomped over to me, and grabbed my hand, tugging me forward.

I tugged back. This wasn't okay.

He let go but said, "Come on. We're going right now."

It was a quick four-block walk, well, march, to Carole's Reading Room, which was in a tiny redbrick house one block off Main Street. There were a couple of bookshelves under the porch roof, with a sign dangling from the ceiling overhead reading Bargain Books! A rainbow flag decal was pasted on the wooden pillar at the top of a short flight of steps leading to the front door. Patrick tried the doorknob. It opened and set off a jangle from the bell attached to the interior header.

We stepped inside. Between the mask and vapor rub, I couldn't tell if the smell was worse inside or not. I didn't see any dead bodies after my first quick scan of the room.

"This way," Patrick said, taking my hand, not too aggressively this time, but not in a boyfriend-type way either. He pulled me deeper into the small, cluttered space, to the back of the room where a brightly painted mural declared this was the Queer Qorner. He stopped at a table with pamphlets and booklets displayed on it and began selecting brochures with titles like *All the Colors of the Rainbow* and *My Truth, Your Truth.*

He picked one up, considered it, and put it back down. He picked up another, almost put it down, then said, "Fuck it," and he strode off to the register, returning with a large plastic bag. He scooped up everything on the table and dumped it into the bag, then began pulling books off the shelves, fiction and nonfiction, and filled the rest of the bag with those. "There," he said, thrusting the loaded bag into my arms. "Let's go."

I hugged the bag to my chest as we hurried back to the plow truck. It was much too bulky to hold by the handles, and I had to continuously shift the bag in my arms to adjust the balance. After two blocks, Patrick slowed the pace a little and said, "Sorry, here," and he took the bag from me.

He was able to grasp the bag to his chest with one arm, and he draped his other across my shoulder and shook me gently, even as we walked. "You are the most *frustrating* man I've ever met." That was funny, because I could easily say the same thing, but I didn't. "You're lucky I love you, man," he said, releasing my shoulder and picking up the pace once again.

*

Once back in the truck, we decided we'd continue on, clearing the road all the way to the Home Depot. We made quick progress, and in just a few minutes we'd reached the urgent care facility where we'd left Patrick's motorcycle on the side of the road on that first day we were together. Ahead of us was the Home Depot. And Pets World.

"Should we rescue those turtles, this time?" I asked.

Patrick glanced over at me, a look of confusion—if I was reading that right—on his face. "Franklin, was that a *joke* you just made?"

"Maybe," I replied. It was intended to be anyway. I remember how he'd relieved the tension when we were here the first time with his comment about the turtles, and I hoped to do the same now after the uncomfortable trip to the bookstore. "Yes, it was," I added with more confidence.

"Well, good job, man!"

Patrick asked me to pull into the Home Depot parking lot. I did, then shut off the truck. I turned to him and said, "But, um, I don't think this is a good time to explore more sex stuff, you know?" Patrick laughed.

"No. Despite what you may think of me, I agree," he said. "But we need to decide what to do next, and I thought you'd like to think about the options without having to operate the truck at same time." I appreciated that and nodded my thanks.

"Okay," said Patrick. "The way I see it, we have three choices now. First, we've done what we came to do, so we could turn around now and head back."

That's what I'd thought we were going to do, and I was ready to do it, but I was also curious about what Patrick thought our other choices were.

He waited to see if I'd say anything, and when I didn't, he continued. "Second, we could head south from here. It's about fifty more miles to the coast. I don't think we should go the entire way today, but maybe we could get a car, and see how far down we make it before we hit a snag. Stan did say a marine center would be a good place for the batteries he needs. Plus, it would be nice, maybe, to have an open road to the ocean. If we get a few miles today, we could always come back with the plow and open it up."

That was an interesting idea. I enjoyed fishing, and Western Bay is protected enough to go out on a small boat. It could be good, too, just to get a better sense of how the roads are beyond Northwood. "What's the third option?" I asked.

"We could go to your house, in case you wanted to go back there for anything. We didn't have a lot of time to plan when we left last time."

I knew what he wasn't saying. He wanted to know if I thought my parents had been back. I considered it. I hadn't even left a note before leaving, I could let them know about Paradise, give them directions on how to get there. It was a nice thought. But...I'd been around now, and I'd seen how things were. They weren't making it back, not anytime soon. Assuming they were alive, that is.

"That's okay. I don't think there's a point in going there. But thanks for asking."

Patrick let out the breath he'd been holding. "That's good, man. I agree. I didn't want to push you, though. So, back to Paradise or onward?"

"Let's go a little farther. See what we find."

Patrick knew of a used car lot two blocks north on Highway 6, so we went there first and snagged a late model Ford Explorer. Once we passed I-27 again, heading south on I-6 this time, I was in new territory. There wasn't much down here, except for a few farms and timber lots, but there also hadn't been much traffic, so we'd been able to go at least five miles before we saw the dog.

It came racing out from a dairy farm, barking at our car as we drove slowly by. It was a medium-sized dog, maybe a beagle mix, with brown-and-black fur.

"Wait, stop," I said.

"Franklin"—Patrick began—"we can't—"

"No, no," I interrupted. "It's not a rescue mission this time. Look at him. He's healthy and well groomed. He doesn't look like a dog that's been fending for himself for weeks."

Patrick pulled the car to the side and put it in Park. The dog ran up to the driver's side door, still barking loudly, but also wagging its tail and staring through the window at Patrick. Patrick turned off the engine.

"Roscoe!" a woman called. "Down, boy. Come." I thought I recognized the voice. "Vet, come get your dog under control before he scares away our visitors." It was Sara, coming from behind a large wooden sign reading, Sweet Pea Dairy Farm. "Hello." She waved to us. "Don't mind the dog; he's friendly. Roscoe! Come."

I had my door open and was already stepping out when a woman appeared behind Sara. She was middle-aged, wearing overalls and farm boots. A patterned yellow bandana covered her head. She was wiping her hands on her thighs, and she looked behind her, calling, "Come on, Vet. There's people here."

"Franklin!" Sara exclaimed when she saw me. "And Patrick too!" she said as Patrick made his way around the front of the car, Roscoe running circles around his legs. "Oh, boys, it's so good to see you. Emily, these are the young men I was telling you about." Before we could be introduced to Emily, however, a young muscular Black man with a shiny, bald head rolled around from behind the farm sign in a wheelchair. His left leg ended at the knee. Roscoe darted to the man, wagging his tail vigorously, awaiting a command.

Sara reached me first and held out her arms. "Is this all right, dear?" she asked.

"Yes please," I said and meant it. I wasn't just tolerating the hug. I think she could tell because she gripped me tightly and whispered into my ear, "I'm so proud of you, Franklin." We broke apart, and she hugged Patrick. I could see Patrick was tearing up, of course, but I knew him better now, and it didn't bother me. Well, not too much, anyway.

After that, Sara made the introductions.

Emily owned Sweat Pea Dairy Farm and was the fourth generation of her family to run the operation. She'd heard Sara setting off Northwood's fire siren and made her way to town to investigate. "I'm looking forward to telling Loris what a good idea she'd had about the sirens," Sara said. "We'll have to try it in other towns too."

Vet and Roscoe had found Sweat Pea Farm just this morning. "Vet was just starting to tell us his story when we heard Roscoe barking," Sara said. She looped her arm around Patrick's and ushered us both toward the farmhouse. "Come in, come in. We'll get to know each other and plan our next steps."

Chapter Twenty-Six

The farmhouse was in rough shape. It wasn't very clean and had piles of junk mixed in with the furniture in every room. It made me very uncomfortable. "Sit," Emily said, waving at a collection of threadbare furniture in what was probably the living room.

Patrick removed a stack of papers and knitting from a two-person love seat. One of its four short legs was broken, and the sofa leaned slightly toward the front left corner. He sat there, nudging me down next to him. I sort of perched on the edge of the seat, not touching anything or looking too closely at the pile of dust-covered electronics—alarm clocks and portable heaters—jumbled together under the adjacent end table. Sara helped Vet through the door and carefully pushed aside another table, balancing the two lamps on it to make room for his chair.

Roscoe stayed outside. Smart dog.

After we'd managed to find seats, Emily came into the room carrying a big glass mixing bowl filled with a white jiggling substance. She plopped it on a table by the wall, pushing aside a bundle of pamphlets to make room. She returned to the kitchen, then reappeared with a stack of small, mismatched, serving bowls and a handful of plastic and metal spoons. "Fresh cheese," she explained. "Help yourselves."

"Uhn," I heard myself say. I felt myself starting to rock, just gently, and stopped when Patrick pressed his knee against mine.

"Oh," said Sara. "That's..." She trailed off.

"Very nice." Vet rescued her. "I'll roll on over there in a minute or two and give it a look."

The cheese gave off a strong, earthy smell, and I swallowed loudly. I felt beads of sweat on my forehead. We all jumped when the top serving bowl slipped from the stack and landed on the tabletop, no doubt resulting in another chip along its ragged lip. It wobbled before knocking a plastic fork onto the floor. No one moved.

"Uhn," I repeated.

"Look, Franklin," said Patrick, directing my attention out the window to the bright-blue sky and open fields. And...cows? They were smaller than any cows I'd ever seen, with thick, shaggy red hair.

Emily followed our gaze. "Those are my Highlands. My pride and joy."

The cheese smell became overwhelming, and I could feel bile rising up my throat.

"It's such a lovely day out," announced Patrick, in too loud of a voice. "Maybe we should head outside and meet your cows."

"What a lovely idea," agreed Sara, leaping to her feet. Patrick and I did the same, and even Vet began rolling toward the door before Emily could respond.

*

Being out in the sun and away from the cheese settled me. Yes, it smelled of cows and manure and hay, but in a clean way. A dozen or so cows clustered together in the nearest pasture, still feeding on hay this early in the season. I could hear their slow, rhythmic chewing and the occasional grunt as one jostled another for a better spot at the feeder.

A bench near the fence rail faced the pasture, and Sara had seated herself there. Patrick was sitting on the arm of the bench, opposite Sara, and Vet had pulled himself from his chair and was standing on his one leg, leaning against a fence rail for balance. He'd offered his "seat" to Emily, and she sat in the wheelchair, rolling it gently back and forth with her heels. I was standing next to Patrick, fidgeting as I recovered from the state of the house indoors.

Sara turned to me and Patrick. "Vet was just beginning to tell us his story and what his plans are when you two arrived."

"Vet is an odd name," I said. Sara frowned slightly and Patrick tensed. I realized that must have come out wrong, and when I replayed it in my head, I saw how I should have waited for Vet to speak first before asking about his name. And I shouldn't have just come out and said it was odd, even though it was. I was getting better about seeing my mistakes, usually afterward though. Oh well.

He didn't seem offended. "Sure is. But since I am one, and that's what everyone called me, I stuck with it."

"When you say you're a *vet*," Patrick began, "do you mean, like, a war vet"—everyone made a point of *not* looking at where his left leg must have once been—"or a veterinarian, like, with animals?"

"Yes," Vet said. Then, after a pause, he said, "Both." Roscoe sat at his side, lazily wagging his tail through the dirt. "I'm an army-trained veterinarian. I made sure all the dogs working with the troops were in tip-top shape. Bomb sniffers, service dogs, whatever."

Emily perked up at this. "A vet? I could sure use help with my stock." She waved an arm to encompass the entire farm. "Everyone's gone."

Sara spoke up, "Emily, we spoke about this, remember?" Emily cocked her head. "We're going to try to get to the Shaker village up north."

"I can't leave my herd," said Emily.

"I know, dear. That's why we were going to think of a way to take them with us. Perhaps if we all put our heads together, we'll be able to think of a solution." Sara turned to us. "Did you boys make it? With Loris? What's it like? Could we bring these cows?"

"They're not all cows," Emily said.

"Yes," Patrick said. "We made it. Stan did too. He's great, and he has a radio we think will allow us to talk to other people."

"And there's plenty of room for the cattle too," I said, looking at Emily.

"That's sounds nice," she responded, sort of absently, like she wasn't paying attention. In fact, she was staring at Patrick. "I know you, don't I? We've met before?"

"No, I don't think so," said Patrick.

"No, I do. I know it. Let me think..."

"Have you lived here long?" I asked, trying to be helpful. "Because, a few years back, you might have seen Patrick's—"

"Franklin!" Patrick interrupted. "Emily and I haven't met before. Really." He gave me a meaningful look, which of course I didn't understand, but I knew enough to shut up about it. "Why don't you tell Sara and Emily about the village?"

"Right," I said. "They have this amazing round barn with two levels, and plenty of fenced pastures," I continued. "Fruit orchards too. And running water and toilets. There's sheep right now, but no cows."

"Sign me up," said Vet. "Roscoe and I have been making our way, very slowly, up the highway toward Northwood. We were hoping to find other survivors. What you guys are describing sounds good."

"But how to get the cows there?" Sara asked. "Sorry, cattle," she said as Emily was about to correct her. "There's a cattle truck here, but I know it couldn't make its way fifty miles up through all the wrecks on the highway."

"We fixed that," I said.

Everyone turned to me. Patrick spoke up. "It was all Franklin's idea," he said. "There was a huge state snow plow left at the village, and we drove it all the way down here this morning, clearing the wrecks from the highway as we went along. We left it at the Home Depot. It's clear sailing from here all the way up to the Shaker village."

"Oh that's fantastic," said Sarah. "We can all spend the night here and head up together in the morning."

I thought of the cheese, and the inside of that house. So did Patrick, evidently. "I think we need to head back up now," he said. "We don't want Loris and Stan to worry, and they're expecting us back today."

"They're expecting me and Roscoe, too, right?" Vet asked.

"How could they be?" I began. "They don't even know..."

"Yes, come with us," interrupted Patrick. "It'll be easier to squeeze you into the Explorer than the cattle truck."

"Do you want to eat first?" asked Sara. "There's soup, not just cheese."

I didn't want to go back in there, and Patrick and Vet seemed to feel the same way, so we decided to hit the road. Vet leaned his weight on the fence rail as he took the few steps back to his chair. He sat and began wheeling his way toward the street. "At least let me walk you out to the car," said Sara.

"Bye, Emily," called Patrick, as he headed out of the yard. "It was nice to meet you. We'll see you tomorrow."

"I'll be sure the barn's ready for your cattle," I added. "And there's plenty of hay, so don't worry about that."

When we got to the car, Vet leveraged himself out of his chair and told me how to fold it so we could put it in the back. He threw his pack into the back seat and pulled himself in after it. Roscoe jumped in behind him.

Patrick and I were lifting the chair into the back when Sara said, "It'll be okay for us at the Shaker village, won't it?" She glanced back at the house. "I think she'll be...more stable once she's settled. She's been alone here the whole time."

"It'll be fine," Patrick said. "There's plenty of space, and the entire setup was built to operate without electricity. You'll like it there, and once the cows are settled in, Emily can rest up and get over the shock of everything."

"That's good," said Sara, taking Patrick's hand and squeezing it briefly. "There's nothing really wrong with her, not that I can tell. I think she just got overwhelmed by everything."

I knew *that* feeling.

"You're a good man, Patrick," Sara continued and turned to me. "You two are taking care of each other?" I must have blushed a deep red and didn't know what to say. Sara smiled. "Well! I guess you are then. Good for you. Be careful with each other."

"That's what Stan said," I managed. Patrick shot me a questioning look. I remembered he hadn't been there when Stan showed me the picture of his grandson and told me hearts were fragile things. "I'll tell you about it later."

"I'm looking forward to meeting him." Sara hugged us both and went back to join Emily.

"I'm starving!" Vet exclaimed from the back seat as soon as we turned around in the farm's driveway and began heading toward Northwood.

"We could go back, you know, for cheese," Patrick said. I knew he was kidding, and I was pleased I didn't even have to think about it to figure that out.

Vet laughed. He had a robust, deep laugh, and Roscoe woofed along with him. "Jesus, that lady is batshit crazy. I didn't know what I rolled into when I stopped there. I almost went right by, but Roscoe knew there were people there. Or maybe it was the cows." Roscoe was sitting up, getting a chest rub, and leaning against Vet. "Glad you guys came along when you did to rescue me."

"What happened to your leg?" I asked.

"Franklin..." Patrick began, but Vet jumped in.

"It's okay," he said. "I get it. Franklin here is a direct kind of guy, right?"

Yes, I was direct. "To a fault," as my father would say. Why did so many people find that uncomfortable?

"I served with a guy like you. His name was George. Luckiest bastard I ever knew. Bullets and bombs missed him all the time. If anyone's still alive over there, it'd be him." He pointed to where I sat in the front passenger seat. "Don't like to be touched either, do you?"

"No."

"That's okay. George hated it too. We'll get along just fine."

Patrick smiled.

"I lost the leg in a roadside explosion in Afghanistan last year. Lost Roscoe's dad in that explosion too." His left leg ended just below the knee, and he rubbed the end of his stump as he told his story. "Roscoe comes from a long line of service dogs. I took him on as a puppy when I got back. I started training him to be a service dog, but maybe I wasn't too good at that, or maybe he just wasn't cut out for that life." He scratched behind Roscoe's ears. "Anyway, he failed out pretty early in the process. Now he's just my best bud."

We continued on and came to the Home Depot. "There's our plow," Patrick said. "Figured we leave it here, maybe come back and clear the road south to the coast."

"Good idea," said Vet. "I imagine other survivors might be traveling by boat along the coastline. Avoiding the cities and highways."

"We'll be downtown in just a few miles. We can grab some food from the market. What else do you need while we're here, Vet? Clothes? Anything from the drug store?" Patrick and I waited for Vet's response, but he was silent for a few moments.

"Uh, guys?" he asked finally. "Anything I need to know here?" I turned around to look in the back seat and Patrick glanced in the rearview mirror. Vet was holding up *Abnormal Sexuality*.

"See, Franklin? You should never have picked up that book."

"I just wanted to learn about things," I protested once again. I turned around and faced Vet. "Patrick says he's—"

"Enough, Franklin." Patrick reached over and tapped my knee.

"No worries. All good, men. Just making sure you're not axe murderers or anything."

Chapter Twenty-Seven

We stopped first at the drug store, just before entering town. It smelled worse inside than it had when Patrick and I had stopped here the morning we met. It could have been the sewage, or it could have been whatever was ripening inside the small, formerly refrigerated, dairy case. But whatever it was, none of us wanted to linger. Vet picked up soap, shampoo and body wipes, as well as deodorant, vitamins, and—condoms? Patrick and I shared a glance. Who were those for?

We made our way back to the medical supplies, and Vet found an adjustable crutch he could use, allowing him to move about out of his chair, which made the rest of the trip through the store much faster. He grabbed a box of energy bars and several bags of mixed nuts and dried fruit, as well as a bottle of water and a candy bar on the way out.

We got back into the close confines of the car. "Jesus, I stink," Vet said, pulling off his shirt and opening the package of wet wipes. He really *did* stink. I was pretty sure he hadn't had an opportunity to clean himself up for days. I snuck a quick look at Patrick, who once again was reading my mind. He winked and took an exaggerated sniff, then shook his head at me and smiled. "Nothing," he said to me.

Good to know it was just *my* stink that turned him on.

Vet grinned when he saw the library, so we made yet another stop. He emptied out much of the science fiction section and said he was impressed by the setup we'd had before the sewer problem drove us out.

We made two more stops. First at Jarrett's, where Vet pulled on a new shirt after having cleaned up with the body wipes and grabbed several others. He also found pants, socks and underwear, and outdoor weather gear and boots. Well, boot.

Finally, we went to the Main Street Food Market, where we filled the Explorer with canned goods, bags of rice and beans, and crackers and chips. We didn't forget bags of dog food and treats for Roscoe and Prissy.

Even though we knew the road was clear, it still felt risky somehow to go very fast, so it took us the better part of two hours to make the trip back to Paradise. We got to know Vet better, and we learned why Roscoe wasn't going to make it as a service dog: he was afraid of children. Patrick thought that was funny, but I thought it showed wisdom on Roscoe's part. Children are scary. And messy.

We told Vet what to expect at the Shaker village, and he said it sounded like an ideal setup, especially when I described Stan's radio. "Oh, sure," he'd said. "It's like shortwave. We used that a lot in the military."

"Can you still drive?" I asked Vet.

"Probably could in an emergency, yeah. But my one working leg doesn't really *work* so well. It was damaged in the explosion, too, and doesn't always do what I tell it."

After a couple more miles, Patrick asked Vet if he was married.

"Nope," Vet said. "Still single." But he didn't elaborate and said nothing about a girlfriend, or a boyfriend.

"What about you guys?" Vet asked.

Patrick responded, "Franklin and I are just starting a relationship." Huh. I guess we're public about it then. Okay.

"Good for you guys. I kind of got that vibe from you." I knew nothing about vibes and always became confused when people talked about them.

And speaking of confusing... "Yes, but Patrick told me he's..." *What was it again? Demigray? Demigrace?*

"Franklin," Patrick interrupted, "Vet doesn't want to hear all about our budding romance."

"Sure I do."

"No," Patrick insisted. "You don't." That sounded final, and we passed the rest of the drive in silence.

The gate was closed when we pulled up to the Shaker village, so we stopped the car and got out to open it. I had swung one of the gates open, and was working on the second, when I heard Vet yell, "Roscoe!" I turned just in time to see the dog fly out of the passenger door and disappear toward the barn. I remembered Prissy doing the same when she'd scented the coyote.

I started to rush back to the car, but Vet had lowered his window and leaned out to call to me. "No worries, Franklin. He'll be fine. He runs off all the time." I waited for Patrick to pull through; then I shut the gates behind him and jumped back into the car for the quick ride to the dwelling house.

"He probably smells the sheep," I said.

*

We pulled up close to the building, left Vet's chair in the car, and headed toward the front door. Patrick supported Vet up the steps while I carried his crutch. Once inside the kitchen, Vet whistled and said, "Nice! Look at those sinks." I gave him his crutch, and he wandered about, checking out cabinets and worktables. "Beautiful construction. And there's running water?"

"Yes," I said.

"Hello?" Patrick called out. "We're back." When there was no response, he disappeared into the dining room; then I could hear him going up the stairs. He returned in a moment. "They're not here. Let's see if they're in the barn."

"I know the barn's like, right there, but do you mind if we drive?" Vet asked. "My working leg isn't doing so well today. I can hobble around in here on the crutch but would hate to have to make my way across a field."

"You got it," Patrick said. "Let's go."

When we arrived at the barn and opened the car doors, I heard a harsh, rhythmic grunting from inside.

"Patrick," I said, reaching for his arm as I remembered the horrible sheep attack when we'd first arrived.

"I know," he replied and turned to look at Vet, who was swinging his leg out the door.

"You guys go," Vet said. "I'll be right behind you."

We did. It was dark in the barn, and we needed to allow our eyes to adjust. "Oh, Patrick, thank god!" I heard Loris call, then: "Stan, no! Here. Shine the light right here."

The moaning was much louder now, clearly one of the sheep in pain. As we got closer to the stall where Stan and Loris were kneeling, I could see a sheep on her side, writhing and breathing out big puffs of steamy breath with each grunt. "I don't know what to do!" cried Loris.

We made our way over, and I saw the animal was giving birth. But there was obviously a problem, and a lot of blood. Her movements and moans were slowing down, not in a good way. Patrick went and knelt next to Stan, while I turned around and headed back to the barn's entrance to help Vet.

"Who are you?" asked Loris.

"He's a vet," I said.

"Oh," she said, pushing herself away and making room for Vet. I helped him sort of collapse in a controlled way onto the ground. Then I gave a supporting push as he pulled himself right up the sheep's hindquarters. The light shook in Stan's hands, sending deep shadows bouncing around the pen's short walls. "Patrick, hold the light," Vet commanded. "And, Stan—I assume you're Stan—" Stan nodded. "—go find another." He turned to Loris. "Sharp scissors and clean towels?"

"Yes, right here," she said.

"Iodine?" he asked.

"Shit. No, it's up in the supply room," she replied.

"Go get it," he said. Loris headed to the central stairwell at a jog.

"Let's see what we have here. Yeah, Patrick, keep the light right there. Franklin, don't let her kick you, but try to hold this leg—" He indicated her left rear leg, which she wasn't lying on."—up in the air for me." I grabbed hold of her and held it up. She seemed to have given up fighting and offered no resistance.

Vet pressed all around her belly, pushing hard, as if moving things inside her with his hands. "This is bad," he mumbled quietly.

Loris and Stan returned at the same time. "Stan, hold on to the iodine and keep a small clean cloth ready. And get ready with the scissors, but don't let them touch the ground. I need them clean." He dragged himself even closer to the sheep. "Loris, more light here please." With the additional light I could see...something...a head maybe?...just sticking out of the birth canal. Nothing was moving though.

The sheep let out a soft moan.

"Okay," Vet said to all of us. "I need to push the lamb back in, twist it, then reach in farther to find its front legs. I may have to cut the sheep open. I need all of you to be calm and ready. Patrick, Loris, she may thrash around a lot; you need to keep your lights where I'm working. Franklin, be very careful, but try to keep her as still as possible." He looked quickly at each of us, then nodded his head.

"Good. Here goes." He took both hands and slipped them around the head, *pushed*, and kept pushing as the head disappeared back into the sheep's body. She let out another moan, even softer this time. Vet was in up to his elbows, and was moving his hands around inside trying to reposition the lamb. "Damn it. Almost."

He leaned forward and twisted his own shoulder to shift his angle, said, "Keep the lights here," and then he *pulled,* slowly withdrawing two front legs, a head, and then suddenly, the rest of the body came sliding out in a wet puddle of fluid and blood.

"Light!" he yelled as both beams began to wobble. He reached his right hand back in. "We're not done here," he said. He twisted his arm, withdrew it, and a second lamb slipped out, landing with a soft plop onto the straw next to its twin.

"Right," he said. "Towel." Stan handed him a clean towel. He began vigorously rubbing and drying both lambs, paying special attention to cleaning noses and mouths of fluid. Loris let her light shift to the face of the ewe. "On the lambs please, Loris." The beam snapped back.

"Franklin, move around to her head and hold her gently. See if you can keep her on her side, with the teats clearly exposed." I let go of the leg I'd been holding and did as he asked, scooting around behind her and brushing pieces of straw and dirt off her belly. I used my fingers to comb back the thick wool from the teats, then moved forward to cradle her head in my lap.

"Loris, any other lambs born this afternoon?" Vet was still rubbing both, cleaning with the towel.

"Yes, two. One was stillborn though."

"Good," said Vet, which I thought was an odd reaction.

"Take this dirty towel and rub it around the belly and head of the sheep that lost its lamb. We might be dealing with orphans." Loris took it and her flashlight and walked a few stalls farther along the curve of the wall. I looked down at the head in my lap. Her eyes were closed, and I couldn't feel breathing. "Does anyone here have experience in milking?" Vet asked, loudly enough that Loris could hear him too.

No one did.

"Okay. Stan, give a clean towel to Patrick. Patrick, set your light down so it shines on her belly, and start rubbing the lambs, gently now that I know their airways are clear, and support them if they try to stand. I'm going to see if I can get milk flowing. They need the colostrum. Stan, get ready with the scissors and iodine." Vet pulled himself around until he was at a good angle to get to her teats, then began massaging one in a rhythmic, squeezing and pulling motion.

"Franklin, reach your hand down here." He took my hand and covered it with his as he continued working. "See what I'm doing? Can you feel the motion?"

"Yes."

"Good. Start doing this to the other one." I moved my hand out from under his and placed it on the other teat. Her belly was warm, and the udder felt full and squishy. "There might be a waxy plug blocking the tip." There was. "Just pick it off, like you would dried ketchup from the tip of a squeeze bottle." I did, and it quickly peeled off. I started massaging the teat. Nothing was coming out.

"Keep trying," Vet said.

We both worked for a minute or two. The head in my lap remained motionless.

Then two things happened at once: Patrick said, "This one's trying to stand." And Vet said, "Got it!

"Patrick, I'm going to keep this up. Bring a finger over here and get it wet with milk, then put it in the mouth of the lamb trying to stand. Keep doing that. We're going to try to trigger sucking." Patrick moved to do what Vet had asked, and for a moment I couldn't see anything because he had squatted between the flashlight and the sheep. Once he shifted, I could see what he was doing.

His finger was slicked with the sticky fluid as he reached toward one of the lambs. "It's thicker than I thought," he said.

"It's colostrum. Normal milk comes later." After a moment, he said, "Is it working?"

"Not yet," Patrick replied. But after another few seconds, he said, "Oh wait. Yes! He's sucking on my finger." Vet looked over at Patrick and smiled.

"Bring the lamb here. Franklin, go to the other lamb and take over the gentle rubbing from Patrick."

The newborn was laid in front of the sheep's teat, and after several false starts, it latched on and start sucking. "Thank god," Vet said. "One at least. Patrick, work your finger magic on the other lamb." Vet sat alongside the nursing lamb, his leg stretched out away from the ewe's body. "Stan, hand me the scissors please; and be ready with the iodine and a clean cloth."

Vet cut the umbilical cord a few inches from the lamb's body before taking the bottle of iodine from Stan and soaking the cloth with it. He used the cloth to clean the cut, then turned to Patrick. "Any sucking yet?"

"Yes," he replied.

"Good. Bring it over. We only have one working teat here, so we'll need to swap them out." Vet pulled the protesting lamb away from its mother's teat and placed the other newborn there. The first lamb wobbled on its feet now, stumbling about. It went to its knees once before pushing back up and shaking itself vigorously. The second lamb was also nursing now, but not nearly as urgently as the first one did. The ewe was not moving.

At some point, both Roscoe and Prissy appeared. They were sitting outside the stall, staying out of trouble but intently focused on their humans.

"I think that's it," Vet said. "We'll get no more from her, I'm afraid. Hopefully, it was enough." Oh, I guess I'd known since I had her head in my lap, but she was dead. "Let's hope the other ewe is willing to take them on. She'll have their scent now from the towel."

Loris had returned and was leaning over the pen's wall.

"She's...dead?"

"Yes, sorry. I did what I could. Hopefully we can save the lambs."

"Oh god...but...how can we hope to...what's going to happen when..." Loris was beginning to cry. Stan moved to her and put an arm around her shoulder. When Patrick cries, I know how to handle it. I don't like it, but it doesn't freak me out anymore. But I don't like Loris, and her crying bothered me. She leaned into Stan and started sobbing in a messy, uncontrolled way. I heard myself let out a soft *uhn*.

"Let's go inside," Stan whispered to her as he began leading her toward the exit.

"Patrick, can you bring these two little guys over to their new mom?" Patrick picked both of them up at the same time. "And let me know if they start nursing."

"Franklin, help me clean up, okay?" I grabbed a couple of the clean towels Stan had left behind and knelt next to Vet. His hands and arms were filthy, and his body was covered in sticky damp straw from lying on the ground. "Are you doing all right?" he asked me. I thought I was. I'd like to talk about this with Patrick though.

"Why was Loris crying?" I asked.

"You know her better than I do."

Not by much, I thought.

"Does she seem to you like the type to cry over a dead sheep?"

I thought about it. Actually, no. She struck me as kind of hardened.

"No."

Vet finished wiping off his hands and tossed the towel aside. "Hand me my crutch," he said. I did, and he raised himself up, stiffly. I helped brush off bits of straw and dirt. "So then, maybe there's something else going on with her."

"Undertows," I murmured.

Vet nodded.

Chapter Twenty-Eight

Immediately after the bloody birthing experience, I took Vet over to the laundry building and began heating water for a bath. While we were waiting, Vet told me about the work he'd done in Afghanistan, both caring for the army's dogs and also helping out local villagers with their goats and sheep. This hadn't been his first difficult livestock birth.

When the water in the heating tank was piping hot, I hooked up the hose and drained it into the bathtub. Vet stripped down, and I helped him climb in; then I went to start heating a new tankful, knowing all the dried blood and dirt would quickly turn the first tubful filthy. I put the soap and shampoo where Vet could grab it. He let out a relaxed groan as he sank in.

He had a series of black and very dark-blue tattoos running across his shoulders and down his arms to the elbows. It was a knotted design, all complex interconnected geometries. They highlighted how muscled he was, and probably meant something in the language of tattoos. He had a series of smaller, starlike tattoos in an arc above his groin, and, finally, a chain-link-shaped tattoo that circled his leg just above the stump. I wasn't sure where to look, or not look, for that matter.

Vet leaned back in the tub and sighed again. "Ever seen a stump before?" he asked.

"No."

"This is a good clean one. I had a great surgeon. She was also a friend. Still over there. Or, dead now, I suppose."

I thought about Puerto Rico.

"Anyway, she was able to nicely tie the extra skin around the cut, no ugly scars or anything. I was fitted for a socket and ready to get my new blade-runner foot, you know? Then the shit hit the fan."

I checked the temperature of the water in the heating tank. It was hot. "Ready for a refill?" I asked.

"Yeah," he said, leaning forward and removing the tub's plug. The dirty water quickly circled down the drain. When the tub was completely empty, he said, "Hit me," and leaned back again. I moved the hose into position and opened the nozzle. As the tub filled, I studied the stump.

"Funny thing," he said. "The leg that's not there hurts more than the one that is, most times." He proceeded to soap up. He washed his hair, and I rinsed it with the hose. "One of these days, I'm going to make it over to Bangor, to the vet health center. I think my new socket and leg are just sitting there in a box. Waiting for me to come get them."

I thought about that. There was no reason we couldn't clear the road to Bangor just like we had to Northwood, and like we planned to do to get to the coast. There would probably be more survivors there too. People who could maybe come help here.

"We can do that," I said. "Would you know where to go?"

"Yes, I've been there for rehab and my fittings."

"I'll talk to Patrick."

Vet sank down into the tub so only his chin was above the water level. It was weird to see the one knee sticking up out of the water. "So, you and Patrick, huh?"

"Yes."

"Nice. It's good to find someone, especially when you're young. Me, I'm an old man already, and not even thirty yet." He closed his eyes and leaned his head back. I didn't say anything. I was puzzling through what he might have meant by being old but not yet thirty. I could ask, I guess. That's probably what Dr. Levy would suggest.

Vet popped open his eyes and looked at me. "This is when you say, 'You're not old, Vet.'"

"Why would I say that if you already said that you are?"

He sighed and sank all the way under the water, so far under that his stump bobbed at the surface. Then he shot back up and shook his head, sending water flying about the room.

"Yep, just like George." He seemed to be talking to himself more than he was to me, so I didn't respond. "I'm going to have to get used to this all over again."

*

Sara and Emily arrived the following day, along with all the cattle, and we spent the next week settling in and getting ourselves sorted.

Vet ended up with a mattress on the first floor, in the small room behind the back stairs, so he wouldn't have to navigate steps to get to the toilet. It was also convenient for him because the handicap ramp entrance to the building was in the rear, so he could more easily get in and out from there.

Emily seemed, well, less confused anyway, but still not entirely *present*, I guess. Of the two lambs Vet had managed to save, only one had successfully imprinted on its new mother. The ewe had rejected the other lamb. It was a tough thing to watch, and we knew the little guy wasn't going to make it.

But Emily saved the day. She knew all about bottle-feeding orphaned livestock and made us go back out to the local market to get a baby bottle. She was able to collect plenty of milk from the nursing ewes, and soon had a baby lamb with her all the time. She would sit for hours with it, feeding it, or just rocking it as it slept. I think it was good for both of them.

No one ever told me why Loris had cried so hard when the ewe died. Patrick didn't know, and both Sara and Stan wouldn't talk to me about it.

*

Later in the week, we connected with the people in Pennsylvania. Stan knew someone was broadcasting on that channel we'd heard in the truck because of the music, and he tried checking in every hour, and it finally paid off. There were ten people together there in a situation similar to ours, living on a horse farm in Amish country near Lancaster.

They'd already made contact with six other groups in the United States and three in Europe. Every other day, at 11:00 in the morning, Eastern time, all who could got on the same channel and shared news and information. We only made it to one group meeting before Stan's radio battery died, but now that we knew how useful the radio would be, we prioritized getting additional batteries and better antenna materials, so we could move it from the barn to the dwelling house.

The one thing we did learn before we lost contact was that the entire world seemed to be impacted, and no one who became infected recovered. Everyone who was alive right now was somehow immune, but no one knew why or how. Best estimates were about one person in a thousand didn't get sick. I did the math and concluded that would leave a couple of dozen survivors in and around Northwood. There were more of us out there then.

And that would also mean more than a thousand people alive in Maine right now, with many of them down near Portland, which isn't safe, given all the health risks. How many Shakers lived here at Paradise, at the height of their movement?

How many people live in Puerto Rico?

Chapter Twenty-Nine

By the end of April, the sheep had stopped birthing. We'd lost two adult ewes and seven newborns. But there were nearly two dozen healthy lambs now, including plenty of males, so the trend was good. Emily's cattle herd had already included four calves when it arrived, and two of those were males, and she hoped they would make good studs next year. I didn't ask what she'd done with all the males born last year.

Loris and Sara had been planting vegetable seeds, which were still in flats inside the greenhouse. They wouldn't be able to go into the ground until late May. Stan said we should take a stab at field crops, knowing the first year would just be a learning curve. "Better to learn now, when there's still plenty of feed available at the farm stores," he said, which was a good point.

So we planted alfalfa and clover, plus plenty of corn, beans, and peas.

I had become "in charge" of the barn, which I liked. It was quiet, useful work, and I understood the setup and the needs of the animals. Every morning I'd hunt around the second level of the barn and collect eggs, check on the sheep and cattle, put down fresh food, and fill the water troughs. In the afternoons, I mucked out the stalls and tended to the compost heap.

Prissy would keep me company, and occasionally Roscoe would join us too. After they'd sorted themselves out during the first few days, the dogs generally ignored each other.

I would occasionally see Emily aimlessly drifting through the barn. She'd become more detached than ever. I complained to Sara one morning. "Emily doesn't do anything *useful*," I said, shortly after I'd spent two hours mucking out all the cow shit from the barn.

"I'm disappointed you'd say that, Franklin. We can't lose our humanity, now more than ever."

Sara had a way of saying things like that. Things that didn't make any sense at first, but once I'd had the chance to think about them for a while, they'd seem really smart. Eventually, I realized Sara was saying it was a mark of a strong community when we care for each other, regardless of what we can or can't contribute. Sara is a smart lady.

"You know, Franklin, in addition to my husband, who was in France when all this happened, I also have a daughter."

I didn't know that. When I thought about it, I realized I didn't know anything about the lives of any of the people who worked at the school. Sara waited to see if I'd say anything, and I knew I was supposed to respond.

"Was she...here?"

Sara sighed. I think she was glad I'd asked, that I knew to engage that way, but now she had to answer, and that was difficult in its own way.

"No," she said. "Hanna left home when she was only eighteen. She fought with addiction for years. I don't know where she's been living. It's been a decade now."

Sara wasn't crying, which I appreciated. I knew I was supposed to say, "I'm sorry," which I did, but without thinking, I kept going. "You've been so good for me though. For all of us." She did cry then, just a little.

"*Thank you*, dear. You have no idea how much that means. Grab onto people, Franklin. *Love them*. Love them as hard as you can. It's the only thing that matters."

*

One morning, which promised to be the first truly warm day of the season, Patrick and I were loading hay bales into the second level of the barn. It was hard work, and we used a heavy handcart to bring the hay in and position the bales around the walls near the drops where they could be lowered down into the animal pens as necessary. Prissy was darting about in piles of straw, following the occasional squeaks and skitterings of mice.

He and I had fallen into a comfortable rhythm. We were both getting good at kissing, and, well...more. Although not *much* more. I kept thinking about the condoms Vet had picked up, wondering when he thought he might use them. I worried, too, about whether or not Patrick would ever want to do anything that would require a condom. I was pretty sure I hoped he wouldn't. And even though we could talk about anything, I did *not* want to ask about that.

I hadn't gotten too far in my reading, either. Patrick had made me promise I'd go through all the pamphlets and novels he'd grabbed for me first before I began reading the medical texts. Since it was important to him, I agreed. But I was regretting that now. Some of the things he'd grabbed from the table were just silly, and I was having a hard time sticking with them. But whenever I tried to explain to Patrick that stories about people's experiences and personal feelings weren't helpful, and certainly not scientific, we would fall into an argument about the "legitimacy of people's lived experiences." It just felt so...soft, somehow. I needed facts.

But I decided to let it be for a while. We were getting good at learning each other's boundaries.

When the last of the bales was in position, I sank down into the straw with my back against the wall and pulled a water bottle out of my pack. I held it out to Patrick. "Come here," I said.

He walked over, wiping his sweaty hair from his forehead. "Thanks," he said, reaching for the bottle. Right before he could take it, I pulled it away from him and lifted my arm above my head. I tilted my nose toward my armpit, where my T-shirt was soaked in sweat.

"Phew," I said. "I stink."

Patrick smiled broadly and dropped to his knees, straddling me. "Do you now?" he asked, moving his head toward my neck. "You're getting pretty bold in your advances, my young man." He was right. I took the lead occasionally now, and we both liked it when I did. I was about to capture his chin and turn his head so I could kiss him, but I didn't because that's when we heard the gunshots.

Three loud shots, with a second or two between them. We froze and looked at each other. "What the fuck?" Patrick asked. Prissy appeared from under a pile of straw and started barking. Patrick and I scrambled to look out the window. We were facing the dwelling house and didn't see anything.

Three more shots followed, clearly coming from outside, on the opposite side of the barn. We hurried around the perimeter to the opposite windows and knelt before one.

In the hay field below, Loris and Vet were target shooting with handguns. Or, more accurately, Vet was teaching Loris how to shoot. His chair was off to the side, and he was leaning on his crutch, standing next to Loris, a bull's-eye target paper ten feet or so in front of them.

Now that we were on this side of the barn, our heads at the window, we could make out some of what they were saying. "Better," said Vet, "but keep your elbows locked so your shoulders take the recoil." He moved behind her, *directly* behind her, then reached his arms around hers and held onto her forearms. "Like this," he said.

Patrick looked at me and rolled his eyes. "Obvious much?" he whispered to me.

Loris backed more firmly into Vet's grip, and fired off three more shots.

"Nice!" Vet exclaimed. Loris let out a girlish laugh.

"Seriously," whispered Patrick.

"Why are they doing this?" I asked.

"Loris did mention she wanted to be able to protect the flock from coyotes." Patrick responded. We couldn't hear what they were saying now, if anything, but Vet seemed to be rubbing his hands up and down Loris's arms. Was that part of the instruction?

Patrick huffed and turned around, sliding down to the floor so that he was sitting with his back to the wall, mostly below the window. I did the same, without the huffing, and sat next to him.

"Does it bother you they're doing that?" I asked.

"No. No, of course not," he replied, rubbing his index finger against the tip of his thumb. So, "yes," he meant.

"Why?" I asked.

"Why doesn't it bother me?"

Now he was just being difficult. "No. Why *does* it bother you?"

Patrick chuckled. "I'm not sure how I feel about this new you, all tuned in to reading my complex emotions and all."

I liked the new me, and I wasn't letting him change the subject. "Talk to me. We said we always would."

"Chill, Dr. F, fine. Let me think a minute, though, so I can make sense of it myself, okay?"

"Sure. I can wait while you think about things." It was nice to be able to do that for him, since I was usually the one needing thinking time.

We sat in quiet, with Prissy softly burrowing through a straw pile, and the chickens making their way toward us in a small group, pecking for seeds and bugs as they went. There were no more gunshots, but occasionally what sounded like a giggle floated up to our window.

"Okay, here's the thing," Patrick said, rubbing his forehead with both hands, then folding them in his lap after he twisted to face me more directly. "I think, maybe, I'm a little bit disappointed she could...like Vet...that way.

When I thought she liked me that way." He'd been looking down at his lap when he said this, but when he finished, he raised his eyes to look at me, to see my reaction.

"But you told me before you *didn't* think she liked you that way."

"I don't think I used those words *exactly*," he said. When I began to protest, he held up a hand. "But you're right, when you said you thought she did, I tried to wave it away."

"Why?"

"Because I knew it would upset you, Franklin. I could see you were becoming obsessed with her, like you are about the fact that I'm ace. I didn't want you getting all anxious about it." So, what, he lied to me to make feel good, because he didn't trust me with the truth? And what *was* the truth? *Did* he like her? Was that why he was bothered about Vet?

"But why shouldn't I be anxious? If you think she likes you, and you think you're asexual—"

"I *am* asexual. Demisexual, remember? I think we may have talked about this a few thousand times already." He actually rolled his eyes.

"Well, then, you could like her back, right? The way you like me?"

"No! I mean, maybe I *could*, but I don't. I only like *you* that way, Franklin. How many times do I have to say this? I don't feel sexually attracted to any *type* of person. I'm only attracted to you, because—god help me—we bonded that way."

We were going in circles. I hated when this happened. I took a deep breath and tried to follow Dr. Levy's advice about breaking bigger problems into smaller ones, making them easier to tackle. First, I reached over and took one of Patrick's hands in mine. I had come to learn he read this as a signal I wasn't too upset.

"Back up. Let's start at the beginning. *Do* you like her?"

"No." he said. I glanced down at his hands but realized he wouldn't be able to rub his fingers together since I was holding one. But I didn't want to let go now. Plus, he sounded sincere. "In fact, I don't think I even *like* her, you know? I mean, as a person."

That was interesting. I didn't like her, either, but I'd always assumed it was because I thought she liked Patrick. But maybe there was more to it? "Why don't you like her? I mean, generally," I asked.

"I don't know exactly. She always seems so *intense*, I guess. I mean, yeah, everything's changed and it's upsetting, but she's always, like, thinking ten years down the road, when I sometimes just want to get by, you know?"

Yes, I could see that. I kept hoping we'd find our way back to civilization, or it would find its way to us. Loris seemed committed to this idea that we need to recreate everything, and we need to do it here. "Yeah, she is intense. I see that. Like how she's always trying to touch you." I nodded up toward the window behind us. "And maybe him now."

"Right, so I guess, maybe what bothers me is she wasn't just that intense for me, but she can just be that way with everyone." Patrick slumped a little, and his hand tightened in mine. "Which is shameful, I know. It's just my wounded ego."

That was honest and seemed less threatening to me, now that I knew Patrick didn't really *like* her. Still, it was disturbing to think he wanted her to like him, in an intense kind of way. That was confusing. And what about Vet? Did *he* like her? Did he know she was treating Patrick the same way, or that she wanted to at least? Thinking about Vet and Loris brought my mind back to the drugstore trip.

"Condoms," I said.

Patrick froze in place. "Uh, right, well, I... I don't have any with me..." he began. "I mean, I wouldn't necessarily be...*totally* against the idea...uh...sometime in the future, maybe...but doesn't it seem a little soon...you know, particularly since we're..."

"No! No! That's not what I meant. God. Gross...oh, no, not *gross*...exactly... I just meant...no. Stop now."

We both silently agreed to forget the last minute and resumed our conversation from right before my condom bomb. "It's curious though," said Patrick. "I wonder why she's behaving this way? She doesn't seem so...sure of herself, I guess...not the kind of woman to get all silly over a man. I mean, generally she seems pretty confident and resourceful. Resilient even. Is this an act? And if so, why?"

His question reminded me of Vet's, when he'd asked me if she seemed like someone who would fall apart over a dead sheep. No, she didn't.

"And I meant to ask you earlier," Patrick continued. "When did she tell you there were plenty of other fish in the sea?"

Oh. I had to think back. That was our first morning at the village. That's right; we'd been talking about Patrick.

"She was asking about you, that first morning. She wanted to know if we were gay."

Patrick's eyes widened. "Seriously? What did you tell her?"

"I told her I was, and then I told her what you'd told me." Or the important part anyway, I thought. No way was I going to try to explain all the demi-ace stuff. Or whatever.

Patrick chuckled. "Oh man, I would have loved to see you try to explain gray ace sexuality."

"I didn't do that. I *still* can't do that. I just told her you'd told me you weren't gay."

"Oh, just...that?" Not good. He was rubbing his fingers together.

"Yes. I told her I was gay, and that I asked you if you were gay. And that you told me you weren't gay. Twice." Was I forgetting anything? "Oh, and she told me I was brave, which doesn't make any sense at all; then she said that bit about the fish." I thought that was all of it.

Patrick gulped. "Gosh, when you put it that way..." He squeezed my hand. "Um...how did she take it?"

"Weird. She seemed excited about the whole thing."

"Oh no," he sighed. "I'm sorry, Franklin; I didn't mean to put you in that position. I'll need to talk to her."

I didn't understand his comment. He hadn't put me in any position. Just more undertows, I guess.

Chapter Thirty

A few days later, I had finished my morning chores and was sitting up on the second level of the barn by a bright window, trying to finish my Patrick-assigned reading so I could finally get to the medical texts. Prissy was napping beside me. The sun warmed my neck and shoulders, and I was dozing as much as reading.

I was in the middle of a short novel, another story of a brave young person defying convention and boldly asserting their identity, overcoming all sorts of hardships, and finally finding love, or at least happiness, in some sort of relationship situation I didn't understand at all. I kept trying, for Patrick's sake, but all these stories were blurring together for me.

To be fair, I wasn't a fan of fiction in the first place. It made no sense to me that people make up these wild stories and present them as if they were true. If it was science fiction or fantasy, I could get into it. That wasn't *supposed* to be true. I'd been obsessed with *The Hobbit* when I read it as a boy. I knew it wasn't real, but I enjoyed the detailed, constructed world, and it was clear about the rules and distinguishing between right and wrong.

These books Patrick gave me were different. I found it difficult to know what was true and what wasn't, and even harder to figure out who was supposed to be right and who was supposed to be wrong. It was all very confusing and I didn't like it.

But still, I had promised I'd read them, so I struggled through it.

I looked down at the book in my lap and realized I'd been on this page for a long time. I'd been thinking about the radio, and the fact that things were organized enough here now that Patrick and I could take a couple of days and try to clear the road to the coast, find a marine center, and get as many deep-cell batteries as we could. Also, now that I knew more about how the radio worked and the different bands, I was developing a shopping list in my head for what we'd need to develop different antenna capacities and where we might be able to find those items.

But I forced my attention back to the book. I tried to find where I'd left off. I was near the bottom of the page. The main character was going to a protest march at their school, something about bathrooms, I thought, and they were painting a sign to carry. "Safe Spaces for ALL LGBTQIAP+ Students," the sign read. In what I *think* was intended to be a funny scene, they were having a hard time finding different-colored paint for each of the letters in the acronym. I was becoming more comfortable with some of the characters using "they" as their pronoun because they didn't think of themselves as either male or female, or at least not one or the other all the time. But I kept tripping up on the grammar. Was it "they were" or "they was"? After all, it was a plural word being used as a singular pronoun. God, more confusion.

But wait a minute. I went back and reread the paragraph. Where the hell did that letter *P* come from? I thought Patrick's *A* was supposed to be the end of the acronym. I looked again. Yes, there was definitely a *P* there. That did it. I was done.

I looked at Prissy. "I am sooo confused," I told her. She rolled onto her back for a belly rub. "Let's go find your other daddy and see if he can help."

I headed back to the house. Patrick had told me earlier in the morning he'd be working in the kitchen today, rigging up the charcoal burner to heat the dish water. Although we wouldn't have hot water on demand, we'd be able to heat enough for washing up after cooking and meals.

Vet was in the kitchen sitting at a table by a sunny window, reading a book. He was taking notes.

"What are you reading?" I asked.

He looked up at me, then glanced into the far corner. I hadn't noticed when I first came in, but Emily had spread a blanket on the floor there and was sitting crossed-legged, bottle-feeding her lamb. Vet held up a finger in front of his lips, nodded to Emily, then showed me the cover of his book: *Livestock Slaughtering for Small Scale Farms*. Oh, right. We were a strange bunch, that's for sure.

"Where's Patrick?" I asked.

"I heard him going upstairs a little while ago," he said, then returned his attention to his book.

That was odd. I hoped he wasn't getting sick and had gone back to bed.

I passed Emily and her lamb on the way to the back stairs. She didn't look at me as she hummed and rocked the animal. I didn't think Sara had been right when she'd predicted Emily would recover from her shock once she was here, but I recalled Sara's words, so I paused and squatted in front of her. "Hi, Emily," I said and reached out to stroke the lamb's head. "He sure looks happy this morning."

She smiled up at me. "He is. We both are today, I think," she said.

I left the kitchen and went upstairs to our dorm room, but saw no sign of Patrick. I assumed he'd gone back down, and out the back of the building, without Vet noticing. I went back into the hallway, and was heading toward the stairs, when I heard a...grunt...or a groan, maybe...coming from the dorm across the hall, the one Loris used. The door was open, so I leaned in.

Patrick and Loris were standing in a tight embrace. Patrick was...oh god...caressing her back. She had her head tucked against his neck, her arms wrapped around his waist. She tilted her head up and...oh god...kissed his cheek.

"Uhn," I heard myself say, right before the panic started to rise in me, drowning out Dr. Levy's tiny, distant voice, calling for my attention. Patrick heard me and turned his head in my direction.

Oh no! I thought. *No! No! No!* A burst of energy ran through me. Even as I felt it building, I spun around to escape. I don't know where I thought I'd go; I'd never managed to run away from a meltdown.

As I whipped around abruptly, I collided with Patrick who'd rushed over to find me. For a few seconds, I thought everything was turning upside down as I watched Patrick spin sideways, then fall face-first onto the floor. The ceiling was moving and the walls shifted up; then I felt my head hit the floor. I rolled to my side and came to my knees, vision blurry and my pulse pounding in my ears.

Fuck! I hadn't had a meltdown since I was a little kid. I screamed my frustration and pounded my fist into the floor.

Patrick was trying to sit up, blood dripping down his face.

No! No! No! Was that out loud? Was it in my head? I didn't know. I saw Vet pulling himself up the stairs, dragging his crutch behind him. He lurched into the hallway with a determined look on his face, ready for anything.

Shit! I punched the floor again. I was shaking as I pushed myself upright. Distantly, I heard myself shouting. "No! Patrick, no!" He was still on the floor, twisting at the waist to brace a hand against the wall, blinking away blood. I moved toward him. Loris stood in the doorway, a look of abject fear on her face.

Chapter Thirty-One

I don't know how long I was in the grip of the meltdown. Thankfully, at some point I shut down, pulling in on myself and disappearing into my head.

I wasn't fully back yet, and I didn't want to be. This was the stuff of my nightmares—that something like this could happen to me again. I'd been so certain those experiences were behind me. I knew I'd been shutting down more since this disaster began, but I never thought I'd have an actual meltdown. God, what would they think of me?

I was lying down, I think, a heavy blanket covering me. I opened one eye. It was too bright, and I had to squint to see where I was. It hurt to turn my head, but I did, and I realized I was in my bed, the covers tucked tightly under my sides. What happened after I shut down? How long had I been here?

Vet leaned against the doorframe, eyeing me.

And, oh god, Patrick. He stood next to Vet, looking...looking...I couldn't tell. He had blood on his face, dripping from a wide cut above his eyebrow. His forehead was swollen. He was rubbing his fingers. Stan was there, too, resting a hand on Patrick's shoulder.

I opened my mouth to speak and tasted blood. "Don't do that," I said to him, or tried to. I think I meant what he was doing with his fingers, but I was confused and not thinking clearly. My lips were too thick, and I had a hard time forming words.

"You're back?" Vet asked.

Was I back? Yes, I guess I was. My head hurt; my side ached.

"Yes," I said.

"Good," said Vet, breathing heavily, trying to catch his breath. "Let's not do that again." He stared at me, hard. "Understood?"

I looked over at Patrick. All that blood. "Yes," I said again.

"Good." He looked at Patrick. "You gonna be okay?" Patrick nodded. "You should let me stitch you up. That's gonna scar." Patrick shook his head, keeping his eyes on me as he dismissed Vet's offer.

"All right. Stan, help me downstairs; we'll let the others know what's going on."

Stan picked up Vet's crutch and handed it to him. He offered his other arm and helped Vet toward the door. Patrick stepped aside to let them through and then came over to me.

"Did I do that to you?" I managed to ask.

"Not directly, no. We sort of did it to each other. Do you remember what happened?"

I thought so. I know I saw him and Loris hugging and kissing. A warmth washed through me.

"I remember I came up here to find you, to tell you about the *P*."

"The *P*? What...? Never mind, go on."

"Then I saw you in there, on the bed, wrapped in each other's arms...kissing each other." I was getting upset again just remembering.

"You're rocking."

Was I? I stopped.

"Go ahead, what else do you remember?"

"Nothing." Just being here, tucked uncomfortably tight in my bed.

"Huh," said Patrick. "So you don't remember the meltdown or knocking me over?" He indicated his bloody face and the swelling developing above his left eye. "Or scaring the shit out of Loris?"

Did I? Sort of. It wasn't a memory I wanted to recall.

"I'm sorry," I said. I knew that was weak, and not nearly enough.

Patrick surprised me though. He sighed and wiped at a trickle of blood dripping down his cheek. "It's okay. It's not your fault."

How did he figure that? "It's not?" I asked.

"Well, it *is*, of course. I mean, it's not like I threw myself onto the floor just to bang myself up." I flinched.

"But what I mean is," he continued, "Sara explained what happens. With you, sometimes. How you had a meltdown."

I was silent, concentrating on my breathing and letting my eyes adjust to the brightness.

"Sara said a meltdown is different than a shutdown."

I nodded in confirmation.

"I've been through shutdowns with you, but never like this before," Patrick said.

"No, you hadn't seen me melt down. Before," I said. "Now you've seen the real me." I closed my eyes, so I didn't see his reaction. When I opened them again, he was frowning. "How long was I out?" I asked.

"It's been over an hour."

Dammit.

"You were pretty agitated, though, at first," Patrick continued. "So we tucked you in tight. To keep you safe, you know?" This was bad, and restraining me wasn't the best thing to do. In fact, it probably made it worse—my sense of panic, I mean—but this wasn't a good time for a lesson.

I wriggled my arms under the blankets. "Would you pull these off me?"

"Oh, right, sorry." Patrick came over and stooped beside me. He tugged the blanket off, and then the sheet. I swung my feet over the edge of the bed and stood, letting out a groan as I did so. "What happened to my side?"

"Vet shoved his crutch into it," Patrick said, letting out his own groan as he stood.

"What?!"

"He misjudged. You were yelling, sort of, and I was struggling to stand, and he thought you'd attacked me."

Oh. I could see how it might have looked that way.

Patrick and I were standing two feet apart. I wanted to reach out to him, at least clean the blood off his face. He backed up a step.

"You really frightened Loris. And me too."

God, what a disaster. I couldn't go around freaking out like that. I couldn't *hurt* people.

I felt tears on my face. Shit. I *hated* when I cried.

Patrick touched me then; he closed the gap between us and hugged me, very lightly. He let me cry for a few minutes, and when I finally stopped, or close enough, he pushed me slightly away so he could look me in the eyes.

Still holding my shoulders, he asked, "What *should* you have done, Franklin? You say you saw us hugging and kissing. I know that...frightened you. What should you have done?"

I remembered now, hearing Dr. Levy's voice trying to break through. "Stop. Breathe. Think." Could I have done that, if I'd tried? I didn't think so. There was no warning. It just came over me. But then I remembered Sara telling me I needed to keep practicing. Every day even, so when it was important it would come to me right away. I hadn't been keeping up on the exercises. I'd thought the meltdowns were behind me, and I'd stopped practicing. I'd been wrong.

"Stop, breathe, think," I said. Patrick smiled, as if he understood, then winced at the pain. "I'm sorry I hurt you," I said.

"You didn't do it on purpose. You're a lot stronger than you look. I felt like I'd been hit by the plow truck," he said, lightly touching his finger to his eyebrow and drawing it away to check for blood. There was a little bit, but not too much.

"I haven't been practicing," I admitted.

"I don't know, as body slams go, that was a pretty good one."

"No," I said. "I mean my coping skills."

"I know," Patrick whispered. He brushed a thick curl of hair off my forehead and then placed a finger under my chin, carefully tilting my head to look me in the eye. "Sara filled me on...things...while you were...out. So, what triggered you to panic like that?"

I didn't have to think about that at all. "Your choosing Loris over me. I'm going to lose you." Part of me—a big part—hoped he'd deny it. But he didn't. I felt the panic rising again, and my face flushing. I darted my eyes toward the door, seeking an escape route.

"No, Franklin, that's not true. Slow deep breaths now," Patrick said. I focused on my breathing, and then Patrick asked, "What did you see when you looked into Loris's room?"

I pictured them, entwined on her bed, kissing each other, touching each other. "The two of you, hugging and kissing." I willed my hands to stay in my lap.

"Uh-huh. What did you actually see, Franklin? Describe it for me."

They'd been hugging. But they hadn't been on the bed, had they? No, they'd been standing, and although they'd had their arms around each other, there hadn't been a whole lot of movement. Patrick had stroked her back. "You were standing. You weren't in bed."

"What else?"

"You were hugging. You rubbed her back." Then they'd kissed. But they hadn't been rolling around on the bed, had they? No. They'd still been standing when they'd kissed. I tried to visualize the scene and continued to breathe carefully. Actually, now that I was remembering it, Loris had kissed *him* and only on the cheek.

"You kissed."

"Did we?"

"Well, she kissed you. Once. On the cheek."

Patrick leaned forward and took both my hands in his. "Good, Franklin. Good. Now, why would losing control like that have helped?"

I took my hand from his and reached forward, touching the trickle of blood still running down his face. My side ached as I leaned forward. "It didn't, obviously," I replied.

He smiled. "Well, right." Then he looked serious again. "But why did you let it happen?"

"Because I wasn't in control." We were going around in circles now. I hated this.

"But what *should* you have done, Franklin?"

I didn't know. We'd already been through the stop, breathe, think steps, so what else was there? I thought back to my sessions with Dr. Levy when we'd gone over this. It was just stop, breathe, think; there wasn't anything else. But then I remembered what Sara had said: "That's just the emergency brake, Franklin. The real work starts when you engage with the person or situation upsetting you. You need to use your social skills tools then."

"Oh!" I said. "Talked to you. That's what I should have done next. Talked to you about what was happening and what it meant."

"Right! We'll need to practice a lot more, though, I think."

Wait? Did that mean he wasn't going to leave me for Loris?

"Are you ready to go downstairs? Everyone was very concerned. They all worry about you too."

I thought I owed everyone an apology. Although now that we'd gotten to this point, what I really wanted was to stay here and have Patrick explain about Loris and what that meant for me, for us. But I knew I had to do this other thing first.

"Yes," I said. "Let's go."

Chapter Thirty-Two

Patrick and I helped each other down the stairs and through the dining room to the kitchen. We were both limping, and Patrick's face was still bleeding. He went in first, and as he did I heard Loris gasp at the sight of him.

"Yeah, but you should see the other guy," he said to the room as he stepped through the doorway. "Oh, here he is now." I followed him in.

We took a few steps into the room and stopped. The others were spread out in the kitchen. Vet sat at the worktable in the middle of the room, studying one of his books. Sara and Loris were both leaning up against the far counter next to the washing sink. Sara was rinsing canning jars, but Loris simply stood with her arms folded across her chest. Emily sat on the floor, in the corner closest to us, bottle-feeding her lamb. Stan sat across from Vet, looking winded, probably from all the excitement. All my fault.

It didn't seem right to sit at the table with Vet and Stan, when the others were scattered throughout the kitchen, so we remained standing. I knew what I had to do. Patrick gave me a very slight nudge, and Sara put down the last jar and sent me an encouraging, soft smile.

"I want to apologize to everyone," I began, "and explain what happened." Vet closed his book and turned his chair to face me. I took a deep breath, following it through my nose and into my lungs.

"You don't need to apologize, Franklin—" Sara began, but I cut her off.

"No. I want to. If we're all going to be together, I want people to understand me. I...I might need people to help me. Sometimes."

Sara smiled and spread her hands in front of her. She nodded at me to continue.

I remembered to make eye contact with each person at least once, which was really, *really* hard for me. I took a deep breath, and began to explain.

"So, I had a meltdown, which I guess you all heard. I got overwhelmed and kind of lost control of myself for a while. I knocked into Patrick, and he fell and got hurt, and I was making a lot of noise, too, yelling and stuff." My knuckles were beginning to throb from when I'd punched the floor.

"The thing is, I haven't had a meltdown since I was little kid. Some people—" I paused; I was just going to go ahead and name it. "—living with autism have to struggle with that all their lives. I'm lucky that way. Or, well, I have been. For me, when I get overwhelmed by stress, well, I usually just shut down, curl up, and disappear into my own head. Not that that's great either, but I prefer that to a meltdown."

Sara offered me an encouraging smile, and she teared up, but I could tell she was trying not to, for my sake. I thought about that, about what a good person she is, and about how surprising it was I knew that about her. I think spending all this time together has allowed me to learn more about people. That was good, right? Maybe the future will actually be *better* than—

I felt Patrick nudge me with his elbow.

"Right. I'm not very good with emotions, or understanding when people have them. Sara—" I nodded to her. "—has helped me with learning coping mechanisms, but I was supposed to practice them all the time; then I thought I was better, so I stopped. But then, everything...happened..." I was beginning to feel overwhelmed again. "I mean, my parents...and...and..." I lost track of what I was saying. I felt tears building in my eyes.

Sara took a step forward, moving to come to me, but Patrick held up a hand to hold her off. He turned to me. "You can finish this, Franklin. What do you want to say?"

I focused on my breathing and counted slowly. Ten, twenty. I let the breath out softly through my mouth.

"I want to say I'm sorry for scaring everyone, especially you, Loris," I said to her. "But when I saw you and Patrick together, I just thought... I thought..." Through my tears, I could see Sara giving Patrick one of those meaningful looks I don't understand. He took a step toward me, reaching out his arms. I put my hand up to stop him.

"Please, I want to finish. I just want to say I promise to practice my skills more. But I also want to ask each of you to help me, be patient with me, and help me understand the emotional things, before I get too overwhelmed. Because sometimes...sometimes..."

"Stop," Loris said. "Jesus, you're killing me." She looked at Patrick. "You didn't tell him, did you?"

Patrick shook his head, reached out, and gripped my elbow.

Loris let out a sigh and rubbed her hands through her cropped, white hair.

"*I'm* the one who needs to apologize," she said.

What?

"I can't believe how fast the world fell apart. I mean, two months ago, I had everything, right? A good job here, plus my blacksmith craft had developed a strong client base down in the city...for decorative items, you know? Gates, railings, candlestick holders...that sort of thing." She looked at the doorway into the front hall. "All those hooks along the wall in there? I made those."

I was following what she was saying, but I couldn't see the connection to why she should apologize.

"Anyway," she continued, "I decided I should become a parent. I mean, I didn't intend on ever getting married, so why not do it all on my own, right? The truth is—" Here she looked directly at Patrick and then at Vet. "—and I'm sorry I misled you guys, but I don't even *like* men. Sexually, that is. I don't really like anyone that way."

"Oh my god—" shouted Emily, suddenly, from her corner.

"Oh my god—" I said.

"—you're pregnant!" Emily exclaimed.

"—you're asexual!" I said.

"Um, yes," Loris said, looking at Emily. And then she turned to me said, "Um, I don't know?"

Vet placed his palms on the table and leaned back. "Fuck. Me," he murmured to himself.

"No, no," I said to him. "That's exactly how it *doesn't* work. Or, at least, it's not supposed to, but then, Patrick *likes* sex, so it gets confusing." I remembered what Patrick had said, and it all started to fall into place. "But that's okay, because he's *demisexual*, which means he likes sex, but only with me." I frowned and continued more slowly, "But then why is that called *asexual*? That doesn't make sense. Wait..." I trailed off, unsure of what I'd been intending to say. Everyone turned to look at Patrick, and he turned a bright red.

"I think we're stealing the attention from Loris's moment here," he said.

We looked back at Loris.

"Right," she said. "So suddenly I'm thinking in terms of twenty or thirty years, you know? Setting something up that would allow me to raise a baby, maybe find other children and give them a future. And I knew this village would be ideal because it sustained so many people before, but I couldn't do it all on my own."

I thought back to all her planning, and it began to make more sense to me. Sure, we could keep foraging for canned goods and dried foods, using up batteries and flashlights, but eventually—if you were talking about a next generation—you'd need something else. Patrick squeezed my arm again.

"But I panicked," she said. "So much of the work here is physical. I can do a lot but not nearly enough, so I— sorry again, but I'm ashamed of this—I decided I needed a man, at least one, to commit to being here. Long-term.

So I pretended to be interested in Patrick and then Vet." She was looking down at the floor.

Sara put her arm around Loris's shoulders. "It's okay, dear. You did what you thought you had to do for yourself and for the baby."

Loris sniffed back a sob. "It's just that I was so afraid—for the baby. What kind of world will she grow up in? And *will* she grow up? I mean, I was immune, but will my baby be?"

Oh. I hadn't thought of that. But I was still trying to figure out what all of this meant—for me and Patrick. Did she not like him?

Then she turned to me. "And, Franklin, you've been nothing but honest with me, even when I asked you those awkward questions about Patrick. I want you to know that just now—upstairs—I told Patrick all of this. He knew I wasn't really interested in him, and he sure wasn't at all interested in me." She looked embarrassed by that. "It's only you he's into."

I let that sink in. I'd misread everything. But why hadn't Patrick told me? He could have simply explained he'd been comforting her, hugging her that way, not the way I had thought at first. He was still holding my elbow. And, evidently, reading my mind again. "You'll figure it out," he whispered to me.

Emily had been staring intently at Patrick, and I turned to look at him. "Oh," I said to him. "You're bleeding more." I pointed at his forehead, where a trickle of blood had started up again and was running down his cheek.

Loris was still talking, which I guess is just going to be a thing she does, even now that I liked her a little bit more. "I hope everyone can forgive me, and most importantly, that you all decide to stay and help make a go of it here. We have everything we need to be—"

"Oh!" Emily shouted, still staring at Patrick and leaping to her feet, the lamb forgotten and tumbling into the corner. "The blood! Of course, *that's* how I know you." She rushed past us and out of the room. I heard her hurrying up the stairs.

We were all stilled by the outburst for a moment. Patrick looked like he'd been kicked. Behind me I heard Emily rushing back down the stairs. Patrick turned to me. "Franklin—" he began.

"I don't under—" I started to say, when Emily barged back into the room, brandishing Loris's gun.

Chapter Thirty-Three

"Patrick Larson!" Emily shouted. "That's who you are. You raped that girl!" She waved Loris's gun about before pointing it directly at Patrick's chest.

A collective gasp went around the room. Loris and Sara stiffened at the counter, clutching each other's arms. Vet calmly, almost unnoticeably, pushed his chair back from the table, angling it toward Emily. Stan looked confused. I reached for Patrick, but he shoved me away. "Go to Sara, Franklin," he commanded. I stood where I was, but Patrick took a few steps away from me, and away from the others too.

"Stay right there!" yelled Emily. "There's no room for a rapist here. Don't you come near any of us, or I swear I'll shoot."

I remembered Patrick telling me about what had happened, how his picture with his bloodied face had been in the papers. But I remembered the rest of it too.

"No," I said. "You've got it wrong. They only *thought* he raped that girl. You know, because he'd killed his father."

"What?" cried Emily, her gun wavering. "He killed his father?"

"Well, yeah, he did do that—" I began to explain.

"Not helping, Franklin," Patrick interrupted, as he slid another half step away from me, causing Emily to pivot farther in his direction, still pointing the gun at his chest. This put me within a couple of feet of her and slightly off to her side, almost behind her. The gun kept shaking, making me nervous. I remembered Sara telling me to be compassionate with her, but to be careful around her too.

Loris looked shocked, her arms resting protectively across her stomach. Sara had inched in front of her. Vet slowly moved his hand to rest it on his crutch, which was leaning against the table. The crutch he'd jabbed into my side earlier. He was trying to tell me something, jerking his head toward Emily while she was focused on Patrick. Sad to say, but he'd picked the wrong guy for subtle signals.

"Oh yeah...I remember all that," said Stan. "Thought you looked familiar. Nothing ever came of it, though, right? Sent away for a time, weren't you?" But his talking set off a coughing fit. He was wheezing and gasping and began to slide from his chair. Vet grabbed his crutch, and Emily, startled, looked over at Stan.

And then, finally, Vet's signals clicked into place. I lunged forward and grabbed Emily, holding her tight to my torso and pushing the hand with the gun skyward. I half expected it to go off into the ceiling. It would have, had this been a movie, but it didn't. Vet swung his crutch around and held it at Emily's side, but she and I were already lowering to the floor. I disarmed her and carefully slid the gun along the floor, away from everyone. Soon, I was sitting with her against the wall, sort of holding her, but mostly just sitting. Her lamb wandered over and tried to climb into my lap.

Sara came and took the gun.

Vet turned to Stan, "Good job, man."

Stan was still on the floor, wheezing. "Yeah...wish I'd...planned...it," he managed to say. Sara rushed over to him and knelt at his side. She picked up his wrist for a pulse. He took a steadying breath. "I'll be fine," he said; then he took a few more breaths. "Not the first time. Just need to rest a minute." His breathing became steadier as he sat with Sara. "Help me up." She frowned but offered an arm and supported him as he rose. He sat back in his chair.

We all just looked at one another.

Finally, Emily spoke up. "I'm not living with a rapist and a murderer. He needs to leave."

Patrick sighed. I opened my mouth to explain. "No, Franklin," Patrick said. "Please."

"Is it true?" asked Loris in a small, soft voice.

"There's a lot here," said Sara. "But I don't think it will help if Patrick *or* Franklin—" She gave me a direct and pointed look. "—tried to explain things right now." She put an arm around Loris. "Why don't we all just—"

"I'll kill him if stays on this property another minute," interrupted Emily.

"I'll go," said Patrick.

"No," I said. "We shouldn't have to leave. You didn't *do* anything."

"Not *us*, Franklin. *Me*. You need to stay here. You need to work the barn, and Stan needs help with the radio."

I was having none of that. "We're sticking together. Always." I would have said more, but there was nothing else to say. It was simply the truth.

Stan looked at Sara. "You know, we could really use those new batteries now," he told her. "Might be we can connect with someone who's had a baby recently."

"Yes!" Sara said. "Thank you, Stan." She turned to me. "You and Patrick should go now, clear the highway down to the coast, and find some of those... What were they again, Stan?"

"Deep-cell batteries. Used a lot with boats."

"Right. Find those and the other radio supplies on your list, and come back. Give us a day or two. We'll figure out what to do next, get everyone on the same page. Okay?"

I felt myself starting to tear up. This felt like goodbye. "Can we really come back?" I asked Sara. "Because, if not, I need to get Prissy and her things too."

Sara walked across the room and hugged me. "You're coming back." She turned to Patrick. "Both of you." Then quietly, just to us, she said, "I know the truth. I'll explain."

I turned to Vet. "Take care of Prissy." He nodded. Patrick and I headed for the door. Loris backed away from us as we passed her.

"Boys," Stan called after us. "If you find yourselves in a pharmacy, look for a drug called digoxin, would you? I've run out."

Chapter Thirty-Four

I hurried back upstairs to grab our backpacks and a few supplies for the road, and then we were off.

We stopped after just a few miles to get gas from an abandoned Jeep on the shoulder. It was a chilly day, cold even, and I regretted not grabbing hats and gloves before setting out. A massive group of starlings was shifting about in a nearby clump of trees, their chattering drowning out all other sounds.

We were standing by the Jeep, Patrick holding the syphon hose in its tank, squeezing the pump to keep the trickle of gas flowing, while I held up the gas can to capture the outflow. The can's metal handle was cold, and I kept switching hands, alternating which one I could keep warm in a pocket. I knew we had things to talk about. But I was still so unclear on what had happened, or how I felt about it. So instead, I asked, "What's the word for a big group of starlings?"

"I don't know. A mob, maybe. A murder? Or is that just crows?" The gas had stopped flowing, and Patrick shook the end of the hose in the gas tank. "I think it's tapped," he told me. "Pour it into the truck, and we'll see how far it gets us. Do you mind driving for a bit?"

"Sure, I'll drive," I said as I emptied the gas can into the tank. "You okay, though?" I asked.

"I will be. Problem is some punk slammed me around, and now I'm a little sore. Oh, and blood keeps dripping into my eye."

Well. "Let me clean you up," I said. I tied the gas can back onto the roof, then opened the back of the SUV. I'd thought to grab a couple packages of cleansing wipes, plus bandages and rubbing alcohol, when I went back for our things. I pulled two wipes out of the container and gently cleaned Patrick's forehead and cheek, holding his chin with one hand while I angled his face for the best light.

When I was finished, I turned my back to Patrick, took a cotton ball, and soaked it in alcohol. I turned to face him again and took his chin, turning his head to the right. "Close your eyes," I told him.

"Why?" he asked even as he followed my instructions. I took the alcohol-soaked cotton ball and pressed it against the cut above his eyebrow.

"This is going to hurt," I said, even as I applied the alcohol to his wound.

"Jesus!" Patrick jerked away. "You could have warned me!"

"Why? Do you enjoy anticipating pain?"

"Oh," he said. "Okay, clever. I see what you did there. I suppose turnabout's fair play." He was silent while I bandaged the wound. We were both probably thinking back to that first day when Patrick had taken care of the abrasions on my wrist in the drugstore. "We've been through a lot together," he said.

"Yes," I agreed. "I understand why you didn't tell me right away about Loris being pregnant."

"Do you?" he asked, lightly touching his forehead, feeling the outline of the covered gauze there.

"Yes. Because it didn't matter. Whether or not you'd chosen Loris over me, I need to be able to deal with things. *We* need to be able to deal with things. Together." I *thought* that was it. I was pretty sure it was because, man, was that a tough lesson! I was still hopeful that's all it was—a learning opportunity. And not that Patrick was *really* done with me.

He looked up into the air, and when he turned his gaze back at me, I could see tears in his eyes. They didn't bother me anymore—it was just who Patrick was. "I honestly have no idea how you did this to me. It makes no *sense*," he said as he pushed me back against the side of the car. He leaned in and pressed his weight into me. My side hurt, but I wasn't going to say anything. Then he kissed me. "Ouch," he murmured as his jaw touched mine.

I lifted my arms to wrap them around his shoulders. He moved his head to my neck and took a deep breath. "You stink," he whispered.

"Gee, where could this be heading...?" I asked.

Without letting go, he reached behind me and opened the rear door. He began pushing me, backward, toward the seat. "Get in," he growled.

"You know, I think I *like* this whole demisexual thing—"

"*Now!*" he commanded.

I did.

*

About an hour later, I reached down to the floor of the back seat and pulled a cleansing wipe out of the package in my bag. "Here," I said, handing it to Patrick. "We should stop wasting all our boxers." He stretched next to me on the seat and took it.

"I think there's enough packages of shorts out there to last our lifetimes, Franklin," he replied, as he began wiping down my chest.

"I know, but I was thinking about what Loris said. About the long-term, you know?"

"So you're a Loris fan all of a sudden?" He was rubbing at the side of my face and then messing with my hair. "I don't know if your hair is just greasy, or if we managed to get some in there too."

"I'm not a *fan*, exactly," I said, ignoring the hair comment. "I just don't mind her so much now that I know she's not after you." Patrick snorted.

"You know—" He gave my nose a final wipe with the cloth, then balled it up and dropped it on the floor. "—I had planned on staying angry with you for flattening me a *lot* longer than this."

"Well, I don't blame you. But think about it. I mean, sure, we could get to a Walmart or something and have plenty of boxer shorts, but other things, like fuel for the cars, batteries for flashlights, gas cannisters for stoves... That sort of stuff won't last more than a few years, right? And then there's the food. The canned stuff is good for what...five years maybe?"

He didn't answer. He didn't have to. We knew we'd need to face it eventually.

"Thinking about the baby changes things, doesn't it?" he asked.

"Yeah, it does. Loris is right; we need to plan for the future, and not just our future. She just figured everything out before we did."

Chapter Thirty-Five

I'd been driving about a half hour before I saw the remains of the bodies I'd crushed a few weeks back with the plow. They were still there in the middle of the road, more scattered and picked apart by animals now. Patrick and I had been in the middle of a discussion of what stores to keep our eyes open for, and how we thought you'd spell the name of the medication Stan needed, when I saw them and slowed to a stop.

"Do you want to switch?" he asked.

"No," I replied, waiting to feel that mixture of fear and revulsion I'd felt last time, sick at the thought of just driving right over them. "Huh," I said. "Nothing." I turned to Patrick. "Ready?"

"If you are..." he replied.

I put the Explorer in gear and drove forward quickly. We weren't so high up this time or separated by massive tires. *Thump, thump. Crunch. Thump.* And then we were through.

"That was surprisingly easy," I told Patrick, turning to him with a grin.

"Dude, welcome to the new normal."

*

We made it to Northwood without incident and stopped at our favorite pharmacy to look for Stan's medicine. The town still smelled awful, and I wondered how long it would take before the sewer stink went away. Patrick opened the drugstore's door and reached down for the lantern. It wasn't there.

"That's odd. I was sure I'd left it." He went back to the car to grab one of our heavy-duty flashlights. There was plenty of light to see in the very front of the store, but the pharmacy was in the back and there were no windows there. It smelled inside too. Worse, I thought, than when we were here last. We'd left our masks and vapor rub in the car, but we'd been in this store so often I knew right where to find them. We just hadn't been thinking about the smell. We were growing used to life on the farm, I guess.

We made our way back to the pharmacy and ducked under the counter to the shelves where the prescription medicines were stored. Patrick went first, and I heard him say, "Uh-oh," as I was stooping to follow him through. I came up on the other side and saw chaos. Patrick played his light across the shelves, their contents spilled onto the floor, with many packages torn open and others crushed.

"Animals?" I asked, but even as I did, I knew that wasn't it.

"Come on," he whispered. "They might still be around. Let's get out of here."

We hurried to the car and quickly drove out of town, heading to the Home Depot and our plow truck. Neither of us said anything. I was scanning the town as we went through, looking for signs of other people, but didn't notice anything obvious. We both let out a sigh of relief when we saw the plow parked where we'd left it.

I pulled the truck in next to it and cut the engine.

"Okay, that was kind of scary," Patrick said.

"Doesn't change our plan, though, right?" I asked. "Switch vehicles here and clear our way down to the coast?"

We were both silent for a minute; then Patrick finally said, "I think that's right. We'll just want to be careful about where we spend the night."

Patrick decided he'd take a turn at driving the plow. He wasn't as good at it as I was, so it was slow going at first. We passed Emily's farm, and Patrick made a point of sniffing. "Do I smell cheese?" he asked. "Fresh cheese?" It felt good to break the tension. We made it another ten miles before we had to do any clearing, and even that was a simple matter of pushing a bus off the side of the road. A school bus, though, so there was that.

At the next intersection with a paved road, there was a small strip mall, and the largest shop on the corner was a grocery store. The sign said it was a pharmacy too. "Dinner?" Patrick asked.

"Yes, let's stop and stock up. Maybe we'll find Stan's meds too." We remembered our masks and vapor rub this time, and after covering up, we grabbed flashlights and headed to the store. It proved more difficult to get in than we'd thought. We couldn't manage to get the door open, so we had to break a large window in the front and climb in.

It smelled *awful* in there, even through the masks. It could have been bodies, or it could have been all the rotting meats in the open cases. Either way, the stench was the first horribly wrong thing we noticed. The second thing was worse.

"Why is it moving?" I managed to ask through clenched teeth, trying to breathe only through my mouth. I shined my light down one of the aisles, but it was very dark, and the flashlight beam only penetrated so far. But the shadows. They seemed to be...*moving*. I looked where Patrick aimed his light down a different aisle and saw the same thing. What was happening? How can the aisles just...*shift* like that?

"Fuck," Patrick said, at the same time I felt something on my foot. I lowered my beam. Rats. Lots and *lots* of rats. So many it seemed like a thick black fog disappearing into the darkness of the store.

Did I scream? I think so, but I can't be sure. I know I dropped my flashlight, its bouncing light illuminating rat head after rat head as it rolled across the floor, bumping across tails and claws. I turned, scrambling for the window behind me, and felt Patrick pushing my ass up and out. I tumbled to the ground and immediately bounced back up, turning to give Patrick a hand, pulling him through.

"Fuck, fuck!" Patrick kept screaming, releasing my hand and frantically beating at his legs as if rats were climbing on him.

"Jesus," I said, willing my heart to stop pounding. We looked at each other, eyes wide. Patrick clasped my hand, squeezing far too tightly. I turned back to the window. A rat popped through, dropped to the ground, then skittered along the foundation. In the shocked silence I could *hear* them inside, chewing and scratching. Another rat scrambled through the window.

"For fuck's sake, run!" Patrick gave me a push to the truck.

I drove. Patrick was too busy having a panic attack to take the wheel.

"Jesus," he kept saying over and over as I pulled back onto the roadway. He kept looking at his legs, then down to the floor, then back to the store, scanning for rats.

"It's not like they're going to come after us," I said, helpfully, I thought.

"Jesus," he said again. He took a deep breath and let it out. "I know. I just have this...thing...about rats. Totally freak me out."

I'd had a pet rat when I was ten years old. He was an adorable little guy I named Zeus. He'd sit on my shoulder and sometimes climb through my hair. I was very proud of the fact that I realized this would not be a good time to mention that to Patrick.

"This is turning into a really dark day," he said glumly.

*

We drove on for a few miles when a warning light appeared on the dashboard. Crap, I hadn't been paying attention to the fuel gauge. "We need gas," I said.

"Perfect timing then," said Patrick, indicating the roadside motel we were approaching. It was set well back from the highway; the long parking lot held half a dozen tractor trailers. It was starting to get dark. "We can fuel up and bed down here for the night. We've got enough food, so we don't need to find a grocery store." He shivered slightly at the memory of the rats. "Plus, there's probably vending machines inside in the office."

I drove into the parking lot and continued around the side of the motel to the service drive heading behind the building.

"You're parking in the back, aren't you?"

"Yes," I said. I knew it was silly, but for some reason I felt the urge to be less visible. The looted pharmacy had freaked me out. I was worried about drug addicts on the loose.

"Good," said Patrick. "I was going to suggest it, but I didn't want to sound paranoid." He was clearly on edge too. "Let's not park *right* next to the dumpsters, though, okay?"

We grabbed our backpacks and flashlights and walked around to the front of the motel, Patrick's light sweeping the ground before us as we went, even though it was still light enough to see. Mostly. We eyed the rigs parked in the lot and decided we could deal with the fuel issue in the morning.

It was a low, straight building, stretched out along the parking lot. It had twenty-four rooms, each with a separate entrance. Next to each room's door, there was a wide window, some with the drapes closed. As we walked past each room on our way to the office, we noted which of the rooms with open drapes appeared empty and clean. About half the rooms had their drapes closed. We ruled those out because there were probably bodies inside.

There were a few rooms with open drapes *and* bodies inside. Gross.

We settled on room 17 for the night. The drapes were open and it was unoccupied, as were the rooms on either side. Hopefully, that would lessen the smell.

The office door was open, and there were no bodies. Patrick was right about the vending machines. There were two, and we broke the glass on both. We stocked up on Pop-Tarts, granola bars, and nuts. I grabbed a couple of personal toiletry kits with toothpaste and toothbrushes. Patrick took several bottles of water. The keys to all the rooms were in a metal cabinet behind the desk. We found the one for room 17 and were out of there less than five minutes after we'd gone in.

The room didn't smell bad at all, and the bed was neatly made up. We set a lantern on the desk and proceeded to dine on the dried fruit we'd brought along, unheated cans of beef stew, and the nuts we'd grabbed from the office. We saved the Pop-Tarts for dessert.

Afterward, we relaxed, stretched out on the double bed. "It says we can watch HBO for free," Patrick observed.

"Dick," I replied, tossing a pillow at him.

"We'll be able to flush the toilet at least once. Even use the ones in rooms 16 and 18 if we wanted. I imagine there's enough water in the tank for a couple of cold showers too," he offered. That was probably a good idea. It'd been a stressful day, and cleaning wipes could only take us so far.

"Maybe the water's still lukewarm from the heat of the day. I'll go see." I got up, went into the bathroom, and turned on the tap in the tub. The water was rusty, but cleared after a minute or two. It wasn't *too* cold. I did the same thing at the sink and then brushed my teeth. I went back into the room. "We'll be able to shower if you don't mind cold," I said.

Patrick had a paper map spread open on the bed, and he was tracing a path on it with a pen. He looked up at me and said, "You'd think there would be a straightforward road right down to the coast. But there's not. We have a least three choices. Look." I went to the bed and lay next to him, reaching up and flattening the map on the mattress so I could see it better.

"Where are we trying to get to?" I asked.

"Here. Hog's Cove," he said, pointing to a town on the eastern side of Western Bay.

"Why not head down to Bar Harbor instead? Wouldn't there be more marinas there?"

"More everything," Patrick responded. "Don't forget the bigger towns will have more dead bodies and disease risks. And based on this map, it looks like's there's several marinas around Hog's Cove. We should be able to find what we need."

That made sense. "Great, pick a route. It doesn't matter to me," I said as I rolled over onto my back. I was beginning to feel exhausted. "How's the cut?" I asked.

"Okay," he said, then gave lie to that by asking, "Which one of us brought the ibuprofen?" I got up, went to my pack, and brought back the pain meds and a vitamin. I handed them and a bottle of water to Patrick. I took the bottle from him when he finished, put it on the bedside table, and stretched out again.

Patrick sniffed. "You smell bad," he said.

"Seriously?" I said. "Now? We just did that, like, three hours ago."

"Uh, no. I mean, you really do smell bad. Go take a shower. I'll take one after you."

Considering how the day had gone, that wasn't a surprise. First there'd been the meltdown; then I'd been forcibly constrained in the bed. I'd been threatened with a gun, wrestled Emily to the ground, and gotten thrown out of the village. Fooling around with Patrick in the back of the truck had been pretty messy too. Oh, and there was the episode with the rats, so...yeah, I was probably a little rank.

We both took showers and remarked on each other's growing bruises. I felt like an old man stepping in and out of the tub. I was so stiff and sore. Afterward, I rebandaged Patrick's cut. Thankfully, the bleeding had stopped entirely, but I suspected Vet was right about scarring, and I would always have to confront the physical evidence of what had happened. Maybe that would help remind me to practice.

We barely made it into the bed before we were fast asleep.

*

I was pulled out of a deep sleep by a noise. Popping? I'd been dreaming of Patrick, and Emily pointing a gun at him. But then it was Patrick who had the gun, and he was shooting rats. *Pop, pop, pop.* I was abruptly wide awake and sat up quickly. *Pop, pop, pop.* Patrick jerked awake, too, and grabbed my arm.

Pop, pop. Far away, I thought.

"Gunshots," whispered Patrick.

Then, the throaty roar of a motorcycle, definitely far off.

We sat still, barely breathing, until the noise faded in the distance.

"What *time* is it?" I asked. Funny how things make no sense when you're woken suddenly from a deep sleep. Who knew what time it was? Who cared? A ghost of an old song drifted through my head and was gone before it settled.

"I don't know," Patrick responded as if the question had made sense. "Still dark out though." We'd left the drapes open, and we both looked at the inky blackness outside. There must have been no moon, or at least a thick cloud cover. I got up and pulled the drapes closed, then went to the door and slid the dead bolt. Once back in bed, I asked, "Should we do anything?"

"I don't think so. I don't know what we'd do. Let's just go back to sleep."

"Okay," I said. But I don't think either of us did.

Chapter Thirty-Six

We got an early start in the morning. I think we were both just waiting for it to brighten enough outside to syphon some fuel. There was no sign of the motorcycle rider, although we both kept our eyes open for anything unusual as we made our way south. Of course, *unusual* was hard to pin down exactly, given the state of the world.

As we got farther from Northwood, the road became clearer with fewer breakdowns and crashes. Patrick was driving, which gave me time to think through everything that had happened in the last twenty-four hours. We were silent for a while, until Patrick said, "Twenty dollars for your thoughts? Especially if they involve you in your boxers." He grinned, and I realized I was okay now with his stupid porn jokes.

"You know, it doesn't annoy me anymore. That thing you do about the porn. Maybe you'll need to find a new thing?"

"Don't think I won't! Seriously, though, what are you working on in that ever-active head of yours?"

"I was thinking," I said. "What if they don't let us stay?"

"Franklin, it's me they're worried about. You can stay." He reached over and gripped my knee. "Seriously. The village needs you."

"We've been over this. We're not splitting up. No matter what."

I noticed his eyes getting teary again, and he tried to hide it by brushing them with his sleeve and then turning it into a pushing-back-his-hair motion.

"Don't worry," I told him. "I'm getting good at my Patrick-is-crying coping skills too."

He snorted out a laugh. "All right then, you and me it is!" In a more serious tone, he said, "Thank you." We were passing through a dense forested area, the early morning sun blinking at us through the canopy. "They'll welcome us back though. Sara will explain what happened."

"Maybe," I said. "But if we needed to, maybe we could go live in the castle?"

"What castle?"

"The one on the hillside across the river from the Shaker village. I'm sure I told you about it. I could see it from the roof of the barn when I was putting up the antenna."

"I don't remember. How far is it?" he asked. "Why would anyone build a *castle* there?"

"At least a few miles away," I replied. "You wouldn't even be able see it if it wasn't set high on the hillside. And it sure looks like a castle. All big gray stones with square corner towers and places on the roof you could hide behind, then shoot arrows from between the gaps."

"Crenellations," Patrick told me. "That's the word for what you're describing. They allowed for defense of the castle in medieval times. Not that anyone was building castles here back then."

"Well, I don't know who built it," I said, "but I asked Loris about it and she said it was a monastery, but not for priests or nuns, but for Buddhists, you know, the ones that shave their heads and wear orange robes?"

"I *do* know, yes. I think they call themselves monks." We drove in silence for a minute. "I used to want to be one. Once."

"A monk!?" I asked. "Oh. They don't have sex, do they?"

"Seriously, Franklin?" He turned toward me just so he could roll his eyes at me. "That's what you think would drive my decision about something so important?" He sighed. "But yes, they're mostly celibate."

"Well, then you have to admit it wouldn't be a bad career choice for an asexual. Although maybe the fact you always want to have sex would make that weird."

"I *don't...argh.* You drive me crazy sometimes!" We passed a stretch of run-down shops. A gun store. A liquor store. A garage. Then the road led back into the woods. "But sure, if we can't stay with the Shakers, let's go join the Buddhists. They were similar in some ways. Spiritually, I mean."

"I wonder if there's a bunch of bodies in the castle? Loris said it was used regularly for retreats."

"We could go check it out someday if you want," Patrick said. "But we're staying at Paradise."

Once we passed the main highway along the coast, the landscape changed. Even this far down east, Maine was built up along the coast. I cracked a window and was surprised to smell the sea and feel a warm breeze. "Wow, that's nice," Patrick said. "Let's roll down the windows and enjoy the day."

We did, but it only lasted five minutes. It was still May after all, and too cold to drive with open windows, at least in the morning.

"There!" I said, pointing to an intersection's road sign. "Granite Way is the road Stan said the electronics shop would be on." Patrick managed to slow down in time to make the turn, and sure enough, less than a half mile in, right after a scrap metal yard, was Radio and TV World. It looked like it had seen better days. Maybe even better decades.

There was a simple lock on the door, easily broken with a rock from the front yard. The inside smelled musty and dry, and I was relieved there were no bodies in it. From the looks of things there may have been nobody in it for quite some time. I wondered if it had even still been in business when everything fell apart.

It was a series of dark narrow shelves, piled high with what I could only describe as *stuff*. Handwritten tags along the shelves read: RF switches, adapters, transformers, attenuators. I recognized some of the names from the manual Stan brought with him, but I had no idea what most of it did.

"I don't think we're going to find any deep-cell batteries here," said Patrick.

"No, but look," I replied. I'd found a large section of the store called, simply, Antennas. "There's all sorts of antennas here. These ones labeled as base station antennas are huge. I know Stan wanted one of those. And these scanning antennas look like they might be useful too. Let's just grab lots of different types."

"Okay," said Patrick. "I'll take some of these mounting brackets and antenna cables too. We can always come back with Stan if they're the wrong things." We loaded the truck and continued our journey.

After another half hour, the truck was grinding its way up a steeply sloping section of road when, suddenly, we were at the ocean, driving along a tall bluff, the rough sea spread out beneath us to the right. Spectacular mansions perched along the cliff top between the road and the sea. We slowed at one expansive estate, all glass and stone, with two driveways and a name—Puffin's Bluff—and decided we had to stop. The manicured drive, although very wide, was still too narrow for the plow, so we left it on the road and walked to the front door.

Surprisingly, the front door was unlocked, and the house appeared to be lived in. Most of these mansions were only occupied seasonally. Perhaps the owners had come to open up early, or maybe they were one of the few wealthy retirees who enjoyed Maine's weather year-round. Either way, there was no obvious sign of dead bodies, and the views of the ocean through the glass walls were breathtaking.

"I could live here," I said.

"Well, we can for a day or two. Let's make it home base while we're here."

After we'd collected our things and brought them into the house, we checked the map and concluded we were about halfway down a wide peninsula on the eastern side of Western Bay. "There's a small village at the end of the road that sticks out into the sea. Plus, several marinas, here and here—" He tapped the map. "—and also right over this bridge, here."

"Great," I said. "I'm hungry. Let's head down there and see what we can find."

We didn't expect the road to be blocked, but we decided to take the truck anyway. For some reason, I felt weird about just leaving the truck in the middle of the road. It turned out we had to pull over and leave it when we came to a narrow, one-lane wooden bridge. We walked the rest of the way into town.

It was a perfect day. Warm with the smell of the ocean hanging in the air. May flowers bloomed in profusion, and as we passed through the historic district, we marveled at the centuries-old wooden houses with their tiny gardens and picket fences. We only saw one body, and that was in a backyard. Neither of us mentioned it.

I took Patrick's hand in mine, and we strolled down Front Street like teenagers on a date.

"We could live here forever," Patrick said and wrapped his fingers through mine.

"No, we couldn't," I said. "No one lives forever."

Chapter Thirty-Seven

Our first afternoon at the coast went well. We found a small village shop stocked with plenty of snacks and beef jerky (and no rats!) and a pharmacy that hadn't been ransacked, but we couldn't find Stan's drugs. We scored a Prius with keys in it and drove around to local marinas, but didn't see where anyone sold batteries. There were plenty of boats still stored for the winter though, so we decided we could always take batteries from them.

Dinner was canned soup on the deck of Puffin's Bluff overlooking the ocean. There was an outdoor gas-fired pizza oven built into an alcove, and we used that to heat the soup. Finally, we made a total mess out of a simple, boxed brownie mix. They were good though, and we ate all of them.

Hours later we were still on the deck, stretched out on chaise lounges under the stars. The Milky Way blazed over the ocean, the breaking waves blinking silver in the starlight.

"This could be our southern outpost, for when we feel like getting away from the Shaker village," I said.

"That's a good idea." Patrick leaned up and poured more peppermint tea into his cup. He held the pot up to me. "No thanks," I said.

"Vet needs to get to Bangor," I said. "He thinks his new leg might be there waiting for him."

"Oh. We can do that. We'd need the truck though. I imagine the interstates are a disaster."

"That's what I thought too. But we know we can do it now." I thought about how difficult it would be to lose a leg. Then I thought again about his condoms. "Did you see his face when Loris told us she was asexual?"

"She didn't *say* she was asexual. She said she 'doesn't really like anyone that way.'"

"What's the difference?"

"I don't know, Franklin." He sighed. "And it's too beautiful out here tonight. I'm not talking to you about asexuality anymore." He stretched and closed his eyes.

I suddenly remembered about the *P*. "Hey, I forgot. Why didn't you tell you me there was a *P* after the *A* in your acronym?"

Patrick grunted. "Oh my god, there are *so* many things wrong with that question."

"What? It's just a question."

He sat up and swung his legs over the side of the chaise to face me. "First of all, it's not *my* acronym. It's your acronym, too, you know—there is a *G* in there." He stopped me from responding by holding up his hand. "Second, there is no *P* after the *A*. That's why there's a plus sign at the end. To encompass all the other possibilities."

"Ha!" I said. "That shows what you know. There *is* a *P*; it was in one of the books *you* made me read."

"The book was wrong, then. There is no *P*."

"Yes, there is," I insisted. I'd seen a reference to it at least twice.

"Okay smarty, what does the *P* stand for then?"

Hm. I realized now, too late, that I probably shouldn't have mentioned this. "I don't know. That's why I was looking for you, to ask you, when I found you...with Loris."

Patrick swung back around. "Huh. Funny how things happen sometimes, isn't it?"

"No," I said.

"Poppycock," he replied.

"Huh?"

"Poppycock," he repeated. "That would be a good sexual orientation word that starts with a *P*." He laughed, because he *always* thought his own jokes were funny.

"Pig," I said, and waited.

"Oh, Franklin's playing now too! Excellent, and I thought he was a *prude*."

"No, just *picky*."

"You're not picky; you're a *pushover*."

"Psycho."

"What? Oh...I see what you did there. That's *good*, Franklin. You win!"

*

The next morning we were in the Prius, on our way to find a boat to break into. We had taken a back road that cut inland across the peninsula. "Look," I said, pointing to a sign above a commercial building reading Arty's Automotive and Marine Supply.

"Worth a try," said Patrick as he pulled into the dirt lot.

The door was open, and I noticed the smell as soon as we stepped inside. I didn't see the body though. Maybe it was in a back office. It wasn't *too* bad. "Is it my imagination," I asked, "or is the dead body smell getting a little better now?"

"Maybe. It's been a couple of months. I think it might be different in each situation. I wouldn't open the office door, though."

Right. I wandered down a couple of aisles until I found batteries. Then I saw them. "Paydirt," I called over to Patrick. Under a ceiling sign reading Boat Power Supplies, there were boxes and boxes of deep-cell batteries.

Patrick joined me and said, "Wow, good call stopping here, Franklin! They must have just stocked up for the summer season." We found a handcart and took several loads out to the car, filling it with as many as we could fit. After transferring those to the plow truck at the wooden bridge, and abandoning the Prius, we headed back to the house.

It was still only late morning, but we decided to stay another day. We were enjoying the sea air, the rocky coastline, and each other's company. We also felt it might be best to give the folks back in Paradise Village the opportunity to settle down a bit more. In the afternoon, we took a long walk along the cliff-top roadway back into town and pretended to be tourists for a few hours.

I found a bumper sticker with an outline of a dog that looked vaguely like Prissy. The sticker read: I love my...whatever the hell it is. It would look great on the back of the plow. We picked up T-shirts and sunglasses, saltwater taffy and peanut brittle. We threw those last ones away when we thought about the risks to our teeth.

We were walking along the docks in the village center, feeding stale crackers to the seagulls and harbor seals. "Check that out, Franklin," Patrick said, putting his arm across my shoulder and turning me slightly to direct my gaze out at the water. He was pointing with his other hand, and I followed it, looking into the harbor. He leaned his head next to mine and whispered, "No, out farther." I lifted my gaze, focusing beyond the harbor, into the ocean.

And then I saw them, a pod of whales passing by, leisurely submerging and resurfacing, spouting plumes of water skyward. A flock of birds circled above them, diving occasionally into the churning waters.

A warmth blossomed in me. I felt...connected...to the ocean, to the whales, to Patrick. It was as if there were no boundary between me and them, between me and everything. We watched together, Patrick's arm still resting on my shoulder. And I realized a truth. "I love you," I said.

He tightened his arm around me, then turned his head and kissed my forehead. A tear dripped from his cheek onto mine.

"I know," he said. "Do you think I'd put up with you if you didn't?"

In the distance, the whales continued on their slow journey. At our feet, the harbor seals scrambled about the docks, slipping in and out of the water. I was one with the universe, and Patrick said, "I love you too."

Chapter Thirty-Eight

We spent the last night at our "summer house"—as Patrick insisted we call it—in a lazy way, reveling in our newly declared feelings for each other. We had a light dinner on the deck again, this time wrapped in blankets because it had gotten colder suddenly, and because earlier in the evening we'd been naked and in bed, and we hadn't wanted to dress again.

Clouds had moved in, so there were no stars lighting the ocean. The sounds of the waves breaking against the stony beach below was mesmerizing, the smaller pebbles rushing back to catch the retreating waves. We listened in the darkness for a while, holding hands across the space between the chaises. We were tired and ready for sleep, but neither of us wanted this perfect day to end.

"How can it be," Patrick asked softly into the silence, "that even with all the horror around us, I've never been so happy?"

"I'm glad we're happy. I'm glad we found each other. I'm glad we made something out of...all of this."

"Bed?" he asked.

We got up, and that's when I noticed the boats. Out in the ocean, two sets of lights bobbed in the inky blackness. There was no way to tell how far away they were from shore. Patrick saw them, too, and he immediately bent over and turned off our lantern.

"I'll get the one in the kitchen," I said and went through the open sliders to turn off the lamp I'd placed next to the sink. Our world was plunged into total darkness, and it wasn't until I carefully felt my way back out to the deck that I even thought to question our instinct to hide. "What should we do?" I whispered, though there was no way the boats were close enough for anyone on board to hear us.

"I don't know. We could signal them, I guess. I mean, maybe we should. We've been trying to meet other survivors. A few days ago, we would have been flashing lights at them."

"That doesn't feel right now, though, does it?" I asked. Not after the looted drug store and the gunshots at night outside the hotel.

"No." We stood on the deck for another twenty minutes, following the steady progress of the boats. They continued south along the peninsula and finally disappeared around the tip. "Well," Patrick said, "they either didn't see our light or don't care, but I doubt they'll be coming to see who we are."

"Let's go to bed," I said, and we did, fumbling our way through the dark house.

*

We woke in the morning to a cold, heavy rain, glad we'd loaded the batteries into the plow's cab yesterday. When we left our summer house, Patrick placed a lantern by the front door, promising the house "We'll be back."

"Vacation's over," he said to me, as we shouldered our packs and dashed through the rain for the truck. I climbed into the passenger seat and slammed the door shut against the blowing rain. "Brrrr, get the heat going," I said, rubbing my hands together briskly. "I miss Prissy."

"Me too!" said Patrick. "Drive straight home? It'll take a few hours, more if Stan's drugs are hard to find."

"Yeah, let's do it in one day. I want to learn our fate. Plus, we need to let the others know there are more people around. Maybe dangerous people."

We set off, going slower than we had on the way down due to the storm. When we reached the highway, Patrick turned and took it south for a couple of miles, looking for a drug store. We were in luck and found a strip mall with a CVS. It was relatively easy to break into, hadn't been ransacked, and it didn't smell bad. But it was very dark, given the gloomy day, and even with our lantern and flashlights it was hard to make sense of the shelves and shelves of prescription medicines behind the back counter.

We spent an hour shining our flashlights at boxes and bags of medicines, but we didn't see anything labeled "digoxin."

"We can't stay here forever," Patrick said. "Let's get back on the road. We'll stop if we see another pharmacy, but otherwise, maybe we should wait until we can take Stan with us."

That made sense to me. On the way out of the store, I picked up two bags of dog treats, small ones for Prissy and big ones for Roscoe. I also grabbed several boxes of condoms. "For Vet," I said in response to Patrick's quirked eyebrow.

We stopped at the same hotel we'd stayed at a couple of nights ago, but this time just to syphon more fuel from the tractor trailers. Shortly afterward, we passed the supermarket with all the rats. Patrick shuddered. "I've been thinking about that," I told him. "That's likely to be happening at all the food markets soon, right? The rats I mean?"

Patrick sighed. "Yeah. I've been thinking about it too. I mean, it makes sense they'd take over like that, but I hadn't thought about how it would ruin a lot of our food supply, the boxed and bagged stuff anyway. I don't think they can chew through cans."

"No, I don't think so either," I said. Although I had once seen Zeus chew his way through a brick, but I decided not to mention it. "Still, they'd leave a real mess behind. You'd have to clean each can thoroughly. And who'd even be able to stomach going into the store to collect them?"

"God. I hadn't thought of that. I'm going to have nightmares now. Thanks, Franklin." It was still raining heavily, and we were beginning to drive through flooded sections of roadway. The drains hadn't been cleared for a couple of months. "I wonder how long it takes for a rat to have a baby, anyway. I guess it's shorter than nine months."

"You'd guess right," I said. "Three weeks."

"What! Are you shitting me?"

"Nope. They're pregnant for three weeks. And they don't have *one* baby. They have, like, ten." I did a few quick calculations in my head. "And the babies are ready to start reproducing in about a month, so, in a grocery store with that kind of food supply, and no predators, even just two rats could swell to over a thousand in a year. And of course, if you start with a few dozen anyway, well, you can see how quickly you end up with a big swarming cloud of rats."

"Stop! Jesus." Patrick was breathing heavily, and I saw beads of sweat breaking out on his forehead. This really *was* a problem for him.

"But it can't go on forever," I said. "Eventually they'll eat all the food, then they'll be forced to venture outside. And lots of things eat rats. Owls, hawks, coyotes, bobcats, mountain lions, snakes." I thought about that after I said it. It was true. It was bound to play out that way. "So, now that I think about it, we'll need to be prepared over the next couple of years for a bumper crop of coyotes. Even wolves will probably start returning. That's going to be dangerous for the sheep and chickens, and even the cows."

"Wow, you're a real buzzkill, Franklin." We splashed through a huge puddle, sending waves of water cresting off both sides of the road. "Love you anyway," he added.

"Love you anyway?" I asked. "Seriously? That's not going to become a thing, is it?"

"I don't know. Does it bother you? I could *make* it a thing."

"No," I said.

"No, it doesn't bother you? Or, no, I can't make it a thing?"

"Oh my god, just...no."

We drove on silently for a while, Patrick occasionally chuckling to himself, probably thinking up clever ways to annoy me.

We saw a sign for a pharmacy ahead, but when we pulled into the lot, we noticed the windows of the store had been smashed open. "Let's not," I said.

"I'm with you on that one," Patrick replied as we pulled back out onto the road. "So," he said, "I've been thinking about what you said about the rats and stuff. I guess we should make an attempt to go collect as much food as we can. Take the trucks to every food market nearby, grab as much of the dry foods as we can. Rice, beans, pastas, that kind of thing. Try to get ahead of the rats."

"Yes, and we should learn to preserve the food we grow. Ultimately, that will be the best solution."

We drove on, and as we were approaching Northwood, we came upon one of the signs Sara had put up directing survivors to the Shaker village. Patrick stopped the truck. "What do you think?" he asked.

"I think we should take it down," I said. "I mean, I know we need a lot more people to work the farm and stuff, but it has to be the *right* people, you know?" We sat in the truck for a few minutes, looking at the sign through the rain.

"I agree," said Patrick. "We should at least let the others know of the risks. We can always put them back up. Plus, once you and Stan get the radio operating again, we can check with others to see what's going on in their areas. Maybe they'll have ideas." So we took the sign down, along with the other three we came across on the ride back.

Chapter Thirty-Nine

We pulled into Paradise, right up to the front door of the dwelling house. We could put the plow truck away later. We were too eager to learn our fate to delay any further. "Remember," I said to Patrick before we got out of the truck, "we're staying together, no matter what."

Sara must have heard us, because she stepped out the front door even as we climbed down from the truck. She looked upset, like she'd been crying. That wasn't a good sign. "Uh-oh," said Patrick, quietly. Prissy came racing over from the barn and squiggled in greeting at my feet. I bent down to scratch her head, but also to avoid looking at Sara when she told us we'd have to leave.

"Sara," said Patrick.

"Oh, boys, I'm so glad you're back. I have horrible news."

Patrick had come over to stand next to me, and he placed a hand on my shoulder. "We're not separating from each other, so don't even suggest it," he told her.

"What?" she asked. "Oh, no. No. Of course, you're staying here. Both of you. We set that straight right after you left." She paused then, and I stood up. "It's Stan. I'm so sorry to tell you this, but he died last night. Vet thinks it was a heart attack."

Patrick reached for my hand. "Oh, no," he said.

"I know," Sara continued. "All this death around us, but somehow this one seems more real."

Yes, she put to words exactly what I was thinking. It was strange. How many bodies had we seen lying around in the open? How many bodies had I *run over*? With the exception of Sara, everyone I knew from before was dead. Tyler. Mrs. Knudson. My teachers and classmates. Maybe even my parents—but I still wasn't ready to completely believe that. But somehow, Stan's death felt...personal. I thought of his grandson, Garrett, in Colombia. Was he alive? Did he wonder about his grandfather?

"We were in the middle of a meeting to decide what to do. With the body, I mean. I'm glad you're back in time to join us."

We gathered in the kitchen where our group of, now six, sat at the large worktable with pots of tea and a plate of hard-boiled eggs in front of us. There was no explicit acknowledgment that they'd decided not to kick us out or had even discussed it. But Loris smiled when we came in, and Emily nodded in welcome, so it was enough, I guess. Vet asked about our trip, and we told them about the batteries and the antennas.

"There's more we need to tell you," said Patrick, "but we'd like to know the plans for Stan first." Vet shot me a look I couldn't read, of course. But if I *had* to guess, I'd say what we were going to share about the destruction at the pharmacy and the gunshots at night wouldn't come as a surprise to him.

"So, back to Stan," Sara said. "He'd been tired all day yesterday," she told us, filling us in on what the others already knew. "He died sometime last night. It seems to have been peaceful. There was no sign of discomfort."

Loris spoke up. "There's a cemetery here the Shakers used. More than three hundred people are buried there. It's in a field on the far eastern side of the property."

I'd noticed that plot of ground, surrounded by a stone wall, overgrown with weeds and bramble bushes.

"I don't think we should do that," said Emily. We all looked at her. She didn't talk much, and rarely offered an opinion about things.

"Why is that, dear?" asked Sara.

"I dug a hole and buried my folks at the end of the hay field. None of us got to do things properly. I think...well, I'm not sure what I think...but whatever we do for Stan should be for everybody, you know?"

Vet was slowly nodding like he agreed. I was confused and I looked at Patrick, but he looked blank too.

"Yes," said Vet. "We should mourn everyone when we mourn Stan. We haven't been able to do that yet for our own loved ones. Communally, at least." Patrick was nodding in agreement now too. So was Sara.

"And the...ceremony...should be different too," continued Emily. "This is all new. We shouldn't pretend we're just continuing how things were. We should decide how we want to do things going forward in our own way."

*

In the end, we decided upon a garden. We converted one of the smaller hay fields, planting fruit-bearing trees and bushes salvaged from a local nursery. Later in the summer, we planned on building a stone wall around the newly sacred space.

I wasn't sure how I felt about food grown where Stan was buried, but the others all felt strongly about the symbolism. Plus, it would be years before the trees bore fruit, and establishing the garden was as much about expressing hope and commitment to future generations as it was about mourning today.

We decided on no stones or markers. It wasn't just Stan we were burying after all, but all of our loved ones, and the billions of others we never knew. That had been challenging for me to grasp, but Patrick walked me through the symbolism, and explained how it would help me mourn my own parents, if I was ready to do that.

We each planted something, speaking or not as we chose. Emily planted a persimmon tree in honor of her parents, who loved to make jelly out of the fruit each autumn.

Patrick planted several blueberry bushes. He didn't speak, but I imagined he was thinking about his father, whom he'd killed, and his mother, who had failed to protect him when it counted. And yet he was there for her at the end.

Vet planted a peach tree and said it was to honor his brothers and sisters, dying in strange lands far from home and family. I thought for a minute about brothers and sisters, and family, chosen or not. I think Vet meant brothers and sisters in a large way, not just siblings.

Sara simply knelt in the garden and opened her arms wide, as if she were hugging the world. She did the kind of breathing exercises she'd taught me to do and then finally stood and stepped out of the garden without having spoken. I'm sure she thought of her husband, though, and her daughter, wherever she was.

Loris planted a walnut tree. She'd told us earlier she wanted something that wouldn't mature for decades, an act of faith that her child and others would be here to benefit from her actions today.

I planted two pear trees, one for each of my parents. They both loved cooking pies with pears from local farmers and putting pears up for winter. Dad even tried a couple of times to make perry. One of the last things I ate before meeting Patrick was the last jar of my mom's preserved pears. She'd put sticks of cinnamon in that batch.

I stood silently for a moment after tamping down the soil, recalling the taste and feel of the preserves in my mouth.

I didn't exactly say goodbye to them, but I did begin mourning them that day.

Chapter Forty

The day after the garden dedication, Patrick and I moved the radio equipment into an empty dormitory room. We set up what Stan would have called a radio shack, and this time both Patrick and I climbed to the roof to set up our new antennas. We put the tall pole-shaped antenna directly on top of the cupula, but there was another antenna that was basically a series of wires spread out like a spider web. That one we had to stretch from the roof to several nearby tree trunks.

Before climbing down, Patrick said, "Show me your castle."

I looked out over the river, to the low hills beyond and the higher ones behind those. There was a thick cloud cover this morning and the view was obscured. "It's too cloudy," I said.

"That's too bad. I'd like to see it. Maybe we can drive over there and check it out some day."

"Sure," I said. "Do you still think about it? Becoming a monk, I mean."

"Sometimes. I think we need something in our lives. Something spiritual." He gave one last check of all the connections we'd made and shook the pole antenna to make sure it was securely bolted in. "We don't have that here. Maybe if we went to the monastery, we could find some materials to bring back. Books and stuff on meditation, maybe some practice guides. We could establish our own Sangha."

I didn't know what that was, and I didn't ask, because we were already making our way down the ladder and had to pay careful attention to our footing. When we reached the ground, we found Vet sitting in his chair, waiting for us.

"Gentlemen," he said, "if you have a moment, you'll want to join me in the barn." Patrick and I looked at each other. It sounded important, and we could set the radio up later, so Patrick nodded to Vet and we followed him to the barn. I'd learned he doesn't like to be pushed in his chair unless necessary, so we took our time getting there.

He navigated a quarter way around the barn to an empty sheep pen. We hadn't used this one since the last of the lambs were confined with their ewes. Vet pushed the tip of his crutch against the pen's gate to swing it open. "After you," he said. But it was empty. I didn't understand.

I stepped in first, with Patrick close behind me. I heard a whining sound and looked down. Oh.

"Prissy!" I exclaimed, dropping to my knees. Something was seriously wrong with her. Why had Vet seemed so calm about this? "Is she sick? Is she dying?"

"Franklin, no," Vet responded. "I'm sorry; I should have warned you first. She's going to have puppies."

Patrick knelt beside me. Prissy didn't get up but vigorously wagged her tail, which we took as permission to scratch her head.

"Puppies," I began, "but how...?"

"The usual way, I'd imagine," Vet said. Patrick laughed.

"Remember she was bleeding a little, before we took the plow into Northwood and found Vet?" Patrick asked me. Yes, oh—she must have been in heat.

"Roscoe!" I said. I remembered how he'd jumped out of the car and darted off as soon as we got to the village. "That rascal." I looked more closely at Prissy. She looked uncomfortable and was breathing heavily. I turned to Vet. "Roscoe is a lot bigger than Prissy. Will she be okay?"

"I hope so," he said. "I wish I could do an X-ray, but I felt around some and there's definitely more than one puppy, which is good. The more there are, the smaller they'll be. I also wish I knew if this was her first litter. Those are usually the most challenging ones."

"What should we do?" Patrick asked. "How long will it be?"

"Nothing to do. She picked this space because she feels safe here. You'll need to get water and some dry food for her, plus clean towels. But at this point we just wait. I think a few more hours, at least."

Turned out to be seven more hours, and it was evening when her time finally came.

Vet said not to crowd her, and to keep the gate closed because it provided her with a sense of protection. We stood outside the pen, peering into the stall, waiting. Loris had insisted on joining us. She wore a T-shirt and sweats, and for the first time I noticed the swelling of her belly.

Vet had his medical bag with him, and we were as prepared as we could be.

I knew it was time, too, even without Vet telling us. Prissy grunted and panted. I tried not to think about the problem birth with the ewe that had died, but I still prepared myself for a bad outcome. Loris was breathing almost as heavily as Prissy, and I had a sudden sympathy for her. Now that I knew she was pregnant, I understood how upsetting it must have been to witness the ewe's death.

Vet was in the pen with Prissy, lying on his side, ready to help if needed. Patrick was in the adjacent pen, managing the lighting, and Loris and I were standing next to each other, almost touching, in order to see what was going on. She was silently crying, soft tears glimmering in her eyes.

Patrick looked over at me. He had the look on his face I now knew meant he was concerned and was checking with me to make sure I was handling things. To see if I needed him to help me.

But I was fine and excited about Prissy having pups. Plus, I could do something for someone else now. I glanced at Loris and moved my hand a few inches, gently placing it on top of hers. She startled, jerking her hand away. Oh, I must have had that wrong. But then she took a deep breath and slid her hand back under mine, relaxing her iron grip on the edge of the wall. She took another deep breath, then another, slower one.

Patrick, who'd been watching me, was also crying now. Good lord. I rolled my eyes at him.

We were all having such a moment we almost missed the puppy slide effortlessly into our world. Vet was still waiting to intervene, but Prissy ignored him. She twisted around and immediately began licking the pup, until it was actively wriggling about, instinctively searching for a teat. Vet helped nudge it in place. Within a minute or two, Prissy let out a grunt, and a slimy dark mass was ejected. "Oh, no," I said. "Was that...?"

"Nothing to worry about," said Vet. "That was the afterbirth. Perfectly normal. She's a real champ. I suspect she's done this before."

Prissy repeated the process twice more, and within a half hour, she chewed through the umbilical cords and had three vigorously nursing puppies at her side.

"See," I said to Loris. "Everything is going to be okay."

Chapter Forty-One

A few days later, on a very wet and chilly late spring morning, when there wasn't much outside work to be done, I was in the radio shack, finally ready to get the radio up and running. Patrick had drilled a hole through the wall under an eave, and we'd snaked the wires from the outdoor antennas through that. I'd already connected the deep-cell battery and was finishing hooking up the antennas

Prissy, along with Dexter, Galloway, and Kerry—it had been Emily's idea to name them after cattle breeds—were resting comfortably in the whelping box Vet had set up in the corner of the room. He said it was too risky to leave them unattended in the barn, and Prissy seemed content with the arrangement.

Several of the straight-backed dining room chairs had been brought up, so any of us could listen in while the radio operator—by unspoken agreement, me—tried to make contact with the rest of the world. This morning it was just me and Patrick. Loris had been here, but she'd gotten bored with all the setup and prep work. Patrick had pulled his chair up next to mine.

"Ready?" I asked.

"Go for it," he said.

I flipped the toggle and the display screen lit up pale yellow, and little green lights glowed above various switches and knobs across the face of the machine.

"Do you know how to use all this?" Patrick asked.

"Enough to get started. I still need to learn a lot. Stan was going to be my Elmer."

"I'm not sure what to do with that bit of information. He was kind of old for you, wasn't he?"

"Ha. Ha." The room was filled with the squelch sound, and I was reducing the volume while trying to find a space on the dial to minimize the noise. "An Elmer is a more experienced teacher, who helps a newcomer learn the ropes."

"Oh, like a sensei," said Patrick, nodding.

"Whatever. I'm trying to find the right high frequency band—"

"Nothing to do about that now, though," interrupted a woman's voice from the radio.

"We've got someone!" Patrick whispered excitedly.

"No need to whisper. They can't hear us until I start sending. Let's listen."

The conversation on the radio continued. "Still, it's a shame to lose that foal, after all that effort," a man said.

"Too right," the woman responded. "I wish we'd had a vet with us."

"Hey, speaking of medical care, have you guys heard from that group in Pennsylvania again? The one with the doctor?"

"No! And there's another group upstate, in Syracuse I think, that was trying to reconnect with them too. I hope nothing happened to them."

"I know," the man replied. "We've heard some scary stories about a sickness spreading around Washington."

"All those bodies..." said the woman.

I turned to Patrick. "I'm going to jump in."

I pressed my microphone button and said, "Hello, this is Paradise Shaker Village in Maine. Can you hear me?"

"There you are, Paradise!" said the woman. "We heard about you from the folks down in Pennsylvania. Glad to finally get to hear from you. I'm Lisa near Albany, and you may have heard Mike here too. He's in the Berkshires. Have you been on here before?"

"Well, Stan was; he knows how to use these radios, but he died. And I had to get batteries and antennas, so, no—it's my first time."

"Hello, son, I'm glad you made it. I'm Mike." He sounded older, so I wasn't offended that he'd called me son. "We normally share about our setups on here and swap information that might be useful. As Lisa said, I'm in the Berkshires in Massachusetts, in North Adams. It's just me and two others, staying at an old house with some off-grid tech out in the woods. We're doing okay, but will need to find something more permanent. Lisa is at a horse farm in Saratoga in Upstate New York. She's got ten people with her and, what, like twenty horses, is it?"

"That's right," she said. "Clean water, too, so no disease here. At least not yet, thank god. What's your name, sweetie? Tell us about yourselves."

"My name is Franklin. There are six of us here at Paradise Shaker Village. It's a fully restored living history museum. We have sheep, cows, and chickens, and a whole set of buildings built in the early 1800s before electricity. Plus a lot of farmland, but it's way too much for the six of us to keep up. It's a good place to be, though, I think. Long-term."

Patrick nudged me and mouthed *Loris*.

"Oh, and I'm supposed to ask about a doctor or a midwife. Loris is pregnant."

It turns out Loris was the only one pregnant in their circle of contacts, but they promised to spread the word and see what they could find. Mike asked about the village and how many people it could sustain. I explained there had been over two hundred people living here at one point and said we could use a lot of additional hands for the farming and animal work.

Lisa asked if we could accommodate horses, and I described the barn and the pasture setup. We promised to meet again in two days, and both Mike and Lisa said they'd talk with their groups about possibly joining us.

After the call, Patrick said, "I guess we shouldn't get too far ahead of ourselves about extending invitations until we've talked to the others."

"Right," I said. "But we really do need more people. We only managed to plant, like, a tenth of our fields, and maintaining that and harvesting the crops will be even more work. We'll need dozens more to have an ongoing operation."

"I know," Patrick said. "You're right. And there's all the other stuff we're not even attempting yet—honey, cheese, fiber. But let's make sure we're all on the same page first, okay?"

"Sure," I said, as I carefully adjusted the radio. I was searching through the high-frequency band, which Stan had said can reach anywhere in the world under the right conditions. I was proceeding slowly, channel by channel, calling out to announce ourselves, and waiting for a response. Then repeating that process again before moving on.

"What do you think happened to that group in Pennsylvania we connected with?" Patrick asked. "I keep thinking about the vandalized drug store and the gun shots," he added.

Into the microphone, I said, "Hello. This is Paradise Shaker Village in Maine. Is anyone there?" I turned to Patrick. "I worry about that too. Should we say something to Mike and Lisa next time?"

"I think so, yeah." One of the puppies began noisily nursing in the whelping box. I looked down into the corner. It was Dexter, the black one, and the biggest of the three. I picked up the microphone again.

"This is Paradise Shaker Village in Maine. Is anyone—"

"Maine? Hello? Can...hear...?"

Patrick and I both jumped. I'd been through quite a few channels and hadn't really been excepting a response.

"Yes, this is Paradise Shaker Village in Maine. I can hear you. My name is Franklin."

The next transmission was garbled, and we couldn't make out anything they said.

"Sorry, this is Maine. We couldn't hear you. There's a lot of static. Please repeat."

It got better, but not much. "...anklin, good to...is USS Vermont, nuc...arine...are you?" Patrick and I looked at each other. He shrugged.

"Hello, Vermont. Very bad reception. Is there a better channel for you?"

Before I could reply, a piercing squeal overwhelmed the band, and we lost them.

*

We had fresh meat that night for dinner. Emily proved quite capable of slaughtering a no longer useful rooster, and we stewed it with root vegetables for hours. I was glad to see Emily coming out of herself and participating more. Not because I thought she needed to be useful, but because I think she was healthier and happier now.

The entire house filled with the homey aroma of a relaxed Sunday dinner. I told Patrick that, too, and I pointed out proudly that I'd used a *metaphor*, because I really had no idea what day it was.

As we ate, I told everyone about the radio calls. Patrick and I put our heads together to recall exactly what we heard on the final call, and concluded it could have been from a United States nuclear submarine. And wouldn't that be exciting? It made sense too. Those subs go out for months at a time, and an isolated crew would have missed the virus's spread. We'd noted the channel and would try to raise them again.

Emily was excited by the idea of Lisa joining us with horses. And everyone generally agreed if we could screen people first, we could use lots more hands. Still, our latest experience in Northwood had made everyone cautious, but especially Loris, who kept placing her hands protectively over her belly whenever we talked about the future.

Chapter Forty-Two

It was the middle of June before I finally had a chance to get to the reading *I* had selected from the library. I told Patrick I was giving up on his novels. He resisted the idea, but after I showed him the dialogue where the nonbinary character talked about the letter *P* at the end of the acronym, even he admitted it might be good for me to a take a break.

He was still just as stumped about the *P* as I was.

"Peppy?" I asked.

"Don't be such a phallus, Franklin," he'd replied.

And so, finally, I went up into the radio shack and began reading, confident in the knowledge I would soon be able to put an accurate, scientific label on Patrick's sexuality. Honestly, I don't know why I was still so obsessed. I mean, things were great between us, and whatever he called himself, I knew I was a gay man, and that Patrick and I loved each other. Still, all of the business about gray sexuality and demisexuality felt off somehow.

It felt to me like maybe people were making up their own definitions.

I started with *Human Sexuality* and skimmed through most of it to get to the asexuality section. As I did so, I casually scanned through the radio channels, listening for a signal.

I was startled to learn that being gay was once considered a sexual disorder. But that made no sense. Everyone knows there are gay people, and very few people think there's anything wrong with that. Not anymore anyway. I kept looking through the book. I wanted to know if asexuality was once considered a disorder too.

But I couldn't find any mention about asexuality at all. Instead, there was a paragraph on a syndrome where people, mostly women, failed to have an interest in sex, but it wasn't described as an orientation, the way Patrick used the label. And it was uncommon.

I forgot about the radio and moved on to *Abnormal Sexuality*. Wow, what an eye-opener. There were all sorts of sick and twisted people out there. "I can't believe some of this shit," I said to Prissy. She was peacefully resting in her box as her puppies slept in a tight bundle next to her. Still, no mention of asexuality anywhere. There was a discussion of something called hypoactive sexual desire disorder, but it wasn't presented as a sexual orientation.

The discussion of the disorder didn't sound at all like Patrick. My "lived experience" with him usually involved a lot of mopping up afterward.

I was about to give up. What Patrick was didn't seem to exist, and I was getting very frustrated. I didn't want to go to him with these questions because he hadn't wanted me to read these books in the first place. But then a smaller pamphlet that had been tucked into the *Abnormal Sexuality* book slipped out onto the ground. I picked it up. It had a blue cover and was cheaply put together, stapled in three places down the middle.

It was produced by an organization called Family Truth Advocates and was titled, *A Conservative's Guide to the Radical Left's Sex Agenda*. That seemed interesting. I began to read.

Chapter Forty-Three

I needed to find Patrick. Right away. He'd been misled! Or *we'd* been misled, I guess. This pamphlet said it was all a lie, maybe even the whole acronym.

I didn't need to go far. He was across the hall in our dorm room, reading up on how to install a solar panel/battery setup to generate and store electricity for heating water.

"Patrick!" I exclaimed, charging into the room, waving the *Conservative's Guide*, in the air.

"Franklin! What's wrong? Calm down. Are you all right?"

"No!" I yelled. "I mean, yes, maybe. I learned something disturbing—about you, I mean!"

"Me? What are you talking about?" He stood and approached me. "What is that you're waving around?"

I handed it to him. "It's the first thing that makes sense. I think what they say in here might be true," I said. "Finally. It explains how people have been misled...about all this sex stuff. How *you've* been misled."

Patrick was reading the cover of the pamphlet, and yes, I recognized the look on his face. Anger. And fear too.

He shook the booklet at me. "Where did you get this *trash*?" he demanded.

"From the library," I said.

"No way," he said. "The library would never carry this. Where did you get it, Franklin?"

"It...it was in the *Abnormal Sexuality* book." I was starting to get worried. "But that doesn't matter. The important thing is it says there's no such thing as asexuality, or most of those other labels." I stopped for a moment. Actually, it did acknowledge there are gay people, but it described that as a behavior, a choice. Not an orientation.

I was about to explain that part to Patrick.

"Goddamn it! Some *asshole* hid it there, so someone like *you* would come along. And of course you'd just believe it." He was red in the face and rubbing his hands through his hair.

"What do you mean 'someone like me'?"

"I mean...oh shit, Franklin...Jesus." He was aggressively rubbing his fingers together. "This would be so much easier if you were just normal."

Normal? I couldn't believe Patrick had just used that word with me. I felt like I'd been punched in the gut.

"Normal?" I cried. "You're the one who's not *normal*. It says so right there. Just read it! It said asexuality is *not* a sexual orientation, but is used by people who are ashamed of their sexual attractions or activities to hide their abnormal desires."

Patrick stepped right up to me then. He was shaking. "What the *fuck*, Franklin? Is that what you think of me?

You'd believe some bullshit piece of paper over what I've told you is my truth? My own personal experience? *Our intimacy—*"

"No," I interrupted. "*Of course* not. It's just the label you're using that's wrong. This says 'lived experiences' don't make things true. It says it's just what people want to believe, but that there really *are* facts and truths, not just opinions. See? You've been wrong all this time...about the label, I think, and...and..." I trailed off because, honestly, it was starting to not make sense to me too.

When I'd first read the pamphlet, the points it made had felt right. It was sensible and scientific. But now I started questioning myself. I mean, after all, it said acting on gay feelings was the worst thing of all those things, and I *knew* that wasn't true. So maybe...maybe...

But Patrick was right up on top of me now. He grabbed my shoulders and *shook* me. Hard.

"Fuck you, Franklin." He shoved me backward, and I almost fell. I thought of how he'd pushed Alyssa, and how'd she taunted him into doing it. I felt sick. "Goddamn it!" he yelled again, clenching his fists and moving to the wall, punching it hard. Twice.

Blackness was pushing in from the sides of my vision. I felt a pull to withdraw.

Patrick moved to the bed and collapsed on it.

I would not, *not,* shut down right now!

He was crying, but not just his usual Patrick tears; no, this was sobbing. "It'll always be like this with you, won't it?" I couldn't tell if he was talking to me or himself. "You with your *obsessive* insistence things be labeled and clear all the time. It's all black or white for you."

This wasn't going the way I expected at all. I'd honestly thought this would be a good thing. That I'd found an explanation.

"No," I said. "It's just...you...you were being misled into believing in things that weren't real—"

"Shut up, Franklin." He wiped at his eyes and sighed. "All the things I've told you about myself. All the things we've *done* together. The times I told you I loved you. The times *you* told *me* you loved me. They were all...what? Some big scam? A radical left agenda to destroy the family?"

Well, no. That's not what I thought at all.

"I can't do this anymore. Go away now. I can't have you *challenging* me like this *all the fucking time*. Go." He turned over and flopped onto his stomach, dismissing me.

But we *did* love each other. Of course, we loved each other. I couldn't imagine being without him. And I knew that was true. But.

But now that I thought about it, the book said that was a lie, too, didn't it? I'd been so excited to see the explanation about asexuality being fake that I forgot all about the part that said being gay was wrong. I mean, it didn't try to say gay people didn't exist, like it said about asexuals, but it *did* say gay people were living an immoral and unnatural life. And I *knew* that wasn't true. So why was I so ready to believe the rest of it?

What if Patrick was right? What if whoever wrote this was just some nutcase with his own agenda, and I'd just ruined everything? Patrick told me he couldn't take it anymore. He told me to leave. Jesus, I was a fool.

"But...but I love you" was all I managed to say.

"Seriously, Franklin. Go. The fuck. Away."

I felt dizzy and sat on the edge of the bed. Patrick let out a frustrated groan when he realized I hadn't left. "Now!" he added, his voice muffled in the pillow. But I couldn't go. I wasn't sure I could stand even if I'd wanted to. I focused on my breathing.

In through the nose, flowing into my lungs, softly drifting out my mouth. Again. And again.

I don't know long I did that, but I eventually reached a steady place where I could think. This was important. It might be too late, but it was important.

I loved Patrick, and he loved me. We needed each other and *wanted* to be together. I knew that to be true. But I kept doubting him. He kept telling me his truth, the way he saw it, and I kept telling him he was wrong. Just because it didn't make sense to me. *Of course* he was through with me.

"I was *so fucking* wrong," I said out loud, surprised by the revelation.

But why? What was my problem? I know I needed to have everything organized and clear. Sensible. Labeled. And I know that's been at the heart of our issues. But did I *need* for things to be that way, or was I just more comfortable when they were?

"What *the fuck* is my problem?" I think I said that out loud too.

Couldn't I find a way to accept Patrick's messy reality of lived experience and allow that to be true? I mean, it *is* true. Just because I didn't understand it, or more honestly, didn't like how *messy* it was, didn't mean Patrick was making it all up. *Of course* it was true.

"Shit!" Out loud again, I think. I had to fix this. At least, I could sure as hell try.

"Whoever wrote that pamphlet was a total fuckup," I said. Patrick didn't say anything, but at least he didn't repeat his demand that I leave. "He almost killed us." Patrick still didn't say anything.

I lay next to him, not quite touching, but close. I tilted my head toward him so I wasn't talking into the pillow. "I don't want us to be dead. I really screwed up." I took a couple of breaths, and I felt Patrick doing the same. This next part was important, and I had to get it right. "I know I'm not like most other people," I began. Patrick tilted his head toward mine and opened his mouth to say something. I didn't let him.

"Let me finish," I said. "I know I can't see some of the things other people see, at least, not always. It's not easy for me to understand things that aren't...*definable*, you know?" I hadn't meant to ask a question because I wasn't done. But Patrick only nodded to me, so I was able to continue. "And I know I don't always react the way people expect. To emotional things, I mean, or even understand when people have deep feelings about things that matter. I wish I did, but I don't."

"Franklin—" Patrick began.

"Shh. But I understand more now, about how I am, and how to make it work. But here's what I really want to say. I *am* just like other people about lots of things. I feel happiness and joy, sorrow and regret, and now, for the very first time, love. I love you, Patrick. I always will. I know I hurt you, and I wish I could undo that, but I can't.

"But I promise you this," I continued. "If you don't kick me out of your life, I will always support who you are.

Even if it's, like, some weird, completely not-understandable acronym, with *P*s and *X*s and *Z*s. Whatever you want. Your truth is your truth; it's *the* truth, and I'll believe you. Always."

Our faces were inches apart. Patrick's cheeks were still wet from his tears. I could feel his breath on my mouth and nose. He leaned forward and kissed me, thank god, and said, "If you turn that last part into a hashtag, so help me god, I'll ban you from Twitter forever." I laughed softly into his mouth, and kissed him back.

"And you know," he added, "for someone who's says he's not, you're pretty good about reading people."

I smiled, and he reached over and grabbed my ass.

"You know, for someone who's asexual, you're pretty—"

He shut me up with his tongue, and as our kiss deepened, I felt that connection again—with the universe and with everything—and I knew this was right, whatever it was called, whatever we called ourselves. Forever.

After a minute we pulled apart, both of us breathless, eager for more. "I'll give you twenty dollars if you let me take your clothes off," he said.

"I'll give you a hundred dollars if you let me watch," Vet said from the doorway. Patrick and I both jumped.

"Vet!" I said, sitting up quickly.

"We didn't see you there," said Patrick, as he pulled himself together and swung his feet onto the floor.

"Obviously," said Vet. "Came scrambling up here again when I heard all the hollering, thinking I'd need to break up a fight, but instead..." He shifted his weight onto his crutch and took a step into the room. "Not that I would have minded the show. You guys are hot. Think you'd ever consider a threesome...?"

Oh my god, no. But what about Loris? And the condoms. Wasn't he straight?

"Uh, sorry," Patrick answered for both of us. "We're still new. We have all we need in each other. Check back in a couple years, though." I punched him on the shoulder.

I was trying to make sense of Vet's comment, running through what I knew of the acronym.

"Oh," I said. "You're bisexual."

Vet smiled. "Me? Bisexual? Nah. That's way too limiting for me. It's so binary you know? Leaves out all the other interesting options." He looked at me, waiting.

I ran through the letters in my head again. *I*, maybe? Could that be it? I forgot what the *I* stood for. I should just let it go, right? Labels don't matter. His truth is his truth. But...but...argh!

"So what *are* you, then?" I caved and asked. Patrick shook his head and sighed.

"Me?" Vet asked. "I'm pansexual."

"Pansexual!" Patrick and I exclaimed at the same time. Then we laughed and laughed and laughed.

Epilogue

"Get those damn dogs out of here!" Loris shouted from her position sitting up in bed, knees raised and spread apart, a light sheet draped across her body. Sara was gripping one of her hands, and Emily had the other. Loris was alternately screaming and panting, sweat drenching her body.

Vet said to me, "Do it, and go help Patrick with the water, tell him to bring it up now; it's almost time."

I didn't know how Dexter, Gally, and Kerry had gotten in here, but at six months, they were always underfoot. I bribed them out of the room with treats, and we went to find Patrick in the kitchen. He was busy at the stove, heating water in several stew pots. "They're ready for the hot water," I told him.

I could tell he was nervous. We all were. "Do they need more towels?" he asked, as he grasped the first pot with oven mitts.

"No. They have an entire Walmart's worth of unopened towels up there. Sheets, too, bandages, blankets, everything they could want. Vet's prepared. He just needs water."

"On it," Patrick said, carrying the heavy pot through the dining room toward the stairway.

It had been a long fourteen hours.

Loris's screams echoed through the house, and Patrick returned, white-faced. "Jesus," he said. "I'll take these others up; then let's wait outside."

The sun was high overhead on a warm autumn afternoon. What could be harvested had been harvested, and the trees in the surrounding forest glowed bright gold. I'd been working in the barn the past week to prepare for the horses. Lisa from Albany, along with all the horses and ten other people, were making their way here on foot.

They'd left three weeks ago, in order to avoid the start of snow season, and estimated it would take between two and three weeks to manage the four-hundred-mile trek.

Patrick and I headed to the barn, followed by a rolling tumble of puppies.

Even in the barn we could hear Loris's agony. "Do you think there's a problem?" I asked. "It's been going on for so long."

He didn't answer immediately. "Vet says it's not unusual for it to take this long, especially the first time."

Prissy was hunting mice. I thought a few times this summer I'd seen her get a rat, but I didn't mention that to Patrick. Roscoe was wisely hiding somewhere, and the puppies were play biting in a pile of snarling fur.

"I didn't gather eggs this morning," I said. "We should do that, especially if the others arrive today." Egg production had been dropping as the days got shorter, and Emily had already identified three roosters who were destined for the pot.

"Good idea," said Patrick. "That'll keep us occupied."

We headed for the stairs in the middle of the barn. The chickens usually laid their eggs on the second floor, away from the plodding hooves of cows and sheep. Halfway up, Patrick pulled me to a stop on the landing.

"Remember the first time we kissed here?"

I sure did. And there had been many since then too.

He pressed me against the post and ground his hips into mine. Loris's distant scream pierced the air, sounding even more frantic than last time.

"Um," I said, "kind of not a good time, right?"

He sighed and released me. "Fine, I mean, it's only been, what, eight months for us? But if it's already time to bring Vet in for a threesome..."

I punched him lightly in the chest.

"Pansexual!" we both said at the same time and started laughing all over again.

We collected the eggs, noticeably fewer than yesterday's haul, and headed back out into the sunlight.

"Hello?" someone called from the front gate.

"They made it!" I said to Patrick. We went to welcome our guests.

*

Half an hour later we were sitting in the kitchen. The screaming had reached a crescendo about fifteen minutes earlier, and there had been nothing but an ominous silence since.

Finally, *finally,* the gusty wail of a newborn could be heard. Wow. Patrick was crying, of course.

"Boys," Sara called down to us, "everyone is fine! Come up and meet our newest member!"

Well, almost, I thought, looking at our guests sitting across the kitchen table from us. They still seemed shell-shocked, taking it all in, I guess. I'd been there.

Patrick and I went upstairs and into Loris's room. She looked exhausted, but so alive. She held her little bundle, already nursing. She looked up at us. "This is Stanley," she said.

He was an ugly, wrinkled little thing, all pink and red and...scrunched. "He's beautiful," lied Patrick. Or, maybe he didn't lie. Maybe it was a metaphor. "Is he ready for his birthday surprise?" he asked. Everyone had remained in the room, Vet wiping down his supplies, Emily bundling up all the wet towels. They all turned to Patrick.

"What surprise?" Loris asked Patrick.

Patrick reached over a ran a hand through my hair. "You tell them, Franklin."

"Well," I said. "When he's ready, there's a couple of Buddhist monks downstairs waiting to meet him."

About John Patrick

John Patrick lives in the Berkshire Hills of Massachusetts, where he is supported in his writing by his husband and their terrier, who is convinced he could do battle with the bears that come through the woods on occasion (the terrier, that is, not the husband). John believes that queer characters in fiction should reflect the diversity of their lives—not just their identities, but all of their struggles, challenges, hopes, and loves. Nonetheless, despite all the conflict and drama John imposes on his characters (spoiler alert!), love will always find a way.

Email
John@JohnPatrickAuthor.com

Facebook
www.facebook.com/JohnPatrickAuthor

Website
www.JohnPatrickAuthor.com

Other NineStar Books by John Patrick

Paradise Series

Undercover in Paradise, Book Two

(Coming December 2021)

Also from NineStar Press

The End by M. Rose Flores

On Cate Mortensen's seventeenth birthday, her family is scattered in a fight for survival, and she and her sister Melody are catapulted headfirst into a world where their phones are just hunks of plastic, they must scavenge for every bite, and they sleep with weapons in their hands. Traveling alone, and then not so alone, they follow the route their family planned to Alcatraz Island where the hope of safety and a real life awaits.

After more than a year on the road, Cate has found three things to be true. One: Zombies are a thing now. Two: Not all zombies are just zombies. Three (the game changer): Cate is immune to the infection.

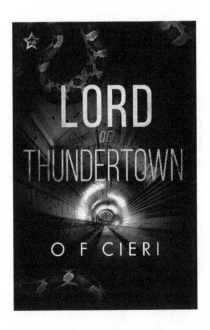

Lord of Thundertown by O.F. Cieri

In the movies, Thundertown was depicted like a real town, with boundaries, Folk-run businesses, and a government. In real life, Thundertown was a block here or there, three businesses on the same side of the street, an unconnected sewer main, or a single abandoned building.

When an epidemic of missing person cases is on the rise, the police refuse to act. Instead, Alex Delatorre goes to Thundertown for answers and finds clues leading to a new Lord trying to unite the population.

No one has seen the Lord, and the closer Alex gets to him, the farther Alex gets from his path home.

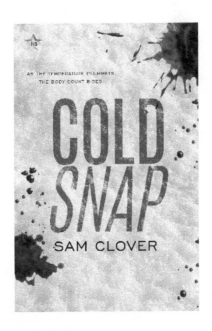

Cold Snap by Sam Clover

A lifetime of bad experiences has left Iddy homeless and wary of shelters.

Rumors of a monster hunting the city streets at night surface, but between the cold and predators of the human variety, Iddy has more important things to worry about. That is until he comes face-to-face with the monster and survives. Now, it has him in its sights.